I AM NOT YOUR PERFECT MEXICAN DAUGHTER

I AM NOT YOUR PERFECT MEXICAN

DAUGHTER

ERIKA L. SÁNCHEZ

ALFRED A. KNOPF NEW YORK

Dwarsligger® is a new book concept created by printer and publisher Royal Jongbloed BV (Heerenveen, the Netherlands).

This book is printed on Thinopaque paper provided by Tervakoski in Finland. Thinopaque is FSC certified, manufactured acid free from environmentally sustainable paper pulp. It is produced following the highest environmental standards.

This is a work of fiction. Names, characters, places, and incidents either are the product of the author's imagination or are used fictitiously. Any resemblance to actual persons, living or dead, events, or locales is entirely coincidental.

 Published in the United States by Random House Children's Books, a division of Penguin Random House LLC, New York. Originally published in a different format in the United States by Alfred A. Knopf, an imprint of Random House Children's Books, a division of Penguin Random House LLC, New York, in 2017. This is a complete, unabridged text.

Visit us on the Web! GetUnderlined.com

Educators and librarians, for a variety of teaching tools, visit us at RHTeachersLibrarians.com

The Library of Congress has cataloged the original edition of this work as follows:
Sánchez, Erika L., author.
I am not your perfect Mexican daughter / Erika L. Sánchez.
First edition.
New York : Alfred A. Knopf, an imprint of Random House Children's Books, [2017]
© 2017
344 pages ; 22 cm
PZ7.1.S257 Iaam 2017
ISBN 978-1-5247-0048-5 (hardcover) — ISBN 978-1-5247-0049-2 (library binding) —
ISBN 978-1-5247-0051-5 (tr. pbk.) — ISBN 978-1-5247-0050-8 (ebook)

ISBN 978-0-593-12617-2 (mini)

Original cover design by Connie Gabbert. Cover design adapted by Jinna Shin.

Design adapted from the hardcover edition. Typesetting by 2K/DENMARK AS, Denmark

Printing and binding: Royal Jongbloed BV, Heerenveen, the Netherlands
10 9 8 7 6 5 4 3 2 1

First Random Mini Edition

For my parents

ONE

What's surprised me most about seeing my sister dead is the lingering smirk on her face. Her pale lips are turned up ever so slightly, and someone has filled in her patchy eyebrows with a black pencil. The top half of her face is angry—like she's ready to stab someone—and the bottom half is almost smug. This is not the Olga I knew. Olga was as meek and fragile as a baby bird.

I wanted her to wear the pretty purple dress that didn't hide her body like all of her other outfits, but Amá chose the bright yellow one with the pink flowers I've always hated. It was so unstylish, so classically Olga. It made her either four or eighty years old. I could never decide which. Her hair is just as bad as the dress—tight, crunchy curls that remind me of a rich lady's poodle. How cruel to let her look like that. The bruises and gashes on her cheeks are masked with thick coats of cheap foundation, making her face haggard, even though she is (was) only twenty-two. Don't they pump your body full of strange chemicals to prevent your skin from stretching and puckering, to keep your face from resembling a rubber mask? Where did they find this mortician, the flea market?

My poor older sister had a special talent for making herself less attractive. She was skinny and had an okay body, but she always managed to make it look like a sack of potatoes. Her face was pale and plain, never a single drop of makeup. What a waste. I'm no fashion icon—far from it—but I do feel strongly against dressing like the elderly. Now she's doing it from beyond the grave, but this time it's not even her fault.

Olga never looked or acted like a normal twenty-two-year-old. It made me mad sometimes. Here she was, a grown-ass woman, and all she did was go to work, sit at home with our parents, and take one class each semester at the local community college. Every once and a while, she'd go shopping with Amá or to the movies with her best friend, Angie, to watch terrible romantic comedies about clumsy but adorable blond women who fall in love with architects in the streets of New York City. What kind of life is that? Didn't she want more? Didn't she ever want to go out and grab the world by the balls? Ever since I could pick up a pen, I've wanted to be a famous writer. I want to be so successful that people stop me on the street and ask, "Oh my God, are you Julia Reyes, the best writer who has ever graced this earth?” All I know is that I’m going to pack my bags when I graduate and say, “Peace out, mothafuckas.”

But not Olga. Saint Olga, the perfect Mexican daughter. Sometimes I wanted to scream at her until something switched on in her brain. But the only time I ever asked her why she didn’t move out or go to a real college, she told me to leave her alone in a voice so weak and brittle, I never wanted to ask her again. Now I’ll never know what Olga would have become. Maybe she would have surprised us all.

Here I am, thinking all of these horrible thoughts about my dead sister. It’s easier to be pissed, though. If I stop being angry, I’m afraid I’ll fall apart until I’m just a warm mound of flesh on the floor.

While I stare at my chewed-up nails and sink deeper into this floppy green couch, I hear Amá wailing. She really throws her body into it, too. "Mija, mija!" she screams as she practically climbs inside the casket. Apá doesn't even try to pull her off. I can't blame him, because when he tried to calm her down a few hours ago, Amá kicked and flailed her arms until she gave him a black eye. I guess he's going to leave her alone for now. She'll tire herself out eventually. I've seen babies do that.

Apá has been sitting in the back of the room all day, refusing to speak to anyone, staring off into nothing, like he always does. Sometimes I think I see his dark mustache quivering, but his eyes stay dry and clear as glass.

I want to hug Amá and tell her it's going to be okay, even though it's not and never will be, but I feel almost paralyzed, like I'm underwater and made of lead. When I open my mouth, nothing comes out. Besides, Amá and I haven't had that kind of relationship since I was little. We don't hug and say, "I love you," like on TV shows about boring white families who live in two-story houses and talk about their feelings. She and Olga were practically best friends, and I was the odd daughter out. We've been bickering, drifting away from each other for years. I've spent so much of my life trying to avoid Amá because we always end up arguing over stupid, petty things. We once fought about an egg yolk, for instance. True story.

Apá and I are the only ones in my family who haven't cried. He just hangs his head and remains silent as a stone. Maybe something is wrong with us. Maybe we're messed up beyond crying. Though my eyes haven't produced tears, I've felt the grief burrow in every cell of my body. There are moments that

I feel like I might suffocate, as if all my insides are tied into a tight little ball. I haven't taken a crapin almost four days, but I'm not about to tell Amá in the state she's in. I'll just let it build until I explode like a piñata.

Amá has always been prettier than Olga, even now, with her swollen eyes and splotchy skin, which is not the way it's supposed to be. Her name is more graceful, too—Amparo Montenegro Reyes. Mothers are not supposed to be more beautiful than their daughters, and daughters are not supposed to die before their mothers. But Amá is more attractive than most people. She hardly has any wrinkles and has these big, round eyes that always look sad and wounded. Her long hair is thick and dark, and her body is still slim, unlike the other moms in the neighborhood who are shaped like upside-down pears. Every time I walk down the street with Amá, guys whistle and honk, which makes me wish I carried a slingshot.

Amá is rubbing Olga's face and crying softly now. This won't last, though. She's always quiet for a few minutes, then, all of a sudden, lets out a moan that makes your soul turn inside out. Now Tía Cuca is rubbing her back and telling her that Olga is with Jesus, that she can finally be in peace.

But when was Olga *not* in peace? This Jesus stuff is all a sack of crap. Once you're dead, you're dead. The only thing that makes sense to me is what Walt Whitman said about death: "Look for me under your boot soles." Olga's body will turn to dirt, which will grow into trees, and then someone in the future will step on their fallen leaves. There is no heaven. There is only earth, sky, and the transfer of energy. The idea would almost be beautiful if this weren't such a nightmare.

Two ladies waiting in line to see Olga in her casket begin crying. I've never seen them in my life. One is wearing a faded and billowy black dress, and the other wears a saggy skirt that looks like an old curtain. They clasp each other's hands and whisper.

Olga and I didn't have much in common, but we did love each other. There are stacks and stacks of pictures to prove it. In Amá's favorite, Olga is braiding my hair. Amá says Olga used to pretend that I was her baby. She'd put me in her toy carriage and sing me songs by Cepillín, that scary Mexican clown who looks like a rapist but everyone loves for some reason.

I would give anything to go back to the day she died and do things differently. I think of all the ways I could have kept Olga from getting on that bus. I've replayed the day over and over in my head so many times and have written down every single detail, but I still can't find the foreshadowing. When someone dies, people always say they had some sort of premonition, a sinking feeling that something awful was right around the corner. I didn't.

The day felt like any other: boring, uneventful, and annoying. We had swimming for gym class that afternoon. I've always hated being in that disgusting petri dish. The idea of being dunked in everyone's pee—and God knows what else—is enough to give me a panic attack, and the chlorine makes my skin itch and eyes sting. I always try to get out of it with elaborate and not-so-elaborate lies. That time, I told the thin-lipped Mrs. Kowalski that I was on my period again (the eighth day in a row), and she said she didn't believe me, that it was impossible for my period to be so long. Of course I was lying, but who was she to question my menstrual cycle? How intrusive.

"Do you want to check?" I asked. "I'd be very happy to provide you with empirical evidence if you want, even though I think you're violating my human rights." I regretted it as soon as it came out of my mouth. Maybe I have some sort of condition that keeps me from thinking through what I'm going to say. Sometimes it's word-puke spilling out everywhere. That was too much, even for me, but I was in a particularly foul mood and didn't want to deal with anyone. My moods shift like that all the time, even before Olga died. One minute I feel okay, and then all of a sudden my energy plummets for no reason at all. It's hard to explain.

Of course Mrs. Kowalski sent me to the principal's office, and as usual, they wouldn't let me go home until my parents came to pick me up. This had happened several times last year. Everyone knows me at the principal's office already. I'm there more often than some of the gangbangers, and it's always for running my mouth when I'm not supposed to. Whenever I enter the office, the secretary, Mrs. Maldonado, rolls her eyes and clucks her tongue.

Typically, Amá meets with my principal, Mr. Potter, who tells her what a disrespectful student I am. Then Amá gasps at what I've done and says, "Julia, que malcriada," and apologizes to him over and over again in her broken English. She is always apologizing to white people, which makes me feel embarrassed. And then I feel ashamed of my shame.

Amá punishes me for one or two weeks, depending on how severe my behavior is, and then, a few months later, it happens again. Like I said, I don't know how to control my mouth. Amá tells me, "Como te gusta la mala vida," and I guess she's right, because I always end up making things more difficult for myself. I used to be a model student, skipped third grade and everything, but now I'm a troublemaker.

Olga had taken the bus that day because her car was in the shop to get the brakes replaced. Amá was supposed to pick her up, but because she had to deal with me at school, she couldn't. If I'd shut my mouth, things would have worked out differently, but how was I supposed to know? When Olga got off the bus to transfer to another one across the street, she didn't see that the light had already turned green because she was looking at her phone. The bus honked to warn her, but it was too late. Olga stepped into the busy street at the wrong time. She got hit by a semi. Not just hit, though—*smashed.*

Whenever I think of my sister's crushed organs, I want to scream in a field of flowers until I'm hoarse.

Two of the witnesses said that she was smiling right before it happened. It's a miracle that her face was okay enough to have an open casket. She was dead by the time the ambulance arrived.

Even though the man driving couldn't have seen her because she was blocked by the bus and the light was green and Olga shouldn't have crossed one of the busiest streets in Chicago with her face in her phone, Amá cursed the driver up and down until she lost her voice. She got really creative, too. She had always scolded me for saying the word *damn,* which is not even a bad word, and here she was, telling the driver *and* God to fuck their mothers and themselves. I just watched her with my mouth hanging open.

We all knew it wasn't the driver's fault, but Amá needed someone to accuse. She hasn't blamed me directly, but I can see it in her big sad eyes every time she looks at me.

My nosy aunts are whispering behind me now. I can feel their eyes latched to the back of my head again. I know they're saying that this is my fault. They've never liked me because they think I'm trouble. When I dyed chunks of my hair bright blue, those drama queens almost needed to be put on stretchers and rushed to the hospital. They act as if I'm some sort of devil child because I don't like to go to church and would rather read books than socialize with them. Why is that a crime, though? They're boring. Plus, they have no idea how much I loved my sister.

I've had enough of their whispering, so I turn around to give them a dirty look. That's when I see Lorena come in, thank God. She's the only person who can make me feel better right now.

Everyone turns to stare at her in her outrageously high heels, tight black dress, and excessive makeup. Lorena is always drawing attention to herself. Maybe that'll give them something else to gossip about. She hugs me so tight she nearly cracks my ribs. Her cheap cherry body spray fills my nose and mouth.

Amá doesn't like Lorena because she thinks she's wild and slutty, which isn't untrue, but she has been my friend since I was eight and is more loyal than anyone I've ever known. I whisper to her that my tías are talking about me, that they're blaming me for what happened to Olga, that they're making me so angry, I want to smash all the windows with my bare fists.

"Fuck those nosy viejas," Lorena says, waving her hand dramatically, shooting them eye-daggers. I turn around to see if they've stopped staring when I notice a dark man in the back crying quietly into a cloth handkerchief. He's wearing a gray suit and shiny gold watch. He seems familiar, but I can't place his face. He's probably my uncle or something. My parents are always introducing me to strangers and telling me we're related. There are dozens of people here I've never met. When I turn around, he's gone, and Olga's friend Angie comes running in, looking like *she* was the one hit by a semi. She's beautiful, but, damn, is she an ugly crier. Her skin is like a bright pink rag someone has wrung out. As soon as she sees Olga, she starts howling almost worse than Amá. I wish I knew the right thing to say, but I don't. I never do.

TWO

After the funeral, Amá doesn't get out of bed for almost two weeks. She only gets up to go to the bathroom, drink water, and occasionally eat one of those Mexican cookies that taste like Styrofoam. She's been wearing the same loose and frumpy nightgown, and I'm almost positive she hasn't taken a shower this entire time, which is scary, because Amá is the cleanest person I know. Her hair is always washed and neatly braided, and her clothes—even when they're old—are patched, ironed, and spotless. When I was seven, Amá found out I hadn't showered for five days, so she dunked me in a scalding hot tub and scrubbed me with a brush until my skin ached. She told me that girls who don't wash their junk get horrible infections, so I never skipped showering again. Maybe I'm the one who needs to throw Amá into the tub now.

Apá works all day, then sits on the couch with a bottle of beer, like usual. In fact, he even sleeps on it now. It's probably molded to his body at this point. He hasn't said much to me this whole time, which is not that different from before. Sometimes he barely says hello. Could it be that my own father hates my guts? He wasn't that much more affectionate toward Olga, but she definitely tried harder. When Apá came home from the factory, she'd bring out his foot bath. She'd kneel down, place his feet gently inside, and massage them. They never said a word during this daily ritual. I can't imagine touching him like that.

The apartment is a disaster, since Amá and Olga were the ones who did all the cleaning. We have roaches, but because Amá mopped every single day, it didn't feel that disgusting. Now the dirty dishes are piled high and the kitchen table is covered with crumbs. The roaches are probably rejoicing. And the bathroom? It should be burned to the ground. I know I should clean, but whenever I look at the mess, I think, what's the point? Nothing feels like it has a point anymore.

I don't want to bother my parents because they have enough to worry about, but I'm so hungry and tired of eating nothing but tortillas and eggs. A few days ago, I tried to make beans, but they never softened, even though I boiled them for three hours. I nearly cracked my teeth on one. I had to throw away the whole pot, which is a sin, according to Amá. I hope my aunts bring over more food. This is the only time I wish I would've let my mother teach me how to cook. But I hate the way she hovers over me and criticizes my every move. I'd rather live in the streets than be a submissive Mexican wife who spends all day cooking and cleaning.

Apá hasn't eaten much, either. The other day he brought home a brick of Chihuahua cheese and a stack of tortillas, so we ate quesadillas for several days, but we've run out now. Yesterday I got desperate and boiled some old potatoes and ate them with nothing but salt and pepper. We didn't even have butter. It's gotten so bad that I've started daydreaming about dancing hamburgers. A slice of pizza could probably make me weep with happiness.

I peek inside my parents' bedroom, and the sour smell nearly knocks me over—a mix of unwashed hair, gas, and sweat.

"Amá," I whisper.

No answer.

"Amá," I say again, louder.

Still nothing.

I finally step inside the room completely. The smell is so awful that I have to breathe through my mouth. I wonder if Amá is ever going back to work. What if the rich assholes she cleans for decide to fire her? Now that Olga is gone and can't pitch in, what are we going to do? I'm not old enough to get a job.

"Amá!" I finally yell. I turn on the light.

She gasps. "What? What do you want?" she says, her voice blurry with sleep. She covers her eyes with her hands.

"Are you okay?"

"Yes. I'm fine. Please leave me alone. I want to rest."

"You haven't eaten or taken a shower in a really long time."

"How do you know? Are you here watching me every hour of the day? Your tía came by and gave me soup yesterday. I'm fine."

"It smells terrible in here. I'm starting to get worried. How can you live like this?"

"Funny how my slob of a daughter is suddenly concerned with cleanliness. When have you ever cared about that before?" Amá has always given me attitude for my messiness, but this is unlike her. "Olga was the clean one," she adds, in case it didn't sting enough. She has compared me to my sister every single day of my life, so why should I expect that to change now that she's dead?

"Olga's gone now. All you have is me. Sorry."

Silence.

I want Amá to tell me that she loves me and that we'll get through this together, but she doesn't. I stand there like a dope, waiting and waiting for her to say something that will make me feel better. When I realize she's not going to, I dig through her wallet on the dresser, take out a five-dollar bill, and slam the door.

After searching every crevice of my room, I manage to find $4.75 in change. I'll be able to buy three tacos and a large horchata, which isn't much, but it will do. If I have to eat one more plain tortilla or boiled potato, I swear I'll cry. I slip out the back door to avoid Apá in the living room, not that he'd even ask or notice. Now I have a ghost father *and* ghost sister.

• • •

The taco place is bright with fluorescent lighting, and smells like grease and Pine-Sol. I've never eaten alone at a restaurant, and it makes me nervous. I can feel everyone watching me. They probably think I'm a loser for eating alone. The waitress gives me a funny look, too. I bet she thinks I'm not going to tip her, but I'll prove her wrong. I may be young, but I'm not dumb.

I order two tacos de asada and one al pastor with extra limes. The smell of fried meat and grilled onion makes my mouth water. When the tacos arrive, I try to eat them slowly, but end up inhaling them with desperation. Not only am I bad at cooking, I'm bad at being hungry. I'm always convinced I'm going to faint when my stomach starts to grumble. Each bite of the taco shoots a rush of pleasure through my body. I guzzle the bucket-sized horchata until I feel sick.

When I get back home, Amá is in the kitchen, with a towel wrapped around her head, drinking tea. She's freshly showered and smells like fake roses. She's finally ditched her nightgown and is wearing her white robe. The sudden sight of her clean and functioning almost scares me. She doesn't ask me where I've been, which has never, ever happened. She always wants to know where I am and who I'm with. She asks a million questions about my friends' parents—what part of Mexico they're from, what church they go to, where they work—but today, nothing. I wonder if she can smell the meat and onion in my clothes and hair.

I can usually predict what Amá is going to say, but this time I'm not at all prepared. She takes a loud slurp of her tea—which always, always gets on my nerves—and tells me I'm going to have a quinceañera.

My heart stops. "Wait, what?"

"A party. Don't you want a nice party?"

"My sister just died and you want to throw me a party? I'm already fifteen!" I must be dreaming.

"I never got to give Olga a quinceañera. It's something I'll always regret."

"So you're going to use me to make yourself feel better?"

"Ay, Julia. What is wrong with you? What kind of girl wouldn't want to celebrate her fifteenth birthday? So ungrateful." She shakes her head.

Plenty is wrong with me, and she knows it.

"But I don't *want* one. You can't make me."

Amá tightens her robe. "That's too bad."

"It's a waste of money. I bet Olga would've wanted you to help me with college instead."

"You don't know anything about what Olga would have wanted," she says, and takes another slurp of tea. Apá is watching the news in the living room. I can hear the news anchor say something about a mass grave found in Mexico. He always turns the volume way up when Amá and I are arguing, as if he's trying to drown us out.

"This doesn't make any sense. I'm already fifteen. Who's even heard of such a thing?" I start pulling on my hair, which is what I do when I feel panicky.

"We'll have it in May in the church basement. I already called the priest. It'll be available by then," she says, matter-of-factly.

"May? Are you joking? I turn sixteen in July. Why would you do that? You can't call that a quinceañera." I start pacing. I feel short of breath.

"You'll still be fifteen won't you?"

"Yeah, but that's not the point. This is so stupid." I shake my head and look at the ground.

"The point is having a nice party with your family."

"But my family doesn't even like me. And I don't want to wear a big, ugly dress. . . . And the dancing. Oh my God, the dancing." The thought of spinning in circles in front of all my idiot cousins makes me want to run away from home and join the circus.

"What are you talking about? Everyone loves you. Don't be so dramatic."

"No, they don't. They all think I'm weird, and you know that." I stare at the cheap replica of *The Last Supper* next to the cabinets. It's so old that Jesus and his posse are starting to fade into light yellows and greens.

"That's not true." Amá furrows her brow.

"Well, either way, you can't call it a quinceañera."

"Yes, I can. It's tradition." Amá's jaw tightens, and her eyes narrow in a way that tells me I'm not going to win.

"Where are you going to get the money?"

"Don't worry about it."

"How can I not worry? That's all you ever talk about."

"I said, it's not your problem. Do you understand?" Amá's voice gets quiet, which is even scarier than when she yells.

"This fucking sucks," I say, and kick the stove so hard the pans rattle.

"Watch your mouth, or I'll slap you so hard, I'll break your teeth."

Something tells me she's not exaggerating.

When I can't sleep, I crawl into Olga's bed. Last week Amá told me to never, ever go inside her room, but I can't help it. I slip in there after my parents have gone to bed and then wake up before they do. I think Amá wants to keep the room exactly as Olga left it. Maybe she wants to pretend that she's still alive, that one day she'll come home from work and everything will be normal again. If Amá knew that I touched Olga's things, she'd probably never forgive me. She'd probably ship me to Mexico—one of her favorite threats—as if that would solve any of my problems.

My sister's bed still smells like her—fabric softener, lavender lotion, and her warm and sweet human scent I can't describe. Olga dressed ugly but smelled like a meadow. I toss and turn for a long time. Tonight my mind won't shut off. I can't stop thinking about the chemistry test I failed yesterday: twenty-four percent, which is the worst grade I've received. Even an intellectually stunted monkey could get a better score. I already hated chemistry, but since Olga died, I haven't been able to concentrate. Sometimes I look at my books and tests, and the words all blur and swirl together. If I keep going like this, I'll never get into college. I'll end up working in a factory, marry some loser, and have his ugly children.

After lying in bed for hours, I turn on the lamp and try to read. I've read *The Awakening* a million times, but I find it comforting. My favorite character is the lady in black who follows Edna and Robert everywhere. I also love the book because I'm so much like Edna—nothing satisfies me, nothing makes me happy. I want too much out of life. I want to take it in my hands and squeeze and twist as much as I can from it. And it's never enough.

I read the same sentence over and over again, and lay the book on my stomach. I stare at the light purple walls and remember the happy times I had with my sister, before we started to flutter away from each other. There's a picture on her dresser of both of us in Mexico. Our parents used to send us every summer, but it's been years since we've been there. Amá and Apá haven't been able to go back because they're still illegal. The two of us are in front of Mamá Jacinta's house. We're both squinting and smiling in the sun, and Olga's arm is around my neck so tight that it is almost as if she's choking me. I remember that day so clearly. We swam in the river for hours, then ate Hawaiian hamburgers from the cart near the park.

Most of my childhood sucked, but our summers in Mexico were different. We'd get to stay up all night and play kick-the-can in the streets until we were filthy and exhausted. Here, we would've been hit by stray bullets. Sometimes we'd get to ride my great-uncle's beautiful black horses, and Mamá Jacinta would spoil us with food, no matter how silly our cravings were. Once, she even made us a pizza with stinky ranchero cheese.

Behind our picture is a poster of Maná, the terrible Mexican rock band that I hate, because all their songs are about weeping angels or something equally lame. On the opposite wall is her high school graduation picture. Olga was a good student, so I could never understand why she didn't want to go to a real college. I've been dreaming of going since I was little. I know I'm smart. That's why they skipped me ahead a year. I was bored out of my skull in class. Now I get mostly B's, with a sprinkle of C's, except for English. I always get A's in English. My mind usually wanders and gets lost in a tangle of worries.

As I look around the room, I wonder who my sister was. I lived with her my whole life, and now I feel like I didn't know her at all. Olga was the perfect daughter—cooked, cleaned, and never stayed out late. Sometimes I wondered if she'd live with my parents forever like that sap Tita, from *Like Water for Chocolate.* Ugh. Such a terrible book.

Olga loved her job, even though she was only a receptionist. What could be so fulfilling about filing and answering phones?

The stuffed animals on the dresser make me sad. I mean, I know they're inanimate objects—I'm not an idiot—but I imagine them all melancholic, waiting for my sister to come back. Olga loved babies, the color pink, and peanut butter cups. She always covered her mouth when she laughed because of her snaggletooth. She was a good listener. Unlike me, she never, ever interrupted. She was also an excellent cook. In fact, her enchiladas were better than Amá's, but I've never said that out loud.

I know Amá loves me and always has, but Olga has always been her favorite. Ever since I was a little kid, I've questioned everything, which drove both my parents insane. Even when I tried to be good, I couldn't. It's as if it were physically impossible for me, as if I were allergic to rules. Things just got worse and worse as I got older. Stuff that's sexist, for example, makes me crazy. Once, I ruined Thanksgiving by going on a rant about the women having to cook all day while the men just sat around, scratching their butts. Amá said I embarrassed her in front of the whole family, that I couldn't change the way things have always been. I probably should've let it go after a while, but I stand by what I said.

Amá and I also argue about religion all the time. I told her that the Catholic church hates women because it wants us to be weak and ignorant. It was right after the time our priest said—I swear to God—that women should obey their husbands. He literally used the word *obey.* I gasped and looked around in disbelief to see if anyone else was as angry as I was, but, no, I was the only one. I poked Olga in the ribs and whispered, "Can you believe this shit?" But she just told me to be quiet and listen to the sermon. Amá said I was a disrespectful huerca, that how could the church hate women when we worship La Virgen de Guadalupe? You can't ever win an argument with her, so why do I bother?

Stuff like that made us hate each other, and Olga was always taking her side. They looked alike, too. They're both pale and thin, with stick-straight black hair, and I'm chubby, short, and dark, like Apá. I'm not, like, super-fat or anything, but I have thick legs and my stomach is definitely not flat. Oh, and my boobs are much too big for my body—two pendulous burdens I've been lugging around since I was thirteen. I'm also the only one in the family who wears glasses. I'm practically blind. If I went out into the world with naked eyeballs, I'd probably be robbed, run over by a car, or mauled by animals.

I read for a little while longer, then try to go to sleep, but I can't. I stay wide awake for what feels like hours. When I hear birds beginning to chirp, I get so angry, I tug at the sheets and arrange the pillow over and over again. I feel something inside it press my cheek. For a second, I think it's a feather, but then I remember I'm not living in the 1800s. I sift through the pillowcase and pull out a folded piece of paper. It's a sticky note with the name of a prescription: Lexafron. Olga probably got it from the pharmaceutical people who always visited her office. On the back, it says, *I love you.* I stare at it for a minute, not understanding. Why the hell is this in my sister's pillow?

My mind is leaping, my thoughts doing somersaults and backflips. Olga only had one boyfriend who I knew of—Pedro, a skinny, little guy who looked like an aardvark, but that was years ago. I seriously don't know what she saw in him, because not only was he ugly, he had the personality of a boiled potato. Even though I was only ten, I often wondered what was going on in that little brain of his.

Pedro was just as shy as Olga, so I don't know what they talked about. When he came to our family parties, my uncles would give him a hard time for being such a dork. I remember tío Cayetano trying to give him a shot of tequila once, and Pedro just shaking his head no. Most of the time, he'd pick Olga up on Friday nights and take her to dinner. Their favorite place was Red Lobster. Once, they even went to Great America (how riveting!). They dated for a year until he and his family moved back to Mexico (oh my God, who does that?). That was the last I knew about Olga's love life.

I tiptoe to her closet and start digging through her things as quietly as possible. One box is filled with photos from school. Most of them are of Olga and her friends during science fairs, field trips, and birthday parties. She was in the science club at school, and, for some reason, felt the need to document every single moment. I mean, there's even a picture of her holding a microscope. Jesus, my sister was boring. I keep sifting through the box when I feel some clothes. I can't be prepared for what I pull out—five pairs of silk-and-lace thongs. Sexy lady underwear, the kind I imagine a very expensive hooker might buy. At the very bottom, I find skimpy lingerie. I have no idea what it's called. A nightie? A negligee? A teddy? Such stupid names for things that are supposed to be sexy. Why would Olga have this in her closet? Why would she subject herself to these forever-wedgies when she didn't even have a boyfriend? Was this what she wore under her senior-citizen ensembles? Olga must have done a good job washing them in secret because, if Amá had found them in the laundry, she would have flipped the hell out.

I have to find her laptop now. I have two hours until my parents wake up.

I look everywhere, even the places I already searched. Finally, when I'm so tired I'm about to give up, I think to check the most obvious place of all—under her mattress, and there it is. Duh.

I know guessing a password is probably impossible, but I have to make an effort. I try a few things—her favorite food; our parents' hometown, Los Ojos; our address; her birthday; and even 12345, which only a complete moron would use. Oh, who am I kidding? This is impossible.

I go back to her dresser. There has to be something else in there. Her junk drawer is full of pens, paper clips, scraps of paper, receipts, old notebooks—nothing even remotely interesting. As I consider going back to sleep, I find an envelope under a pile of notecards. It feels like there's a credit card inside, but it's not. It's a hotel key. *The Continental,* it says. Except for our trips to Mexico, Olga has never, ever slept anywhere else. Why would she need a hotel key? Angie works at a hotel, but it's called something else. . . the Skyline, I think.

I hear someone open a door. Maybe Amá or Apá got up to pee. I flick off the light as quickly as possible and try not to move or breathe. If Amá catches me, she'll make sure I never get in here again.

The next thing I know, I wake up to the sound of someone in the kitchen. My pillow is wet. I must have fallen asleep before I could set an alarm on my phone. Holy shit, Amá is going to kill me. I make Olga's bed as fast as I can and press my ear to the door to make sure no one is near when I sneak back into my room.

Amá must have been wearing ninja shoes because, when I open the door, there she is with her hands on her hips.

THREE

I didn't know things could get any worse at home, but apparently they can. The apartment feels like the play *The House of Bernarda Alba,* but much less interesting. Just like the crazy and grieving mother, Amá keeps all the blinds and curtains drawn, which makes our cramped apartment even more stuffy and depressing.

Because of my punishment for going into Olga's room, all I can do is read, draw, and write in my journal. Amá also took away my phone. I can't even close my bedroom door because she opens it as soon as I do. When I tell her I need privacy, she laughs and tells me I've become too Americanized. "Privacy! I never had any privacy when I was a girl. You kids here think you can do whatever you want," she says.

I don't even know what she thinks I might do if I'm alone in my room. There's no way I'd try touching myself with her yelling and lurking all the time. I don't bother looking out the window because all I can see is the building next door. And now I can't go into Olga's room, not even at night when they're sleeping, because Amá installed a lock and I can't find the key. I've looked *everywhere.* As soon as I can bust out of here, I'm going to the Continental Hotel to see if I can find anything about Olga. I've tried calling Angie about a million times from a land line, and she still hasn't called me back. She has to know something.

I usually go inside my closet to cry so my parents don't hear me. Other times I just lie on my bed and stare at the ceiling, imagining the kind of life I want to have when I get older. I picture myself at the top of the Eiffel Tower, climbing pyramids in Egypt, dancing in the streets in Spain, riding in a boat in Venice, and walking on the Great Wall of China. In these dreams, I'm a famous writer who wears flamboyant scarves and travels all around the world, meeting fascinating people. No one tells me what to do. I go wherever I want and do whatever I please. Then I realize that I'm still in my tiny bedroom and can't even go outside. It's like a living death. I almost envy Olga, which I know is completely fucked up.

If I tell Amá that I'm bored, she tells me to pick up a mop and start cleaning. She doesn't believe in boredom when there's so much to do around the house, as if cleaning the apartment were as entertaining as a day at the beach. When she says stuff like this, I feel the anger bubble in my guts. Sometimes I love her and sometimes I hate her. Mostly, I feel a combination of both. I know it's wrong to hate your parents, especially when your sister is dead, but I can't help it, so I keep it to myself, and the resentment grows through me like weeds. I thought deaths were supposed to bring people together, but I guess that's just what happens on TV.

I wonder if other people feel this way. I asked Lorena once, but she said, "No, how could I possibly hate my own mother?" What was wrong with me? But that's probably because her mom lets her do whatever the hell she wants.

• • •

I don't like most of my teachers because they're as interesting as buckets of rocks, but English with Mr. Ingman is always fun. There's something about Mr. Ingman that I liked right away. He looks like a dorky suburban dad, but his eyes are friendly and his weird, jagged laugh is kinda funny. And he treats us like we're adults, like he actually cares about what we think and feel. Most teachers talk down to us, as if we're a bunch of immature dummies who don't know anything about anything. I don't know if anyone's told Mr. Ingman about my dead sister, because he doesn't look at me like he pities me.

As soon as we sit down today, Mr. Ingman makes us write down our favorite word and says we'll have to explain it to the rest of the class.

I've loved words since I learned how to read, but I've never thought about my favorite ones. How can you choose just one? I don't know why such a simple task makes me so nervous. It takes me a few minutes to come up with anything, then I can't stop.

Dusk
Serenity
Flesh
Oblivious
Vespers
Serendipitous
Kaleidoscope
Dazzle

Wisteria
Hieroglyphics
Sputter

By the time Mr. Ingman gets to me, I finally decide on *wisteria.*

"So what's yours, Julia?" Mr. Ingman nods toward me. He always says my name exactly how I pronounce it, the Spanish way.

"Yes, well, um. . . I had a lot of words, but in the end I picked *wisteria.*"

"What do you like about that word?" Mr. Ingman sits on his desk and leans forward.

"I don't know. It's a flower, and it. . . it just sounds beautiful. Also, it rhymes with *hysteria,* which I think is kinda cool. And maybe this sounds weird, but when I say it, I like the way it feels in my mouth."

I regret that last part because all the guys start laughing. I should have known.

Mr. Ingman shakes his head. "Come on, guys. Let's show Julia some respect. I expect you all to be kind to each other in this class. If you can't do that, I'll ask you to leave. Understand?"

The class quiets down. After we get through everyone, Mr. Ingman asks us why he made us do this exercise. A few people shrug, but no one says anything.

"The words you choose can tell us a lot about yourself," he says. "In this class, I want you to learn to appreciate—wait, no—I want you to *love* language. Not only will I expect you to read difficult texts and learn how to analyze them in smart and surprising ways, I expect you to learn hundreds of new words. See, I'm teaching you standard English, which is the language of power. What does that mean?" Mr. Ingman raises his eyebrows and looks around the room. "Anyone?"

The room is silent. I want to answer, but I'm too embarrassed. I see Leslie smirk next to me. What a jerk. She always looks like she's just sniffed a dirty diaper.

"It means that you will learn to speak and write in a way that will give you authority. Does that mean that the way you speak in your neighborhood is wrong? That slang is bad? That you can't say *on fleek* or whatever you kids are saying these days? Absolutely not. That form of speaking is often fun, inventive, and creative, but would it be helpful to speak that way in a job interview? Unfortunately not. I want you to think about these things. I want you to think about words in a way you've never done before. I want you to leave this class with the tools to compete with kids in the suburbs, because you're just as capable, just as smart."

After Mr. Ingman gives us a short lesson on the importance of American literature, the bell rings. This is definitely my favorite class.

On Saturday morning, Amá is making flour tortillas. I can smell the dough and hear the rolling pin from my bedroom when I wake up. Sometimes Amá lies in bed all day, and other times she's in a cooking-and-cleaning frenzy. It's impossible to predict. I know she's going to make me help her, so I stay in bed reading until she forces me to get up.

"Get up, huevona!" I hear her yelling from the other room. Amá calls me huevona all the time. She says I don't have the right to be tired, because I don't work cleaning houses all day like she does. I guess she has a point, but it's a weird thing to call a girl if you really think about it. Huevos means "eggs," so it means that your eggs (balls) are so big that they drag you down and make you lazy. Telling a girl her balls are too heavy is bizarre, but I never point this out because I know it will piss her off.

After I brush my teeth and wash my face, I go to the kitchen. Amá has already covered the table and counters with rolled-out tortillas. She's bent over the table, stretching a little ball of dough into a perfect circle.

"Put on an apron, and start heating these up," Amá says, pointing to the tortillas scattered throughout the kitchen.

"How do I know when they're done?"

"You just know."

"I don't know what that means."

"What kind of girl doesn't know when a tortilla is done?" She looks irritated already.

"Me. I don't. Please just tell me."

"You'll figure it out. It's common sense."

I study the tortillas as they heat on the comal and try to flip them before they burn. When I turn the first one, I see that I've left it too long. That side is almost burned. Amá tells me that the second one is too pale, that I have to leave it on longer, but when I do, it gets too crisp. When I burn the third one completely,

Amá sighs and tells me to roll them out instead, while she heats them. I take her rolling pin and try my best to shape the little balls into circles. Most of them end up in weird shapes, no matter how much I try to fix them.

"That one looks like a chancla," Amá says, looking at my worst one.

"It's not perfect, but it doesn't look like a slipper. Jesus." I feel myself grow more and more frustrated. I take a deep breath. I don't want to fight with her because I heard her crying in their bedroom last night.

"They have to be perfect."

"Why? We're just going to eat them. Why does it matter if they're not in perfect shape?"

“If you’re going to do something, you have to do it right, or else you shouldn’t do it at all,” Amá says, turning back to the stove. “Olga’s were always so nice and round.”

“I don’t care about Olga’s tortillas,” I say, throwing off my apron. I’ve had enough. “I don’t care about any of this crap. I don’t see the point of going through all this trouble when we can buy them at the store.”

“Get back here,” Amá yells after me. “What kind of woman are you going to be if you can’t even make a tortilla?”

After two weeks of no TV, no phone, and no going out whatsoever, Amá says maybe she’ll end my punishment today. Little does she know that I’m going to the Continental after school.

I'm tired of waiting for permission to go anywhere, and something about Olga is driving me crazy. Maybe I can convince Lorena to go with me.

I put on bright red lipstick, my favorite black dress, red fishnets, and black Chuck Taylors. I flat-iron my hair until it falls straight down my back. I don't even care that I look kinda fat or have a giant pimple throbbing on my chin. I'm going to try my best to have a good day. Well, as good as it can be when your sister is dead and you feel like you might lose your mind at any moment.

When Amá sees me come out of my room, she makes the sign of the cross and doesn't say anything—that's what she does when she hates what I'm wearing or I say something weird, which is always.

I put the leather journal Olga gave me for Christmas in my backpack. It was one of the most thoughtful gifts I've ever received. I guess even when it didn't seem like it, Olga was always paying attention.

When Amá drops me off at school, she kisses me on the cheek and reminds me that we have to start looking for a dress, that I can't show up to my party looking like I worship Satan.

Lorena meets me at my locker and gives me a hug before class. Sometimes I don't know how Lorena and I are still best friends. We're so different and look like complete opposites. People even look at us funny when they see us together. She likes spandex, and bright and crazy patterns and colors. She wears leggings as pants. I prefer band T-shirts, jeans, and dark dresses. Most of the clothes in my closet are black, gray, or red. When I started listening to New Wave and indie, Lorena got into hip-hop and R & B. We always argue about music—and everything else, for that matter—but I've known her forever and we understand each other in a weird way I can't describe. She can tell what I'm thinking just by looking at me. Lorena is ghetto, loud, and acts ignorant as hell sometimes, but I love her. She'll fight anyone who even looks at me funny. (One time, Faviola, a girl we've known since grade school, made fun of my pants, and Lorena knocked her desk over and told her she looked like a scared Chihuahua.)

The bell rings before I can ask Lorena to go downtown with me after school. I run to algebra before I'm late. Not only do I hate math with every fiber of my being, I suspect my teacher Mr. Simmons is a racist Republican. He has a handlebar mustache, and his desk is covered with American flags. He even has a tiny

Confederate one he probably thinks we don't notice. What kind of person would have something like that? He also has a dumb Ronald Reagan quote about jelly beans taped to the wall, which is another obvious clue: *You can tell a lot about a fellow's character by the way he eats jelly beans.* What does that even mean? How exactly do people eat jelly beans differently? Is that supposed to be deep or something? No one else seems to notice or care about these kinds of things, though. I tried to explain it to Lorena, but she just shrugged and said, "White people."

While Mr. Simmons goes on and on about integers, I work on a poem in my journal. I only have a couple of pages left.

Red ribbons unraveling
with the noise of my chaos.

A light beating like a drum.
I opened my wings and took
a swim in a warm, euphoric dream
of hands pressed to faces,
opened to the mad dancing
and combusted into a new constellation.
The dream too warm
for the flesh, too rough for the soft
touch of fingertips, holding my universe
in a single grasp. Everything sank, falling
to the ground, became blue.
The sunsets raining behind me
like a monsoon.

As I'm daydreaming about more images for my poem, Mr. Simmons calls on me, of course. He probably noticed my hatred for him pulsing around me.

"Julia, what is the answer to problem four?" He takes his glasses off and squints at me. He says my name the wrong way (*Jewlia*), even though I already told him how to pronounce it. Amá has never let me say it the English way. She says she's the one who named me and that people can't go around changing it for their own convenience. We agree on that, at least. It's not like it's hard to pronounce.

"I'm sorry. I don't know," I tell Mr. Simmons.

"Were you paying attention?"

"No, I wasn't. Sorry."

"And why not?"

My face feels hot. Everyone is watching me, waiting for my humiliation like vultures. Why can't he just back off? "Look, I said I was sorry. I don't know what else to tell you."

Mr. Simmons is really pissed now. "I want you to come to the board and solve the problem," he says, pointing at me. I guess he was never taught that it's impolite to point at people.

I want to get all Bartleby about it, tell him I don't fucking feel like it, but I know I shouldn't. I've gotten in enough trouble lately. But why does he have to pick on me? Doesn't he know my sister is dead? My heart is racing, and I can feel a thick pulse in my left cheek. I wonder if my face is twitching.

"No."

"What did you say to me?"

"I said no."

Now Mr. Simmons is pink as ham. His hands are on his hips, and he looks as though he wants to bash my skull. Before he says anything else, I shove my stuff into my backpack and run out the door. I can't deal with this today.

"Get back here right now, young lady," he yells after me, but I keep going. I can hear everyone screaming, laughing, and clapping as I walk out the door.

"Damn, son!" I hear Marcos yell.

"Oh hell no, she told *you*!" I think that's Jorge, which makes me almost forgive him for having a rattail.

The sky is clear—a blue so bright and beautiful that it hurts to look at it. Maybe I should've waited until the end of the day to see if I could convince Lorena to go with me, but there's no way I'm going back inside now. The birds are carrying on, and the streets smell like frying chorizo. Cars are honking. Men and women are selling fruit and corn from carts. Mexican music is blaring from every direction. Most of the time I hate walking through my neighborhood because of the gangbangers and guys whistling from their cars, but today nobody even looks at me.

I know I shouldn't have left school, but Amá is always talking about how it's a sin to waste this and that and it feels like a sin to waste a day like this. Besides, now I don't have to wait all day to go to the Continental.

As I walk to the bus, I watch a helicopter fly toward downtown until it disappears into a tiny black speck. I can see the hazy skyline in the distance. As long as I can find the Sears Tower, I know I can't get lost.

A green balloon floats past a power line, then gets tangled in a tree. I remember a movie I watched in first grade about a red balloon that chased a French boy throughout the streets of Paris. I imagine this balloon coming loose and chasing a little Mexican girl throughout the streets of Chicago.

I walk into the most unappetizing diner in the whole entire city. The counters are avocado green, and most of the stools are torn. Even the windows look greasy. It makes me feel like I went into a time machine. It reminds me of the painting *Nighthawks*, but even more depressing. I'm not sure where I am exactly—I think I'm near the South Loop.

I sit down at the counter, and the waitress asks me what I'll have in a thick European accent. Maybe she's Polish or from one of those other countries in Eastern Europe. I can't tell exactly. She looks tired but pretty in a way that doesn't call too much attention to itself, in a way that doesn't say, "Hey, hey, look at me!"

I only have $8.58 in my pocket, and I still have to get back on the bus or train, so I have to choose carefully. What I really want is this meal called "The Hobo," which is made of eggs, hash browns, cheese, and bacon—practically everything I love—but it's $7.99. I won't have enough left to get back home. I order a cheese Danish and a cup of coffee, even though the smell of bacon makes my mouth drip.

I read the newspaper on the counter while I drink my coffee, which is so awful I can barely stomach it. It tastes asif they boiled old socks and dumped the liquid into a coffeepot, but I gulp it down anyway because I'm not about to waste my two dollars. And the Danish is stale, of course. I should have seen that coming. I scoop out the cheese and eat it with my finger.

"Shouldn't you be in school?" the waitress asks as she refills my mug.

"Yeah, I should be, but one of my teachers was being a total jerk."

"Hmmm." She raises an eyebrow; she seems suspicious.

"He was, I swear."

"What did he do?"

"He called on me to solve a problem on the board. I didn't know the answer, but he kept insisting. It was so embarrassing." I realize how stupid this sounds when I say it out loud.

"That doesn't sound too bad," she says.

"Yeah, I guess it doesn't, huh?" We both laugh.

“Well, I think you should probably go back before you get in trouble.” She smiles.

“My sister is dead,” I blurt out.

“What?” she asks, as if she’s misheard.

“She died last month. I can’t concentrate. I guess that’s the real reason I left.”

“Oh no,” she says, her pretty face now sad and severe. Why did I tell her this? It’s not her problem. “You poor girl. I’m so sorry.”

“Thank you,” I say, still not knowing why I just told her about Olga. She squeezes my hand, then walks to a table behind me.

I write in my journal for a little while and try to figure out what to do next. Might as well make a day of it since I’m already going downtown. Whatever I do has to be free or close to it, or else I'll have to walk home. After some brainstorming and doodling, I decide on the Art Institute, which is one of my favorite places in the whole world. Well, in Chicago. I haven't seen much of the world yet. They have a suggested donation, but I never pay it. Key word: *suggested.*

When I ask the waitress for my bill, she tells me someone's already paid for me.

"What? Who? Wait, I don't understand."

"The man who was sitting over there." She points to an empty stool at the end of the counter. "He heard you were having a bad day."

I can't believe it. Why would someone do something like that without asking for anything in return? He didn't even hit on me or stare at my boobs or wait around for me to thank him. I run out to the street to find him, but it's too late. He's gone.

I take out my notebook and stare at the address for the Continental. I'm not very good with directions, but I think I can probably figure it out without a map. I walk northwest. It's not that hard when you know where the lake is. The buildings are blocking the sun, so it's starting to feel cold. I wish I would have brought a jacket.

A homeless man with no legs screams in front of a Starbucks. I think he's drunk because I can't understand what he's saying. Something about a llama? A mother and daughter brush past me with two giant American Girl bags. I've heard those dolls cost hundreds and hundreds of dollars. I can't wait until I have enough money to buy whatever the hell I want without worrying about every single penny. I, however, would never spend it on something as stupid as a doll.

The Continental is small but lavish, lots of blue and off-white. It's called a "boutique hotel," whatever the hell that means. The woman at the front desk hangs up the phone when I approach her. "Can I help you, miss?" Her hair is drawn into a slick, tight ponytail that looks like it hurts, and her perfume smells like a dusty flower in summer twilight.

"Did you ever see this girl come in here? She was my sister." I give her a picture of Olga at tía Cuca's barbecue a month before she died. She's holding a plate of food and smiling with her eyes closed. I figured it was best to use the most recent one I could find.

"I'm sorry, but we're not allowed to give any information about our guests." She smiles apologetically. I see a tiny smear of pink lipstick on her teeth.

"But she's dead."

She winces and shakes her head. "I'm so sorry."

"Can you at least tell me if you've seen her?"

"Again, I'm so, so sorry for your loss, but I can't. It's against our policy, sweetheart."

"Why would a policy matter if she's dead? Can you just look up her name? Olga Reyes. Please."

"The only people we're allowed to give information to is the police."

"Fuck," I mutter under my breath. I know it's not her fault, but I'm so frustrated. "Okay, well, can you at least tell me if this hotel is connected to the Skyline? Are they owned by the same company?"

"Yes, they're a part of the same conglomerate. Why do you ask?"

"Thanks." I walk out the door, without bothering to explain.

Before entering the museum, I take a walk around the gardens outside. Everyone is desperately trying to hang on to the sunshine, enjoying the unexpected warmth before winter takes a cold gray crap on the city and makes us all miserable again.

Though the trees are changing colors, flowers are still in bloom, and there are bees everywhere. Everything is so perfect I wish I could keep it in a jar. A young woman in a flowered dress is breastfeeding her baby. A man with long gray hair is lying on a bench, with his head on his wife's lap. A couple is making out against a tree. For a split second, my mind tricks me into believing the girl is Olga, because they have the same long ponytail, skinny body, and flat butt, but when she turns around, she looks nothing like my sister.

When I tell the woman at the counter that I will pay zero dollars instead of the suggested donation, she eyeballs me as if I were some sort of criminal.

"Don't we all have a right to art? Are you trying to keep me from an education? That seems very bourgeoisie, if you ask me." I learned that word in history class last year and try to use it whenever it's appropriate, because Mr. Ingman always tells us that language is power.

The woman just sighs, rolls her eyes, and hands me the ticket. She probably hates her job. I know I would.

I walk over to my favorite painting, *Judith Slaying Holofernes.* We learned about the artist, Artemisia Gentileschi, in art class last year. My teacher Ms. Schwartz told us something bad happened to her, but wouldn't tell us what, so I looked it up after class. It turns out that her painting teacher raped her when she was seventeen. What a scumbag.

Almost all the Renaissance and Baroque paintings we studied in class were of baby Jesus, which is not very interesting, so when I saw Artemisia Gentileschi's paintings of biblical women killing all those horrible men, my heart trembled. She was such a bad ass. Every time I see *Judith Slaying Holofernes*, I notice something new. That's what's so great about art and poetry—right when you think you "get it," you see something else. You can find a million hidden meanings. What I love most about the painting is that Judith and her maid are slicing off the man's head, but they don't even look scared. They're totally casual, as if they're just washing dishes or something. I wonder if that's how it really happened.

When Ms. Schwartz said that one of her paintings was at our museum, I decided I needed to see it right away. This is my fourth time this year. I love art almost as much as I love books. It's hard to explain the way I feel when I see a beautiful painting. It's a combination of scared, happy, excited, and sad all at once, like a soft light that glows in my chest and stomach for a few seconds. Sometimes it takes my breath away, which I didn't know was a real thing until I stood in front of this painting. I used to think it was just some saying in pop songs about stupid people in love. I had a similar feeling when I read an Emily Dickinson poem. I was too excited and threw my book across the room. It was so good that it made me angry. People would think I'm nuts if I try to explain it to them, so I don't.

I crouch down to get a better look at the bottom part, which I never paid much attention to before. The blood is dripping on the white sheet, and the fibers of the silk are so delicately painted that it's hard to believe they aren't real.

I can't get enough of this place. I can be here forever and ever, studying all the art and walking up and down the dramatic marble staircases. I love the Thorne Miniature Rooms, too. I can spend hours imagining a tiny version of myself living in those fancy, little houses. I always have to come to the museum alone, though, because no one will ever join me. I tried dragging Lorena once, but she just laughed and called me a nerd. I suppose I can't argue with that. I asked Olga one time, but she was going shopping with Angie that day.

As I wander around, I find a painting I've never noticed before—*Anna Maria Dashwood, later Marchioness of Ely* by Sir Thomas Lawrence. I gasp when I see the woman's face, because my sister's eyes are staring back at me. I never paid attention to that expression before—neither joyous nor somber, but as if she were trying to tell me something.

I walk around and around, and lose track of time. I look at my favorite paintings again—*The Old Guitarist* by Pablo Picasso, the *Cybernetic Lobster Telephone* by Salvador Dalí, and the one made of dots by Georges Seurat. Every time I see it, I promise myself

I'll go to Paris some day. I'll roam through the city by myself, eating cheese until I burst.

It's rush hour when I finally get on the train to go back home. The bus is too unreliable at this time. All the men and women in suits are all sweaty and tired. If I end up being an office lady who wears slacks and changes into white sneakers to walk home from the train, I'll just jump off a skyscraper.

The train is crammed with people, but I find a window seat facing backward, next to a man in a filthy coat, who smiles and says, "Good evening," when I sit down. He smells like pee, but at least he has good manners. I take out my journal to make some notes. I love to watch the city from above—the graffiti on factories, the honking cars, the old buildings with shattered windows, everyone in a hurry. It's exciting to see all the movement and energy. Even though I want to move far away from here, moments like these make me love Chicago.

A couple of black kids near the doors start beat-boxing, which makes a man frown and shake his head. I think it sounds amazing, though. I wonder how they can make that kind of music with their mouths. How can they sound exactly like machines?

I go back to the poem I started in Mr. Simmons's class, when a woman with a burned face makes her way through the crowded aisle, asking everyone to spare some change. When she gets closer, I see that her green T-shirt says *God Has Been So Good to Me!* The letters are so bright and shiny, they feel like they're yelling. She puts her hand in front of me, and I reach into my backpack to pull out the rest of the money I have left. The mystery guy at the diner paid for my food today, so why not?

"Have a blessed day," she says, and smiles. "Jesus loves you."

He doesn't, but I smile back anyway.

I look out the window and watch the skyline lit up by the evening sun. The buildings reflect a dazzling orange-red, and if you glance, it almost looks like the buildings are on fire.

I bet the school has already called my parents and I'm in some deep shit again. It was worth it, though. I open my journal to a blank page and write, *God Has Been So Good to Me!* before I forget.

FOUR

On Saturday afternoon, I tell Amá I'm going to the library, but I walk to Angie's house instead. I've called her a million times and she hasn't called me back. It's pissing me off. I'm not sure what I'm going to say, but I need to talk to her. I keep thinking of Olga's underwear, the hotel key, and that strange smirk on her face when she died. For weeks, I've had this feeling that won't leave me alone, like tiny needles in the back of my head. Maybe Angie can tell me something about my sister that I don't know.

It's beginning to get chilly now. The air smells like leaves and the promise of rain. I hate this time of year. When it begins to get dark earlier in the day, I start feeling more depressed than usual. All I ever want to do is take a scalding shower and read in bed until I fall asleep. The long, dark days feel like endless black ribbon. This year will be even worse now that Olga is gone.

Angie and Olga met when they were in kindergarten, so I've known Angie my whole life. I used to admire her because she's so stylish and pretty, with her wild, curly hair and wide green eyes that look forever surprised. In high school, she drew pictures of exotic landscapes that Olga taped to her walls. Though she is poor, like us, she has a sharp fashion sense, matching unusual colors and patterns in ways that somehow make sense. She makes outfits from the flea market look good on her. She smells like vanilla, and her laugh reminds me of wind chimes. I always thought Angie would grow up to be something awesome, like a designer or an artist, but it turned out she was another Mexican daughter who didn't want to leave home. She works downtown and still lives with her parents.

Angie's mom, Doña Ramona, answers the door and gives me a wet kiss on the cheek. Although I've known her forever, I still get startled, because she looks old enough to be Angie's grandma. I'm guessing that on top of having Angie late in life, she also had some tough times. "Está acabada," Amá always says, a word that makes me think of an old, dirty dish sponge. Every time I see Doña Ramona, I swear to God, she's wearing an apron. She probably goes to church in it.

The house smells like roasted chiles, and it's so warm that my glasses fog. My eyes begin to water, and I cough uncontrollably. It happens every time Amá is making a certain kind of salsa.

"Ay, mija, que delicada," Doña Ramona says, slapping me on the back. "Let me call Angie and bring you a glass of water." Everyone likes to remind me how sensitive I am, as if I didn't know. "How are you feeling these days?" she yells from the kitchen. "Angie has taken this very hard, pobrecita."

"I'm better, thank you."

I think Angie's family may be the last on earth to have plastic covers on their sofas. On top of that, there are porcelain dolls on doilies on nearly every surface of the house. Mexican ladies are always knitting doilies for everything—doilies for the TV, doilies for vases, doilies for useless knickknacks. Doilies as far as the eye can see! How pointless. This is what Amá would call "naco." We may be poor, but at least we're not this tacky.

When Angie finally comes out of her room, she's wearing

a ratty gray robe and her hair is matted and greasy. Her eyes are bright red, as if she'd been crying all night. It's been several weeks now, and she still looks like a disaster. She doesn't seem pleased to see me.

Angie hugs me and tells me to sit down. The plastic cover squeaks under me. Doña Ramona gives me a glass of water and shuffles back to the kitchen to continue her cooking.

"How have you been?" I ask, though she probably looks the way she feels.

"Jesus, Julia. How do you think?" she snaps. Angie is nice to me most of the time, but I guess Olga's death has scrambled her up, too. No one is the same anymore. "I'm sorry. I didn't mean that. It's just. . . I can't sleep. Look at me. I look horrible," she says.

Angie is right. The dark purple rings under her eyes make her look like someone punched her out. "Ojerosa," Amá would say.

"No, you're fine," I lie. "Just as pretty as always." I try smiling, but it's so fake, it hurts my face.

Angie glares at me, and the silence grows like a web around us. I hear something in the kitchen crackling in grease, which almost sounds like rain. The clock ticks and ticks. At moments like this, the concept of time confuses me. A minute lasts an hour.

"Can we go to your room?" I finally whisper. "I want to ask you something in private."

Angie looks confused, but says okay and leads me down the hall.

I can tell Angie isn't wearing a bra, and I try not to stare, but I can see her nipples through her robe, which reminds me of the time I walked in on her touching Olga's boobs when I was seven. As soon as they saw me open the door, Olga pulled down her shirt and looked down at the floor. All I remember is that she seemed ashamed and that her boobs were small and pointy.

I sit on Angie's unmade bed. It smells like she hasn't washed her sheets in a few weeks, and the floor is covered with clothes. There are pictures of her and Olga all over her walls and dresser: at the park, in a photo booth, grade school, prom, graduation, dinners. She also has the program from the wake and funeral on her nightstand. It has an angel and some stupid prayer about heaven. I threw mine in the garbage because I couldn't bear to look at it anymore.

"You miss her, huh?" I ask.

"Yeah, of course." Angie stares at the picture of her and Olga in their graduation gowns. "What did you want to ask me?"

"Why haven't you returned any of my calls?"

Angie sighs. "I haven't wanted to talk to anyone these days."

"Well, I'm not exactly feeling social myself, but I'm her sister, and the least you could've done is call me back."

Angie stares at her pictures and says nothing.

"Was it you that Olga was texting when she died?"

"Huh?"

"Was it you?"

"Look, I don't know." Angie rubs her eyes and yawns. "Why does that even matter? She's gone."

"Either it was you or it wasn't. It's not that complicated. She was hit at about 5:30. You would know by looking at your phone. It's not like my sister had that many friends."

"What exactly are you looking for, Julia?"

"I just feel there's something I don't know."

"Like what?"

"I have no idea. That's what I'm trying to find out." I feel exasperated. Maybe this was a mistake. What can I tell Angie? That I went through Olga's room and found slutty underwear and a hotel key? That I never had a real interest in her until she died because I'm a horrible and selfish human being?

Angie looks up at the ceiling, as if she's trying not to cry. I've done that a million times. I'm the master of keeping my tears inside my ducts.

"I found some weird underwear and a hotel key," I say. "The Continental."

Angie tightens her robe and looks down at her chipped pink toenails. "And?"

"What do you mean, *and*? Call me crazy, but that's pretty strange."

"Julia, you're always exaggerating. I don't know what you mean by 'weird' underwear."

"*Weird* as in 'skanky.'" I'm starting to lose my patience. "And a hotel key? When did Olga ever go anywhere? Why would she have that?"

"How would I know?" Angie rolls her eyes, which pisses me off.

"Because you were her best friend, duh."

"You know, Julia, you're always causing trouble, creating

problems for your family. Now that she's dead, all of a sudden you want to know everything about her? You hardly even spoke to her. Why didn't you ask her anything when she was alive? Maybe you wouldn't have to be here, asking me questions about her love life."

"Love life? So you're telling me she was dating someone?"

"No, that's not what I'm saying. You're putting words in my mouth."

"But you just said—"

"Julia, you need to get going. I have things to do." Angie gets up and opens the door.

If I weren't so dark, my face would be a dazzling red. It feels as if someone dumped a bucket of boiling water over my head. Angie doesn't understand how hard it's been for me to speak to anyone in my family. She hasn't seen how the silence and tension have been smothering us for years. She doesn't get that I feel like a three-headed alien in my own home. And why is Angie so defensive? Something isn't right, but I don't know what to say. What exactly should I demand? I just keep sitting in her grimy room, with the taste of chile lodged in my throat, while the guilt and anger spread through me like lava.

"Okay, this is pointless," I say. "Thank you so much, Angie. Thank you for being so nice and supportive."

"Julia, stop. Look, I'm sorry. This has been hard for me. I feel like I'm falling apart." Angie puts her head in her hands.

"You lost your best friend, but I lost my sister. You think I'm just some selfish, narcissistic kid, but my life fucking sucks right now. Every night I expect Olga to come home, and she doesn't.

I just stare at the door like a fool."

Angie doesn't respond. As I leave her room, Doña Ramona comes rushing toward me, her slippers flap-flap-flapping on the linoleum. That has to be one of the most irritating noises I've ever heard.

"Aren't you going to eat, mija? Come, sit. I'm making sopes," she insists.

"No gracias, señora. I'm not hungry."

Her worn brown face crumples with worry. "What's wrong, criatura? Are you crying?"

"No, the chiles are burning my eyes," I lie.

FIVE

After school, Lorena and I go to her house to do some Internet snooping, so I call Amá and tell her that I'll be home late because we're working on a project. At first, she says no, because she's still mad about me ditching school, but when I explain to her that my (imaginary) group assignment is due tomorrow, she gives in. Amá doesn't let me go anywhere unless I have a specific reason. If I tell her that I want to spend some time with a friend, she asks me what for and says she doesn't want me in other people's cocinas, which is stupid. First, I don't understand why she thinks it's so scandalous to be in other people's kitchens. Second, most of the time we're not even in the kitchen—we're in the living room.

Amá doesn't have any friends and sees no point to having any. She says all a woman needs is her family. According to her, only orphans and whores run around in the streets by themselves. If Amá isn't working, shopping for groceries, or cooking and cleaning at home, she's usually with my aunts or her comadre, Juanita, who is also her cousin. Oh, and on Saturdays and Sundays, she's at church. She hardly leaves our neighborhood. Her world seems small, in my opinion, but that's how she wants it. Maybe it runs in the family, because Olga was like that, too, and Apá's favorite place is our couch.

Instead of trying to convince Amá that I need to go out and talk to people I'm not related to, I often make up homework assignments. Sometimes it works. Sometimes it doesn't.

Lorena dumps the hot chips we bought at the corner store

into a big bowl and squeezes lime juice over them until they're completely drenched. We eat them quickly, as if it's some sort of race. Our fingers are stained red and our noses are runny by the time we're finished. Even though I eat half a giant bag, I still want more. I ask Lorena if she has any more food, but she says no. My stomach grunts.

I can only eat junk food in secret because it's forbidden in our house. I guess it's ironic that Apá works at a candy factory. Amá says Americans eat nothing but garbage, which is why everyone here is so fat and ugly. She has the perfect body and expects everyone to be as lucky as she is. She's never taken us to McDonald's, not even once, but no one ever believes me. Sometimes, when I walk home from school, I buy a dollar cheeseburger and eat it in three bites before I get to our door. That's probably why I've been getting kind of porky. My boobs keep getting heavier and heavier, and sometimes hurt my back. Amá says there's no need for burgers and fries when we have a pot of beans and packets of tortillas at home. Whenever I ask her if we can order pizza or Chinese food, she says I'm spoiled and tells me to make myself a quesadilla. Other times she pinches my stomach and walks away from me without saying anything.

"So, what do you want to look for?" Lorena takes a pitcher of water from the fridge.

"I'm not sure, to be honest. I haven't told you, but I went through her things the other day."

"And?"

"I found some underwear. Like, *hooker* underwear."

"What are you even talking about?" Lorena seems annoyed.

She says I exaggerate everything.

"They were scandalous. Thongs and this lingerie-type thing."

"Hello? I wear thongs, too." Lorena rolls her eyes.

"But this is Olga we're talking about. She didn't even swear. Amá would've snapped if she'd found them. She hates stuff like that. She doesn't even like it when women wear shorts."

"So what if she wanted to feel sexy? She was a grown woman."

"Okay, well, how would you explain the hotel key I found?" I pull it out of my backpack. "This," I say, and I throw it on the table.

"I don't know. Maybe she used it as a bookmark or something. Doesn't Angie work at a hotel?"

"Yeah, but not this one. Something's not right, I'm telling you."

"I think you're probably wasting your time." Lorena walks to her room and brings me her laptop from her bedroom. It weighs about a hundred pounds. It was a hand-me-down from her cousin, and it's old as hell.

"What do you want to look for?"

"I don't know. Facebook, I guess, but I don't know if Olga even used it. I'm telling you, she was an old lady trapped in a twenty-two-year-old's body."

"You're not on it, either."

"Yeah, because it's stupid. People are boring enough in real life without having to see how boring they are online. Plus, I don't have Internet, so what's the point? I'm not about to go to the library to use it."

Lorena shakes her head and enters her password.

I search for Olga's name, but there are twelve Olga Reyeses. I click on each one, but none of them resemble my sister.

"Maybe she used a different name?"

"How would I know what name she used?"

"I don't know. Why don't you look through Angie's page and see if you can find her or go through her pictures or something?"

We find Angie, but when we click on her profile, everything is private. All we see is the profile picture of her and Olga when they were kids. The caption says, *I miss you, friend.*

"Damn it, Angie's useless."

"Do you know any other friends, like, from work or something?"

"Not really. She used to have lunch with this girl sometimes. Denise, I think. But I don't know her last name." Defeated, I close the laptop.

While Lorena fiddles with her phone and begins playing her horribly sexist rap songs, I walk over to the altar her mom has set up in the corner of the living room. I like to see the way it changes every time I come over. Lorena's mom worships Santa Muerte, the scary skeleton saint, and if Amá knew about this, she'd never let me see Lorena again in my life. She already dislikes her mom because she thinks she wears way too much makeup and dresses like a teenager. I guess she's right—Lorena's mom's eye shadow is heavy, and her eyeliner curls up from the corners of her eyes. She kind of looks like a homely Cleopatra. Most of the time, she wears skintight spandex dresses that make her body resemble a soft-serve ice cream cone. Not at all flattering.

Lorena takes after her mom when it comes to makeup. She also dyes and highlights her hair, so it ends up a mixture of yellow, orange, and red. The colors remind me of flames, and when she wears her hair in a ponytail, she almost looks like a torch. She's prettier with dark hair, but she doesn't listen to me. She says I don't know what the hell I'm talking about, that why should she listen to me when I dress like a homeless lesbian? She ignores me about her hazel contacts, too. Anyway, Lorena and her mom make questionable choices when it comes to their looks, and Amá always feels the need to point them out, as if I didn't already notice. "That old lady shouldn't be running around like a quinceañera. She has no shame," Amá whispers to me. Although Lorena's mother isn't the best parent, and she looks lumpy and nuts, she's always been nice to me, feeding me cookies or cake whenever I see her. A few days after Olga died, she took Lorena and me out for ice cream.

Today Santa Muerta is wearing a red satin dress. Last time she wore a black cloak, which wasn't as scary, because what else would a skeleton wear? In front of the doll, there are three fresh candles, a pack of cheap cigarettes, an open can of Tecate, a bowl of apples, and a white rose starting to brown at the edges. There's also a new framed picture of Lorena's dad riding a brown horse. Lorena looks exactly like him when she smiles. Even though Lorena's mom has been with her boyfriend, José Luis, for years now, she still has her dead husband's pictures hanging everywhere. When Olga died, Lorena's mom asked for a picture of her so she could pray for her soul, but I thought it was too bizarre, so I pretended I forgot.

Lorena never talks about her dad, and I never ask about him, because it's really none of my business. It's up to her if she wants to talk about him. I don't like to pry. The only reason I know what happened to him is because, a few months ago, she and I got shit-faced after school, and it spilled out like a sack of fallen beans.

After about the fourth glass of Alizé, which her cousin had bought for us, Lorena started crying out of nowhere. Maybe it was the mariachi song with the sad trumpets that was playing on the radio, I don't know. I asked her what was wrong, and between sobs and gulps of the syrupy booze, she told me that she missed her dad. She was crying so hard that I could barely understand her. Her mascara started streaming down her face, which made her look like a grotesque clown. It would've been funny under different circumstances, like the time we got caught in the rain and her makeup smeared like a gasoline rainbow and we had to go back to her house to fix it.

I didn't know what to say, so I kept rubbing her back and smoothing her hair. After she calmed down a little, she was able to tell me the story, but I think I missed some bits and pieces because of the crying. Lorena said that when she was seven years old, her dad went back to Mexico for his mother's funeral, even though everyone told him not to. He had lived in Chicago for ten years, but still didn't have his papers. In order for him to return to the U.S., he had to cross the border with a coyote, just like he had the first time. Lorena's mom even dreamt about it the night before he left, so she knew something bad was going to happen. In the dream, an eagle pecked at his heart while he sat there watching it. She begged him not to go, told him he'd die, but he didn't listen. He said he loved his madrecita too much.

After his mother's funeral, Lorena's dad took the bus from Guerrero all the way to the Arizona border, where he met a man from his hometown who everyone had recommended. This coyote took all their money and then abandoned the entire group of mojados while they walked through the desert. They got lost for two days, and the seven in the group, including a baby, eventually died of thirst. Border Patrol found them all two weeks after they were supposed to arrive on the other side, and shipped his decomposed body to his hometown in Mexico, where they buried him. Lorena and her mom never got to see him again. That's when I started to understand why Lorena is so fucked up. My parents crossed the border like that, too, and even got robbed, but at least they made it here alive.

As I study her dad's pictures in the living room, Lorena starts rolling a joint at the kitchen table. She's so much better at it than I am, basically a professional.

"What are you doing?" she asks, without looking up. "Why do you keep staring at pictures of my dad?"

I don't know how to answer because I'm not sure why—curiosity, I suppose. "Doesn't José Luis feel weird about all of these pictures still here?" I finally ask.

"I don't care what that motherfucker thinks," Lorena says, and licks the joint. "You want some or what?" She hands it to me.

I've smoked weed a total of five times now, and every single time, I start worrying about the stupidest things. The last time we smoked I thought the police were knocking on the door. The time before that, Lorena was on her phone and I was convinced she was texting mean things about me. But I keep smoking because I'm hoping that one day it will feel good, that I'll be all floaty and calm, like everyone says.

"I wonder if Olga ever smoked weed," I say.

"Olga? Are you kidding me? No way. That girl was practically a nun."

"Yeah, I'm not sure about that anymore." I take a hit, and it makes me cough so hard my eyes water. I run to the kitchen for a drink. Lorena laughs and throws a couch pillow at my face as I walk back to the living room. It nearly knocks the glass out of my hands. I start laughing, too, and dump the rest of my water on her head.

"You're such a bitch!" Lorena screams. "You wet the couch!" She's still kinda smiling, though, so I know she's not really mad.

"You started it!"

Lorena walks to her room and comes back wearing a different shirt. She changes the music to narcocorridos, those horrible Mexican songs about drug traffickers who buy diamond-encrusted guns and cut each other's heads off.

When the first song winds down, the feeling suddenly clicks inside me—everything is in slow motion, and my body is light and heavy at the same time. It's different from the times before. I'm not paranoid, just a little confused and unfocused. My contacts are so dry it's hard to keep my eyes open.

Lorena takes a few hits before passing it back to me. I shake my head no.

"That's it?"

"I can't."

"You can't be high already."

"I am, so leave me alone, and if I go home like this, my mom is going to ship me to Mexico for the rest of my life. . . . God-damn it, this quinceañera. What a pain in theass."

"Oh my God, get over it. I wish I could've had one, but my mom is always broke as hell."

"I don't even know where they're getting the money. All they ever do is complain about how poor we are. It's like they want to pretend everything is fine. They just want to put on a show for the rest of the family."

"I can't imagine you in one of those dresses." Lorena laughs. "I don't know what your mom is thinking. It's like she doesn't know you at all. Or she doesn't care."

"I know. The party isn't for me; it's for my sister. It's not even my freaking birthday. Can you believe that?"

"Come on, let's look at some dresses. Maybe you'll find one you like," she says, and reaches for her laptop.

"Doubt it."

Lorena pulls up some websites and begins scrolling through dresses. All of them are atrocious, a few even rainbow-colored. When we get to a ladybug-pattern abomination, I'm done. I just can't. They should be classified as crimes against humanity. They should be tried in a court of law. "Stop, please. Before I vomit my chips."

Lorena sighs and begins plucking her eyebrows in front of a small hand mirror. I close my eyes for what feels like minutes, and when I open them again, I become hypnotized by the cheetah-print pattern on her leggings, which I hadn't noticed before. I am soooooo high. The more I look, the more shapes I see—faces, cars, flowers, trees, babies, clowns—and then, for some reason, I start imagining Lorena as a cheetah running through a forest. It's her same head but on a cheetah's body. This weed must be excellent. I laugh so hard I can hardly speak. It hurts but feels good to finally laugh again.

"What is it? Why are you laughing?" Lorena is confused. I try to explain, but I can't catch my breath. Tears are streaming down my face. "What is wrong with you?"

I try to tell her, but I can't get the words out. My face is hot, and my stomach muscles are aching. "You're a cheetah," I finally manage to say, gasping for air.

"A what?"

"A cheetah!"

"I don't know what you're saying!"

"A cheetah!" I say.

Maybe the laughter is contagious or Lorena is high now, too, because she starts laughing harder than I am. I try to think of things that are not funny—socks, cancer, sports, genocide, my dead sister—anything to get me to calm down before I pee my pants. Lorena puts a pillow over her face to control herself and muffle the noise, but it's no use. She's silent for a moment, and then a loud cackle escapes from her, which gets me going again. I cross my legs hard. I hope I can make it to the bathroom.

That's when we hear the door open.

Lorena said that her mom was working, and that José Luis wasn't supposed to come home for several more hours because he was picking up an extra shift, but here he is, walking in as we lie on the couch, high as hell. Lorena looks as if she's about to commit murder.

"What are you doing home already? I thought you were working." Lorena doesn't seem worried about the weed, just pissed that he's there.

"Business was slow, and the boss told me to go home," José Luis explains in his singsongy style. He's Chilango, which means he's from Mexico City, which means he has a super-annoying accent.

"What are you girls doing?" he asks, as if we're all sharing a secret. It makes me feel gross.

Neither one of us bothers to answer.

José Luis has been Lorena's stepdad—step-boyfriend—for about four years now. She said that when he and her mom met, he'd just crossed the border, so he was the freshest kind of mojado. Now José Luis works as a busboy at a few different restaurants on Taylor Street, which is why he's always talking shit about Italians, always going on and on about how cheap they are. He and Lorena's mom are the most mismatched couple in the world, because he's fifteen years younger than she is, making him only ten years older than Lorena. Weird. He'd be handsome, if he weren't so sleazy. Every time I know he's going to be home, I wear my baggiest shirts and sweaters so he can't gawk at my boobs. Sometimes it feels like he's undressing us with his eyes.

José Luis is always lounging around the house in an undershirt, listening to norteñas and polishing his pointy crocodile-skin boots. Instead of leaving us alone like any normal dad, he's always asking us dumb questions about music, school, and boys. I wish he'd just shut up and leave us alone. I know José Luis is a creep, because last year Lorena told me he saw her going to the bathroom in the middle of the night and pushed her against the wall and kissed her. She said he crammed his tongue inside her mouth all nasty and she could feel his penis against her leg.

"I would have cut his balls off," I told her, but Lorena looked more depressed than mad, and didn't respond. The next day Lorena told her mom what happened, but she just said that she was probably dreaming and went back to cooking dinner.

José Luis makes himself a sandwich, then goes into his bedroom. Lorena and I watch a reality show about a bunch of rich kids living in New York. It's stupid, but I try going along with it for Lorena's sake. I'm also curious because I want to move to New York for college. Ever since I was little, I imagined myself living in an apartment in the middle of Manhattan, writing late into the night.

I keep watching until one of the blond girls cries because her mom won't buy her a pair of shoes that cost more than my entire life. It's too much to take. I feel spiritually nauseated.

"This is garbage," I tell Lorena. "Isn't there anything else more enlightening we could watch? Is there anything on PBS? Any documentaries?" But she just ignores me.

When the show is over, Lorena goes into the bathroom for

a long time. I can hardly stay awake. I close my eyes, and, after a few minutes, I feel something near me. Maybe their cat, Chimuela, finally came out from under the bed. When I open my eyes, though, I see José Luis crouched in front of me. He looks like he's doing something with his phone, but I'm not sure. Am I imagining this? Am I that high? I don't know what's going on. I cross my legs and pull my skirt down, and when I open my eyes, I'm alone again.

Every Saturday night, Amá and Olga attended a prayer group in the church basement. Mostly, it's a bunch of Mexican ladies sitting in a circle, complaining about their problems and talking about how God will help them endure. The few times

I did go, I was so bored I wanted to tear out all of my hair. We were there for three hours, and I couldn't take it anymore. I asked Amá if I could read the book I had in my bag, but she said it was impolite. When it was her turn to speak, Amá started telling the group about missing Mexico, her mother, and her dead father. She cried a lot, which made me feel guilty for complaining. Olga held her hand and told her everything was going to be okay, while I sat there like a slug, not knowing what to do.

Amá was always trying to force me and Apá to go to these meetings, but we refused. Who in the world would want to spend their Saturday night talking about God? It's bad enough that she drags us to mass every Sunday morning. After hounding us for a few years, she finally gave up. One Saturday night, Apá let me order Chinese food, which was gloriously greasy. We had to throw the boxes away in the alley so Amá wouldn't find out. We lied and told her we had eaten eggs for dinner.

Amá hadn't been to the prayer group since Olga died. There is no way I'd go, but I'm glad Amá decides to attend tonight and is out of the house. On her days off, she lies in bed for hours and hours, and I worry that she'll never get up again.

As soon as Amá leaves, I always ask Apá if I can go out, because he usually shrugs and tells me that if Amá found out, she'd be angry, but I just assume that means yes. I run out the door before he can protest.

Lorena and Carlos, the new guy she's talking to, are supposed to pick me up at 7:30. She promised she'd make Carlos take us to his cousin Leo's house because he's a Chicago cop and might be able to help with Olga. I'm going to ask him how I can get more information about Olga at the Continental.

Carlos is seventeen and drives an old and battered red car with giant silver rims, which seems ridiculous to me. Why would you spend so much money on rims, when the car is about to fall apart? But I'm not complaining. At least it's a ride.

When I get close, I notice someone in the backseat. A guy. Lorena didn't tell me anyone else was coming. I get nervous and tug at my ponytail. I'm not wearing any makeup, and my hoodie is old and faded. I didn't even bother to look remotely attractive.

Lorena gives me an apologetic smile. "There was a change of plans. Leo had to work. And he said he couldn't help. We asked him, I swear to God. Julia, this is Ramiro, Carlos's cousin from Mexico. He's cute, right?"

"Are you serious, Lorena? Goddamn it, you're unbelievable sometimes," I tell her, then turn to Ramiro to say hello. It's not his fault, after all.

"Nice to meet you," he says in Spanish, and kisses me on the cheek the Mexican way.

Ramiro has long, curly hair, which I don't care for, but I guess his face is okay. I do my best to ignore his pleather pants, too. He's trying so hard it's embarrassing.

He only speaks Spanish, which makes me nervous. I speak it fine, of course, but I sound ten times smarter in English. My vocabulary is just not as extensive, and sometimes I get stuck. I hope he doesn't think I'm dumb, because I'm not.

Lorena and Carlos tell me we're going to the lake. This was not the plan, and it's freezing outside. It doesn't seem like a good idea, but I don't argue because I don't want to piss off Lorena.

When we arrive at North Avenue Beach, Lorena and Carlos run off, leaving Ramiro and me standing awkwardly by ourselves. Ramiro blows on his hands. I wrap my arms around myself under my jacket. After a few minutes, he starts playing with his phone, and I watch the beautiful lights reflected on the water. I kind of wish I were there by myself.

When the silence becomes almost unbearable, Ramiro asks me about my favorite music. I tell him I mostly like indie and New Wave, but he doesn't know what those are, and they're hard to explain in Spanish.

"You've never heard of Joy Division?"

He shakes his head.

"What about New Order?"

"No."

"Neutral Milk Hotel? Death Cab for Cutie? Sigur Rós?"

He shakes his head and smiles.

"What do you like?"

"Spanish rock. My favorite band is El Tri," he says, unzipping his jacket and showing me his T-shirt.

"Ugh. Are you serious? I'd rather listen to dogs barking for ten hours than listen to him for five minutes. I can't believe that's your favorite band." Geez, what a turnoff.

"Wow. Okay, then," he says, turning away from me and looking toward the skyline.

Lorena says I'm always blowing it with guys because of my big mouth. She thinks I need to give people a chance and be less of an asshole. I guess she's right because I think I hurt Ramiro's feelings.

"I'm sorry. That was so rude," I say. "El Tri is a very well-respected band. Although they're not really my style, I'm sure they're talented. Sometimes I don't know when to shut up. It's a medical condition. They say it's incurable, like AIDS."

This makes him laugh. "I hope everyone continues to fight for the cure," he says.

"Yes, me too."

Ramiro and I watch the water for a few minutes without speaking. The sound of the waves is soothing, and for a while, I forget everything—who I'm with, who I am, where I live.

All I can think of is that sound. I think that's what meditation is supposed to be. I remember reading that in a book once. I stay in that trance until an ambulance races down Lake Shore Drive behind us. I search for Lorena and Carlos, but they're nowhere in sight. I bet they're probably fucking somewhere, even in this cold, and most likely without a condom, even though I've told Lorena a million times that she's out of her mind.

"Lorena tells me your sister died," Ramiro says out of nowhere. "That must be really hard."

"It's okay," I say, even though it's not. That's just what you're supposed to say. I'm fine! I'm fine! I'm fine!

"How did she die? If you don't mind me asking."

I do mind, but I tell him anyway. “She got hit by a semi. It ran right over her. She wasn’t paying attention.”

“Damn, I’m sorry.” Ramiro looks like he regrets the question.

Every time I think about my sister, I feel like something clamps down on my chest and I can’t get enough air. Why did he have to bring her up? And why did Lorena have to tell him?

I see a man walking in the distance when I turn to the buildings.

“That guy is kind of freaking me out,” I tell Ramiro.

“Who? That guy?” he asks, pointing in his direction. “He won’t do anything.”

“How would you know?”

“Umm . . . I guess I don’t know.” He laughs. When I turn

back, the man is walking away. "What if I protect you?"

Sappy but sweet in a way, I guess. I don't know what to say, so I mumble, "Okay," and shrug. Then Ramiro puts his hand on the back of my head and leans into me. I never imagined my first kiss to be this way, but I guess it could be worse. When will I ever find someone I really like? Probably never. I bet I'll be a virgin until I go to college.

Ramiro's breath is slightly minty, and at first the kisses are soft and feel all right, but after a while, he spirals his tongue against mine, which totally grosses me out. Is this really how people kiss? It feels like my mouth is being accosted. Right when I'm about to put an end to it, Lorena and Carlos come toward us, hooting and whistling. I'm so embarrassed, I want to bury my head in the sand like an ostrich.

"Damn, girl. It's about time," Lorena says, smiling. I don't bother responding.

Carlos fist-bumps Ramiro and says, "Good job, hermano," which annoys me. It's not like he won a motherfucking prize or anything.

SIX

My cousin Victor is turning seven today, and my tío Bigotes (yes, "Uncle Mustache") is throwing him a big birthday party to celebrate, but I think it's just an excuse for him to get drunk. As Amá is brushing her hair in the bathroom, I tell her she looks pretty and ask if I can stay home. I want to figure out how to get back inside Olga's room. The key must be in the apartment somewhere. But Amá says no without even bothering to look at me. Maybe she thinks that if she leaves me alone, I'm going to orchestrate a giant orgy or overdose on heroin. I don't know why she doesn't trust me. I keep telling her that I will never get pregnant like my cousin Vanessa, but it doesn't matter to her.

Even if I don't find the key, at least I'd be alone. I'm hardly ever by myself in the apartment because Amá is always all up in my business and won't leave me behind. Sometimes, when my parents go to bed, I open all the windows—which Amá hates—and let the breeze flap the curtains open. I sit in the living room with a cup of coffee, journal, book, and reading lamp. I like the late-night sounds of traffic, even if they're disrupted by the pops of gunshots.

I decide to keep begging. "Amá, please. I just want to stay here and read. I hate parties. I'm just going to sit somewhere by myself. I don't want to talk to anyone."

"What kind of girl hates parties?"

"This kind," I say, pointing to myself. "You know that."

• • •

Tío's house always smells of old fruit and wet dog, which I don't understand because Chómpiras has been dead for three years. The stereo is blasting Los Bukis, and screaming children are running in and out of the house. Though I really hate kids, the part I hate most about these parties is arriving and departing. If I don't kiss each and every relative on the cheek hello and goodbye, even if I don't know them, Amá calls me a malcriada, a badly raised daughter. "You want to be like those güeros mal educados?" Amá always asks. In that case, yes, I do want to be like an impolite white person, but I just shut my mouth because it's not worth arguing about.

I kiss everyone in the house hello, including tío Cayetano, even though I can't stand him. When I was a kid, he used to stick his finger in my mouth when no one was looking. The last time he did it was during Vanessa's communion party when I was twelve. I was in the bathroom while everyone was in the backyard. As I came out, he forced his finger in my mouth much deeper than the times before, so I bit him. I clamped my mouth and wouldn't let go. I think I wanted to reach bone.

"Hija de tu pinche madre," he yelled. When I finally released his finger, he walked back outside, shaking his hand, letting the blood drip onto the floor. He told everyone the dog had bitten him and left the party with a paper towel wrapped around his finger. I sat in a corner for the rest of the night, drinking cup after cup of pop to get the salty, metallic taste of his blood out of my mouth. I wonder if he ever did anything like that to Olga.

Tío Bigotes's wife, Paloma, rushes to get us some food once we finish greeting every single person at the party. Tía Paloma is a woman so big that her stomach hangs low and everything wiggles when she walks. Every time I see her, I wonder how she and tío have sex. Or maybe they don't even do it now that tío has that new mistress we've heard rumors about. Amá says Paloma has a thyroid problem, and I feel bad for her, but I've seen her eat three tortas in one sitting. Thyroid, my ass.

After I finish eating, I'm so full, my pants nearly cut off my circulation. I'm uncomfortable no matter how I sit or shift. I almost want to lie down and let the food spread out. I don't know why I do this. Sometimes it's like I'm eating to drown something yowling inside me, even when I'm not really hungry. I pray that I never get as big as tía Paloma.

"Buena para comer," tía Milagros says, eyeballing my clean plate. Normally, I wouldn't be offended by a comment like this—Mexicans are always saying that about kids. It's meant as a compliment. "Good eaters" are people who'll eat anything put in front of them with no complaints; they eat with enthusiasm. It means they aren't picky or entitled brats. But this time, I know it isn't meant as praise because tía Milagros is always talking shit. I used to like her when I was younger, but she's become a bitter, resentful woman over the years. Her husband left her for a woman half her age a long time ago, and she's been salty ever since. It's hard to take her seriously, with her red perm and eighties bangs, but it pisses me off that I've become a target of her passive-aggressive cracks. Something about me just makes her angry. She is always sucking her teeth at what I'm wearing or making some comment about my weight, even though she's more floppy and misshapen than a sack of laundry. She loved Olga, though. Everyone did.

I watch my cousin Vanessa feeding her daughter mashed-up beans. Only sixteen and she already has a baby. That would be the worst thing that's ever happened to me, but Vanessa seems happy somehow. She's always giving Olivia kisses and telling her how much she loves her. I wonder if she'll ever finish high school. What kind of life can you have when you live with your parents and have a baby to take care of? Olivia is cute and all, but I never know what to do with babies.

I walk outside and see my cousins' cousin Freddy and his wife, Alicia, arrive as the piñata is being set up. I've always been fascinated by them. Freddy graduated from the University of Illinois and works as an engineer downtown, and Alicia was a theater major at DePaul and works at Steppenwolf. They are always dressed like they stepped off a runway. Alicia has the most interesting outfits—dresses made of bright, crazy fabrics and earrings that look like they belong in museums. Today two silver hands dangle from her ears. Freddy wears dark jeans and a black blazer. There's no one in my family like them. No one has ever gone to a real college. I always want to ask them a million questions.

"Hey, guys. How are you? What's new?" I feel like a frumpy dork when I talk to them because they seem so sophisticated. I get shy.

"We're good," Freddy says solemnly. "I'm so sorry about your sister. We were in Thailand and couldn't make it to the funeral."

Everyone in the house begins to come outside for the piñata. Victor suddenly starts crying because it isn't ready yet. Jesus, what a baby.

"Yeah, we're so, so sorry," Alicia says, taking my hand.

That's what everyone says about Olga. *Sorry, sorry, sorry.* I never know what to say. Is *thank you* the right answer?

"Thailand! How cool. What's that like?" I don't want to talk about my sister.

"It was beautiful." Freddy smiles.

I see tía Paloma wiping Victor's face with the end of her blouse. He's hysterical.

“Yeah, we got to ride elephants,” Alicia adds. “It was *a-maz-ing.*”

“So what are you thinking for college?” Freddy looks uncomfortable. He can probably sense that they shouldn’t talk about Olga anymore. I think I might visibly recoil every time someone says her name.

“I don’t really know. I want to move away to New York, I think. Somewhere with a good English program. But my grades haven’t been great lately, so I’m kind of worried. I really have to get my GPA up, or else I’m screwed.” When I remember the C I got on my last algebra test, it feels like snakes hatching and slithering in my stomach.

“Well, listen, if you ever need help with your applications or have any questions, please let us know. We need more people like you in college,” Freddy says.

"Totally." Alicia nods, her silver hands swinging. "I can probably get you a summer job at my company when you're old enough. It would look great on a college application."

"Thanks," I say. I don't know what Freddy means by *people like me. . . .* What am I like? Why would anyone care if I go to college or not?

There's no one else I feel like talking to, so I go to the living room to read *The Catcher in the Rye,* which I had to smuggle in my bag because Amá always complains when I read at parties. Why do I have to be so disrespectful? she wants to know. Why can't I just be at peace with my family? But I don't feel like talking most of the time, and today everyone is going to be asking about my quinceañera. Besides, all of my little cousins are still trying to break the piñata, and I doubt anyone will notice that

I'm gone. I just hope tío Cayetano doesn't come in here when I'm alone.

I get to read for a solid half hour before I'm interrupted. When I get to the part where Holden drops and shatters his little sister's record, my dad and uncles pile into the dining room to bust out the expensive tequila from the liquor cabinet. I should've known. This happens at every party.

Today the bottle tío Bigotes takes out is bright green and shaped like a gun. Like always, they sit around the dining room table, passing the tequila and talking about how great it was to live in their hometown of Los Ojos.

"How I miss my little town, chingao." Tío Octavio closes his eyes and shakes his head, as if reminiscing about a lost love.

"Remember how we used to skip school and go swimming in

the river?" tío Cayetano asks as he pours himself another shot.

"I wish I never would have left," Apá says quietly.

If they love that town so much, why don't they just go back and live there? I wonder. Always crying about Mexico as if it were the best place on earth.

I go back to my book, but tío Bigotes motions for me to come near him. "Come here, mija."

I walk to the table and stand a few feet away, but he tells me to get closer. He pulls me toward him and puts his arm around my neck. His breath smells like tequila, cigarettes, and something deeper and more disgusting I can't figure out. I try to pull back subtly, but it's no use—his arm is locked around me. I wish Apá would save me, but he just looks down into his drink.

"What were you doing here in the living room by yourself?"

"I was trying to finish my book," I explain.

"What do you want books for at a party?" he slurs. "Family is what's most important in life, mija. Go outside and talk to your cousins."

"But I like to read."

"For what?"

"I want to be a writer. I want to write books."

Tío Bigotes takes another gulp of his drink. "Are you excited about your party?"

"I guess."

"What do you mean, you guess? You should be excited. Your parents are making a big sacrifice for you."

Right, a sacrifice I don't want.

"You know, without family, you won't make it in this life.

And now that you're older, you have to learn how to be a nice señorita just like your sister, may she rest in peace." Tío nods his head dramatically, then looks me straight in the eye to see if I've understood his point.

"But I want to finish my book, tío." I stumble over my Spanish and feel my face get hot.

Tío Bigotes takes another shot of tequila and lets go of my neck as Amá comes into the living room. She purses her lips like she's just bitten into an onion and calls them all a bunch of sorry drunks.

"Look at this one." Tío Bigotes ignores her and gestures toward me with his glass. "With a cactus on her forehead, and she can barely speak Spanish. This country is ruining your children, sister." He points at Amá as he gets up from the table.

No one seems to know what to say. Apá is still looking into his drink, as if searching for some sort of answer. Amá crosses her arms and glares at tío Bigotes as he walks out of the room. Tío Cayetano pours himself another. This is number four—I've been counting.

Everyone is silent until we hear the violent puking coming all the way from the bathroom. I touch my forehead and imagine a spindly cactus pressed there, my face bloody, like Jesus.

That night I dream I'm sleeping in Amá's old room at Mamá Jacinta's house when it catches fire. I run out into the street barefoot in a bright blue nightgown before it all burns down. I stand there watching the house as it crackles and sputters, the cool mud under my feet. Suddenly, Papá Feliciano, Amá's dead father, is standing behind me holding a dead goat in his hands, its head hanging from its neck by a long, thin nerve. There is blood splattered all over his face and clothes.

Everything is off, in the way dreams are—the house is much bigger than I remember, and there are giant oak trees everywhere. Some things are in reverse or upside down, like an empty car driving backward. I know I'm in Los Ojos, but it is so different, so deserted. The house across the street has been replaced by a field of sunflowers.

"Where is Mamá Jacinta?" I scream at my grandfather, but he doesn't answer. He offers me the limp goat in his arms. I scream and scream while he stands there, blinking at me. I don't know if Mamá Jacinta is dead or alive.

The fire begins to grow, so I run toward the river. I feel the heat on my back, singeing the ends of my hair. Rocks cut my feet. It's night, but the sky is still bright somehow. The sound of crickets is almost deafening. It smells like wet earth.

I jump into the water when the fire finally reaches me, near the abandoned train station. When I open my eyes, the water is thick and dirty, and a group of mermaids tangled in garbage and seaweed swim toward me, their long hair floating all around their faces. Their tails are iridescent green, and their breasts are small and bare. The one in the middle turns toward me and waves. It's Olga. She has the same smile she had on her face when she died, and her skin is glowing, as if something were lit inside her.

"Olga!" I yell, my lungs filling with cloudy water. "Olga,

please come back!" The other mermaids gently take her away. I try swimming toward them, but my legs won't work. It's as if they're chained to the bottom of the river. I wake up crying, gasping for air.

SEVEN

Lorena has a new friend at school who's gay as a rainbow-colored unicorn. She met him in the lunch line when he complimented her ridiculous green heels. They started talking about clothes, makeup, and unfortunate fashion choices of the rich and famous, and that was that—best friends forever! He told her about the wild and crazy parties he frequents with his entourage of drag queens, which got Lorena worked up. All she ever wants to do is party. Now they talk all the time and even hold hands when they walk down the halls.

When Lorena tells me his name, I refuse to believe it because it's so utterly stupid. His name is Juan García, but he goes by

Juanga, which is the nickname of Juan Gabriel, Mexico's most beloved singer, who is *flaming* but has never officially come out of the closet. How can he compare himself to him? I mean, it's like calling yourself Jesus Christ or Joan of Arc. So of course I hate him immediately. I can't deny that I'm jealous. Lorena and I have been Siamese twins since the day we met. Juanga better watch himself.

Our history teacher is sick today, which means it'll be a free period. Our sub, Mr. Blankenship, breathes loudly through his mouth and wears a pilling green sweater two sizes too small. I can see his hairy belly when he lifts his arms. I don't know where the hell they find these people. The last substitute had a lisp and wore a fanny pack.

Instead of continuing to work on our research projects, he pops in a documentary about World War II, which we've already covered. Not even ten minutes into the movie and he's fast asleep, snoring wetly. The whole class slowly sprouts into chaos. Some people play music on their phones. Jorge and David throw a miniature football back and forth across the room, and Dario climbs on his desk and starts dancing, flipping his hair, and pouting his lips. He does this every single time a teacher leaves the room. Something about the way he moves reminds me of a flamingo.

"We have to go to a masquerade Juanga invited me to." Lorena turns to me, her eyes wide. "Everyone, and I mean *everyone*, is going to be there. It's at this fancy loft in the West Loop."

Just hearing his name chafes me. "Who is this 'everyone' you refer to? You know I hardly even like people. Plus, my mom would have a heart attack. No way." Part of me is intrigued by the party, but the other part of me doesn't want to spend a night hanging out with Juanga. He hasn't reached arch-nemesis status, but I certainly don't want to be friends.

"Oh my God, just lie to her, stupid. You never learn, do you? Tell her we're going on an overnight field trip to visit a college."

"That doesn't make any damn sense. We're juniors, remember? How would she believe that?"

A bomb suddenly explodes in the video, and Mr. Blankenship wakes up for about half a second.

"Here. Take this to your crazy-ass mom," Lorena says,

handing me a sheet of paper. "I already thought ahead. We *have to* go to this party."

According to the form, we're visiting the University of Michigan to see what college life is like. We'll be staying in the dorms, eating meals at the school cafeteria, watching a play, and taking a tour. Lorena translated it into Spanish on the back. She was even able to get it on the school letterhead, somehow.

I'm in awe. "Where did you get this?"

"Don't worry about it," Lorena says, smiling.

"Seriously, this is really impressive. I had no idea you were this smart."

"Bitch!"

"Well?"

"Okay, I stole the letterhead from Mr. Zuniga's desk and made up the rest."

"I guess you only play dumb, huh?" I try patting her on the head, but she ducks and swipes at my hand.

"If you miss this party, you're going to be sorry."

When I give Amá the permission form after school, she says no without even looking at me. That's what she always does. It's like I don't even deserve the dignity of eye contact. But I'm not surprised, of course not. I was prepared for this. I even wrote notes beforehand to help guide my argument. I beg and plead and tell her how much I want to go to college, how this will be a great opportunity, how I need this for my emotional and intellectual development. After about ten minutes of groveling, though, it's clear she's not having any of it.

"No daughter of mine is going to be sleeping in the streets."

"The streets? That doesn't make any sense. I'm going to be in a *dorm*."

"You think you're all grown-up. You're only fifteen. You don't even know how to make a tortilla."

I'm beginning to froth with fury. Amá is so dramatic. Sometimes I want to run out of our apartment screaming and never come back. I don't know what tortillas have to do with anything. "This is ridiculous. I want to go to college. I want to see the world. I never get out of this stupid neighborhood." My bottom lip quivers. I'm almost starting to believe my own lie.

"You can live here and go to college, you know? That's what Olga did."

"Absolutely not. Never. I'd rather live in a barrel than stay here and go to community college." Olga went there for four years and never even graduated. I'm not entirely sure what she was studying. Business something.

"How come Olga never felt the need to be out in the streets like some sort of Gypsy? She was always so comfortable here at home, spending time with her family. Bien agusto, mi niña." Amá looks up at the ceiling, as if she's trying to talk to my sister in heaven.

"She was not a girl. She was a grown woman!" I don't know why that pisses me off so much. I run to my room and slam the door. I hate when Amá sees me cry.

• • •

The night of the masquerade I try to read in the living room, but I can't concentrate because I'm so jittery. I'm just waiting until my parents go to bed so I can slink out of the apartment. On Fridays, they usually go to sleep at about 9, which is so depressing. I'd hate to be old and lame and never do anything fun on weekends. That's why I won't ever get married or have kids. What a pain in the ass.

Half an hour after they've gone to sleep, I tiptoe to their door and listen. I hope to God I never, ever hear them having sex, because if I do, I might have to put poison inside my ears. Maybe they don't have sex anymore, though. Who knows? Thankfully, I can hear them both snoring. I don't understand how Amá sleeps through Apá's terrifying growls.

I creep back to my room and stuff my bed with pillows and an extra blanket. I take one of my old dolls and put it where my head would be. I cover most of it, but leave some strands of her dark hair out to make it look more realistic. I'm pleased with myself for being so clever. If Amá opens the door and doesn't turn on the light, it will definitely work. I've caught Amá peering in here some nights. She is so paranoid. If, for some reason, she decides to lift up the blanket, I've left a note saying I'm with Lorena because she's having a crisis and that I'll be back soon, don't worry. I doubt it would help much, but it seems better than nothing.

Once I put on my only decent black dress, I text Lorena to come get me, and she says she and Juanga will be here in five minutes. I walk toward the door as quietly as possible. I'm afraid to even blink. It takes me an eternity to turn the doorknob because I don't want to make any noise. When I shut it, I pray that I haven't woken my parents.

Now I have to wait on the steps in the cold until they arrive. The sidewalk in front of our building has been crumbling for years, and no one has ever bothered to fix it. The few trees on the street are scrawny and have already lost most of their leaves. I hope no one passes by right now. I'm so tired of being harassed by pervs around here. They'd probably bother anything with the semblance of boobs, human or not. I keep checking the time, silently cursing Lorena for lying to me about how long it'd take. What if Amá wakes up and sees me outside? What if someone notices me and rats me out? Our next-door neighbor, Doña Josefa, is always peering out the window and is the biggest chismosa I've ever met. I keep thinking and thinking of all the worst-case scenarios until I feel like a tornado of worry and consider going back to bed. This party better be the best thing that's ever happened to me.

Finally, I see them pull up.

It turns out that Juanga doesn't have a license, but he's "borrowed" his dad's car anyway.

"Don't worry, bitch, I'm not going to kill you," he says, cackling like a maniac when he sees my worried face.

We park in front of a gigantic warehouse just west of downtown. The street is dark, and the building looks ancient and abandoned. I'm convinced we'll be raped and/or murdered, but I don't say anything because I don't want to be a buzzkill. The only thing that comforts me is that there are a ton of cars parked outside, nice ones, too. Before we enter, Juanga hands us both masks. Mine is covered with peacock feathers and rhinestones, which is not really my style, but I'll go with it.

I'm totally wrong about the apartment. It doesn't look like a crime scene. In fact, it's unlike anything I've ever seen before. I wonder what these people do for a living because this place belongs in a magazine—Chinese lanterns, what appears to be real artwork, and intricately designed rugs. God, I would love to live in a place like this all by myself. I can't wait to get out of our dilapidated apartment one day.

Everyone turns to look at us. We're definitely the youngest people here. They can probably tell, even though we're wearing masks. After a few minutes of awkward lingering, a large woman in a tight leather dress and red mask comes running toward us.

"Hey, bitch!" she says to Juanga, and gives him a kiss on the cheek.

"Hey!" Juanga squeals, and turns to us. "This is Maribel, our beautiful host this evening."

"Such a pleasure," Maribel says, giving a dramatic bow. Her dress is cut so low that I'm afraid one of her boobs will pop out. "Make yourselves at home. Don't be shy. There are drinks in the dining room."

The three of us make our way to the liquor. Lorena and Juanga pour some shots of I don't know what. I refuse because the last time I drank shots of vodka with Lorena, I threw up so hard it came out of my nose. I open a beer instead, which I regret immediately. This must be what pee and bile taste like. The only other time I tasted beer was when I was twelve and secretly took a sip of Apá's Old Style when he was in the bathroom. It was disgusting then, and it's disgusting now. I drink it down fast without breathing through my nose.

The mask is uncomfortable on top of my glasses, and it's making me sweat and itch. I would have worn my contacts, but I ran out. I'm afraid it's going to give me a pimple, so I take it off. I zone out, watching the skyline, when a man in a *Phantom of the Opera* mask pulls me out to the dance floor. I have no idea who he is, but I don't have to worry because everyone here is queer or trans. It's nice not to have to deal with creepy-ass dudes for once.

The DJ is playing James Brown, and everyone is going wild, flailing their arms and screaming the lyrics. I'm not a good dancer, but I like the beat. Besides, I can't look any worse than the man next to me, dancing like a *Tyrannosaurus rex.* After a few songs, I begin to loosen up. When I shake my shoulders like the drag queens, they laugh and clap. I'm fascinated by the women here. Even if they're fat, they move as if they think they're fabulous. I wish I could be like that.

As I spin around with a lady in a catsuit, someone taps me on the shoulder. A small woman, wearing a silver mask, tilts her head, as if she's trying to figure out how she knowsme.

"Yes?"

"Wait, are you Olga's little sister? Julia?" she yells over the music.

"What? Who are you?" I shout back, giving her major side eye. I have no clue who she is.

"You don't remember me?" She takes off her mask.

"Obviously not."

"I'm Jazmyn, remember? Olga's friend from high school. Look at you! All grown up."

Then it comes to me—Jazmyn, with the overbite and droopy eyes. I remember her name was spelled stupid, too. Even as a kid, I thought she was insufferable. "Kind of," I say, uninterested. I don't feel like talking to her. I don't want to explain.

"Aren't you a little young to be at a party like this? How old are you again?" There are nosy people everywhere I turn, apparently.

I pretend not to hear.

"Oh man, I spent so much time at your house. Olga, Angie, and I were inseparable sophomore year. I remember you were such a sensitive little girl. Always crying about something."

I roll my eyes. Why does everyone remind me how much I sucked as a kid?

"You know, I haven't seen Olga in years. I ran into her when I was shopping a few years ago. She kept going on and on about this guy she was in love with. She was all excited. I had never seen her so happy."

The music gets louder, and I can feel the bass thumping throughout my body. "Wait, what? Do you mean Pedro the aardvark? Or was it someone else?"

"What?" Jazmyn cups her hand to her ear.

"The dude that looked like an aardvark! Pedro!" I use my hand to illustrate a snout since she can't understand, but she is still confused. Jazmyn moves in closer. I can feel her hot breath on my face. "So how is Olga? We didn't keep in touch after I moved to Texas. I come back every once in a while. This is my cousin's party." She points to Maribel, who blows us kisses.

"She's dead." I refuse to say *passed away*, like everyone else. Why can't people say what they mean?

"What?" Jazmyn looks confused.

"I said, she's dead!" I feel the beer slosh around in my stomach. The room is twirling now.

"I can't believe this. . . . We. . . we. . . were friends." Jazmyn looks like she might cry. Maybe I shouldn't have told her. "How did it happen? She was so young. Oh my God."

"She got run over by a semi. It happened in September."

I can't go anywhere without talking about my dead sister, and every time I do, I think I might pass out or throw up. Jazmyn's eyes well up with tears.

I leave her standing there, and run to the bathroom. When I bend over the toilet, nothing comes out. I splash cold water on my face, which smudges my eyeliner and mascara. I try wiping my makeup with a piece of toilet paper, but I still look like the Joker. I'll just have to put my mask back on. I take a few deep breaths before I go back outside. I'm having a hard time breathing at a normal pace, like my body suddenly forgot. Maybe Jazmyn wasn't talking about Pedro. I rush out and look for her all throughout the loft. I even look outside, but she must have left. I don't see her anywhere. I find Juanga and Lorena doing shots in the kitchen.

"Here, take this. You need it." Lorena hands me a glass.

The smell of it makes my stomach flip, but I drink it anyway. It burns my throat and sends a pleasant warmth all throughout my body. My muscles begin to soften. No wonder so many people are alcoholics.

I'm drunk by the time Juanga and Lorena are ready to go home. I don't know exactly how many drinks Juanga had, but I'm one hundred percent sure he shouldn't be driving. What choice do I have, though? How else would I get home?

I can barely keep my eyes open, but I can feel Juanga swerve all over the expressway. When we get off the exit ramp, he slams on the brakes so hard I nearly hit my head on the back of Lorena's seat.

"Sorry, sorry, sorry," he slurs.

I hope to God that Juanga doesn't kill me, because then Amá would truly go crazy. It's nearly time to wake up and start the day again. The sky is still dark, but it's beginning to brighten. There are beautiful, faint streaks of orange over the lake. It looks like it's been cracked open.

I think of Jazmyn's face when I told her about Olga. Everywhere I go, my sister's ghost is hovering.

EIGHT

Amá asks me to clean houses with her today. Scratch that. She *forces* me to clean houses with her today. The lady she usually works with pulled a muscle in her back and can't get out of bed. Not only that, Amá says I should earn my quinceañera, even though I would rather eat a bowl of amoebas than go through with it. Now that I'm almost a woman, it's time I learn to be responsible, Amá says. Not exactly the way I want to spend a Saturday, but I have no choice. What am I going to say? "Go clean those mansions by your damn self. I feel like writing and taking a nap!" That would not be acceptable, especially since Olga, my angelic sister, was our mother's reliable helper.

All the houses we have to clean are in Lincoln Park, one of the richest neighborhoods in Chicago. The first one belongs to a man who isn't home. It's already spotless, so it only takes about an hour. Easy breezy. People really do spend money on the dumbest things.

The second house is a few blocks away, and the owner is an uptight lawyer who peers over our shoulders the whole time, talking to us in her horrible high school Spanish, even though I can guarantee my English is better than hers. I hate her and her beige furniture from the start, but I just play along and pretend me no espeak English. Amá says it's best not to talk to them if it can be avoided. It takes us three hours to finish because we have to do laundry, too. I don't know why she can't do it herself. I mean, she was there the whole entire time. Some people are so lazy.

The last place is a two-story brownstone near the DePaul campus. The owner tells us he's a professor of anthropology, as if we care. A real prig, too. He introduces himself as Dr. Scheinberg and uses the word *propitious*. I know what that means, of course—I read, duh—but why would you use words like that with a Mexican cleaning lady? As Mr. Ingman says, "Know your audience."

Dr. Scheinberg tells us he'll be back in three and a half hours. When he says *farewell* instead of *goodbye*, I want to punch him right in the throat, but I just smile and wave back.

The house looks like a museum. It's filled with multicolored rugs, brown-and-black African masks, and statues of men and women in weird sexual positions. Everything looks like it costs thousands of dollars and belongs in a glass case. At first glance, it appears to be clean, but when you look closer, there are crumbs and filth everywhere—dust bunnies the size of rabbits.

"Ave María purísima," Amá mutters, and makes the sign of the cross. She probably thinks he's a Satanist. She's always assuming people are Satanists.

Amá says we should begin with the most disgusting parts of the house—the bathrooms, better to get them over with. The master bathroom is covered with piles of wet clothes and towels. The sink is smeared with gobs of toothpaste and little black hairs. Gross. I kick everything to the side and approach the toilet. It only makes sense to start with the worst of the worst. I put on the gloves Amá gave me, take the brush from its stand, and hold my breath.

“Go on,” Amá says.

This is what I was dreading the most. I can deal with filth, but toilets. . . other people’s toilets always upset me. I once got a urinary tract infection after holding in my pee for hours because I couldn’t find a suitable bathroom. The other two we scrubbed today were easy because they were already relatively clean, but I doubt that’s going to be the case here.

I lift the lid, and it’s worse than I expect. Much worse: a giant black turd. Is this real? Is this some kind of joke? Is there a hidden camera somewhere? I jump back and begin to gag. My eyes water. What the hell does this man eat? Coal?

“Don’t be so delicate! Flush it and clean it,” Amá says, rolling her eyes, as if she sees this kind of biological warfare on a daily basis. Well, she might, actually.

I breathe through my mouth and try to clean it as quicklyas possible. When we're finished with the master bathroom, we move on to the guest bathroom, which seems like a walk in a beautiful garden in comparison. Thank God. Why does one man need more than one toilet? I have no idea.

I'm afraid the bedroom is going to be full of sex stuff, but the grossest thing we find is crumpled tissue on the floor next to the bed and nail clippings on his dresser. There are clothes and shoes strewn everywhere, too. I thought *I* was messy, but this man is a complete barbarian.

Next is the kitchen. The fumes burn the inside of my nose as I scour the stove. I wonder how many chemicals Amá is exposed to every day. I wish we had music because the silence is making me restless. All I hear is squeaking, spraying, and wiping. How does Amá do this day in and day out?

"So. . . did Olga like to clean with you?" I don't know what else to say, but I can't stand that it's so quiet.

"Like it? Who likes cleaning? No one *likes* it. It's just what you do."

"Okay, I'm sorry I asked."

Amá looks a little ashamed for being so harsh. "It's okay, mija." It seems like she's really trying to think of something to say. "How is school?"

"It's okay," I lie. The truth is that school is excruciating. I love reading and learning, but I can't stand everything else. I don't have many friends and feel lonely all the time. Ever since Olga died, it's gotten even worse. It's like I don't know how to talk to people. That's why I'm always trying to lose myself in books. “I love my English class. Mr. Ingman says I’m a good writer.”

“Mm-hmm, that’s good,” Amá says, but she’s not paying attention. She doesn’t say much whenever I tell her anything about school. She doesn’t know a lot about it because she had to drop out when she was in eighth grade to help with the family business. Apá quit when he was in seventh grade in order to work in the fields. It’s strange not being able to talk to your parents about something so important.

As I look at a painting of a woman with a large butt, hanging in the dining room, I remember Olga’s friend Jazmyn, who also has a large butt.

“Amá, do you remember Olga’s friend Jazmyn?”

“¿Esa huerca? How can I forget? She was always at our house, never wanted to go home. She drove me crazy. Why? What about her?"

"I was just remembering her, that's all. Do you remember her last name?"

"Why? Did you see her or something?"

I get a little panicky, as if somehow she can see inside my brain and know that I went to that party.

"No, of course not. Didn't she move to Texas? Where would I see her?" I probably sound too defensive. I let the silence hang for a while. With a repulsed look on her face, Amá dusts all of the statues.

"Did Olga have a boyfriend?" I finally say.

"The only boyfriend she had was Pedro, such a nice young man."

If by *nice*, she means ugly and dull, then sure.

"So, she *never* had a boyfriend after that?"

"Of course not. What kind of question is that? Did you ever see her running around with boys?" Amá looks annoyed, but I can't stop asking questions.

"Okay, okay, sorry. It's just . . . how was it that she was twenty-two and didn't have a boyfriend for so many years? That seems weird."

"What's so strange about a young lady who doesn't sleep around, who enjoys spending time at home with her family? Girls here have no morals. You're the weird one, you know that?" Amá's face is starting to get splotchy, and her big eyes look inflamed, so I shut up and keep cleaning.

• • •

Dr. Scheinberg arrives right as we're finishing. When he hands us the money, he says, "Gracias," and bows with his hands pressed together, and oh my God, he's not even joking. I don't like the way he stares at Amá when he says goodbye. There's something about him that makes me feel as if I'm smeared in an awful, warm goo. No wonder he's not married.

It's dark and the ground is covered with snow. Everything looks beautiful and still, as if it were a photograph and not real life. Usually, winter makes me glum, but every once and a while, moments like this are peaceful and pleasant—the icicles, the glittering snow, the silence.

By the time we get on the bus, my back aches, my hands are cracked, and my eyes burn from all the cleaning products. I smell like bleach and sweat. I've never been this tired in my whole life. Who knew rich people could be so disgusting? Now I understand why everyone calls work la chinga and why Amá is always in a bad mood. I wonder what else she sees in people's houses, and if other men look at her the way Dr. Scheinberg does.

NINE

I decide to go to the school dance because the after-party is at Alex Tafoya's house. His parents are in Mexico for a few weeks, and Lorena says his sister, Jessica, who went to school with Olga, will be there. It might be completely useless—I'm not sure how well they knew each other—but I don't know what else to do.

Amá lets me go to the dance, which I think might qualify as a miracle, though she tells me I better not act volada, which means "flirtatious." Every time she says stuff like this, I feel ashamed, and I don't know why because I haven't done anything.

I have to buy a new dress, and Amá says she'll take me to the mall. I hate shopping, but now I have no choice because I have absolutely nothing to wear—the only three dresses I have are literally falling apart. One has a giant hole in the armpit. Amá says it makes me look like an orphan, that I should throw it away, but I like the way it fits. She also says I can't wear jeans or any of my band T-shirts she hates so much. No Chuck Taylors, either. I have to look like a "proper woman."

Thanks to my upcoming quinceañera, my budget is only forty-five dollars, practically nothing.

The Sunday before the dance, Amá and I drive to the outlet mall in the suburbs. After driving west in snow flurries for about an hour, we finally arrive. I thought our neighborhood was bad, but if I had to live in the suburbs, I think I'd just lie down and die. I don't care that the houses are big and expensive; everything is exactly the same, and the only restaurants I see are Chili's and Olive Garden.

The first store we go to is full of white women who look at us funny when we enter, which is already a bad sign. I glance at the price tag on a ridiculous pink sweater and see that it's on sale for ninety-nine dollars. If that's what they think a sale is, then we probably can't even afford their socks. No thanks. "Let's go," I say.

We walk around for half an hour, looking for a store that's affordable, and I just want to give up and bury my face in a Cinnabon, even though they always make me sick. I sit down on a bench and tell Amá that I'm not going to find anything, that she can go on without me.

"Come on," Amá says, yanking me by the arm. "We're going to find you something. Don't be so dramatic. If not, we'll go somewhere else."

"I'd rather buy the worst dress here than go to another mall. Let's get this over with," I say, getting up with a new sense of determination.

After trying on about twenty dresses at five different stores, I finally find one I want. It has a black-and-red-checked pattern and falls right above my knee, which is the perfect length for me, because anything longer makes me look stumpy. The dress is what I imagine a career woman wearing when she goes out for drinks after work. I bet no one at school will have a dress like this. I'm lucky, too, because it's a size 10 and it's on clearance. At seventy-five percent off, it costs $39.99.

When I come out of the dressing room, Amá shakes her head.

"What?"

"It's too tight."

"No, it's not. It fits perfectly!"

"It shows your chest too much," Amá says, scrunching her face as if she's just smelled something gross.

Amá hates it when women wear revealing clothing, but this dress is not sexy at all. It's not even low cut, doesn't show any cleavage whatsoever. Every time my parents turn on the TV, there are women dressed like strippers, even the news anchors, yet I'm supposed to be embarrassed of my boobs? I don't get it. Even the time she found out I had shaved my legs, she was hysterical. Am I expected to cover myself with cloaks and let my body be covered in dark fur?

"I think it looks good on me," I tell Amá. "I like it, and it's the perfect price."

"Why do you always have to wear black? Why don't you try a different color, something nice, like yellow or green?"

A woman comes into the dressing room with an armful of black pants. She gives me an awkward smile, as if she somehow knows this is torture for me.

"Yellow or green? Are you serious? Amá, that's disgusting."

"It's not proper, Julia. Why can't you understand that? I'm not going to buy it."

"So you will only buy me a dress that you like even if I hate it?" I should've known shopping with Amá would be a mistake.

"Yes, that's right."

"I can't believe this. Why do you always do this? Why can't I wear what I want? It's not like I'm wearing a pair of Daisy Dukes and a see-through tube top."

"Remember, you're not the boss here. Why are you always making everything so difficult? Why aren't you ever happy? I try to do something nice, and this is how you act? Dios mío, who would have guessed I would have such an ungrateful daughter?" Amá is highly skilled in the art of guilt trips. She could win a gold medal.

"Jesus Christ, don't buy me anything, then."

I go back into the dressing room, my eyes already brimming. I try to wipe away the tears, but they keep coming and coming. I feel a sob traveling up my body and stop it before it gets past my throat. I'm so frustrated, I don't know what to do with myself. Sometimes, when I feel like this, I want to break things. I want to hear things shatter. My heart beats so fast and hard that I can hardly breathe, and I wonder if anything will ever get better. Is this really the way my life is going to be?

I look at myself in the mirror one last time. I can't help if my boobs are big. What am I supposed to do? Strap them down with bandages? I'm tired of people telling me how I should act and how I should look. Only a year and a half left until I leave home. Then no one will be allowed to tell me what to wear or what to do. Ever.

I have to borrow one of Lorena's dresses, which isn't easy because her closet is full of glittery clothes with wacky patterns. And most of them are way too small. Lorena and I are the same height, but she's skinny enough to buy clothes from the kids' section sometimes. The one I finally pick is black and stretchy. It barely fits, but it will have to work. It also has a slit up the side, which I think looks elegant. I have to borrow a pair of black flats, too, because heels are for suckers, I've decided.

Lorena and I go to the dance with a group of girls—no dates allowed. She tells Carlos he can't come, and Juanga has been MIA for a week, now that he ran off with some old dude from Indiana. I wonder if he'll get kicked out of school. I try to act disappointed when Lorena tells me he isn't going to join us, but she sees right through me.

We meet Fátima, Maggie, and Sandra from our gym class by the entrance. They all have horrifying grammar, but they're really friendly. Besides, I shouldn't judge people for saying *yous* instead of *you* or *mines* instead of mine. A lot of people at school speak like that, so I should get over it already. Lorena tells me I'm too uptight, which is why I hardly have any friends.

The flashing lights and smoke machine make it hard to see. When my eyes finally adjust, I notice people dancing so close they're practically dry-humping. Someone's going to come out of here pregnant.

Lorena and the girls go nuts over a song I don't recognize and run to the dance floor. I decide to stay behind, and after a few minutes, I start worrying about where I should look and where to put my hands. What if I stare at someone too long? What if I look like Frankenstein with my arms hanging stiffly at my sides? What if people think I'm a loser for standing by myself? As all of these stupid thoughts run through my head,

Chris comes toward me, wearing sunglasses and a *Scarface* T-shirt, completely oblivious to how idiotic he looks. I've known him since grade school, and he's always been an unbearable little numskull.

"You look nice, for once," he says, eying at my dress, but mostly my boobs.

"Is that supposed to be a compliment?"

"Yeah."

"You need to learn how to talk to women," I turn away from Chris, but he keeps talking.

"You, a woman? Ha." He gets closer and lifts his sunglasses, as if trying to get a better look, as if I'm some chunk of beef on clearance he's evaluating. "Why you gotta dress stupid all the time?"

“Are you serious? You’re such an asshole, Chris. Don’t ever, ever talk to me again. Don’t even look in my direction, I swear to God.”

“You’re conceited. That’s your problem. You think you’re better than everybody. You think you’re all smart, talking like a white girl and shit.”

“Who do you think you are, talking to me like that?” I’m so angry, my hands are shaking. I want to slap his sunglasses off his face, but it’s not worth it. He’ll probably end up living in his mom’s basement until he’s forty. That should be punishment enough.

I find the girls dancing like it’s their last day on earth, their hands flying in the air and their hips swinging back and forth. They form a circle and shake their butts against me, which makes me laugh.

• • •

When they finally turn on the lights, Lorena tells me that we can walk to the after-party because it's only two blocks away.

"Are you absolutely sure his sister is going to be there? Because you know I'm going to get in trouble, right? I didn't tell my mom because she'd never let me go."

"That's what Alex said. She's supposed to be here."

I text Amá that I won't be home until later. Not even three seconds later, I feel the phone buzzing, but I don't pick up because I already know what she's going to say.

• • •

People think Alex is so cool because he's tall and good at basketball, and all the girls think he's hot, but I would give him a C+ at most. He has nice teeth, but I don't really see what the big deal is.

Alex's house is already bursting with people, which makes me think I've made a mistake. I don't do well in crowds. Once, when I was little, I freaked the hell out during a parade, and my parents had to carry me home kicking and screaming. And sometimes I have trouble breathing in crammed elevators.

The windows are steamy from so much body heat, and everyone is clogging the doors and hallways, making it almost impossible to get through. For a second, I think I might have a panic attack, but I calm myself down. I breathe slowly and tell myself it's going to be okay. After getting past the crowd of people in the living room, we finally make our way to the drinks in the kitchen. The table is covered with all sorts of bottles, and there's a keg next to the sink. Alex and the rest of the basketball team are smoking weed near the window. He asks us if we want to smoke or if he could make us a drink, which is nice of him because he probably has no idea who I am.

The girls all choose Malibu rum, but I go for the Hennessy and Coke. I'm not sure if you're supposed to mix the two, but the drink tastes okay. I finish it in three gulps. When I go for another cup, though, Lorena grabs my wrist and tells me to slow it down.

I cut to the chase. "Where's Alex's sister?"

"I don't know. I haven't seen her yet. Try to have fun, at least. She'll be here." Lorena walks away and gets lost in the crowd before I can follow her.

I spend most of the night searching for Jessica. I don't really remember what she looks like. I'm guessing she resembles Alex in some way. Lorena says her hair is dyed dark red, but I don't see any girls with red hair.

After about three more drinks, I start feeling a little more relaxed. Even though sometimes I have a big mouth, I find it hard to strike up conversations with people I don't know. I guess that's one thing Olga and I had in common. When I wait in line for the bathroom, I ask the cute guy in front of me who the funny-looking man on his shirt is, and he just mumbles something and walks away. Amá always says that women should never approach men, that we should be the ones pursued and courted, and maybe she's right because this is totally embarrassing.

After I pee, I find Maggie in the living room by herself and ask her if she knows where Lorena is. She shrugs and says she hasn't seen her in a while. Maggie is sweet and cute, but there's not much going on in her head. No matter what you're talking about, even if you're not asking her a question, she has a confused look on her face, and there's a sort of blankness in her eyes I can't explain. It's not like Lorena, who only pretends to be dumb. Maggie's stupidity is totally sincere.

"Are you enjoying yourself?"

"Yeah, it's okay. I guess," Maggie says, fixing her ponytail. "No cute guys, though."

"No. None. That dude over there looks like a scrotum," I say, pointing to a bald guy with big jowls slumped on the sofa.

Maggie laughs. "You're crazy."

I nod. "Unfortunately."

As I look around the party, trying to spot Lorena, I see a couple making out in a bedroom through a cracked door. Not just kissing, though, I mean *really* going at it.

"Whoa. Check that out," I whisper to Maggie, and tilt my head in their direction.

The girl is sitting on the guy's lap with her legs wrapped around him. Maybe it's because she's totally drunk, but I don't notice any shred of shame or embarrassment, which I admire in a strange way. Their kisses are wet and sloppy, and you can see their tongues going in and out of each other's mouths. The girl rubs herself on the guy as he starts kissing her neck and chest. The girls next to us are now scandalized, call her a slut, skank, whore, and so many other synonyms in both English and Spanish that it seems like they've consulted a bilingual thesaurus. A group of guys gather and try to snap pictures with their phones. The couple either doesn't notice or doesn't care.

"That's disgusting," Maggie says. "She is so nasty."

"Yeah, so gross," I say, but I'm wondering if anyone will ever touch me like that.

After I use the bathroom for the billionth time, I finally find Lorena in the back porch, surrounded by a circle of cretins who are way too old to be at a high school party. They probably went to school with my sister, too. It doesn't surprise me because Lorena loves attention from men, no matter how old or ugly. What kind of losers come to a party like this once they've already graduated (or dropped out)?

"Where is Jessica? I've been looking for her all night. That's the only reason I came."

“I don’t know. Alex said she’d be here.” Lorena shrugs. “Just chill, okay?”

“No, I want to go home. Now.”

“Yeah, baby, relax,” says a guy wearing a backward baseball cap.

“Mind your business. And my name is not baby,” I tell him, and turn to Lorena. “Look, if I get in trouble, it’s going to be your fault.”

“Give me five more minutes. Come on, don’t be like that.” Lorena is definitely drunk. I can tell by the way her mouth moves, as if it’s suddenly too heavy for her face.

The house is beginning to clear out a little, so I give up and find a spot on the couch.

Next thing I know, Lorena is shaking me and telling me to

wake up, that we have to leave because someone called the cops. When I ask her what time it is, she says it's 3 a.m., which means I'm screwed.

I've done the calculations and have figured out that from the ages of thirteen to fifteen, I've spent about forty-five percent of my life grounded. Seriously, what kind of life is that? I know I mess up sometimes, I know I can be a sarcastic jerk, I know I'm not the daughter my parents wanted, but Amá treats me like I'm a degenerate.

Sometimes, when I'm punished like this, Amá doesn't even let me go to the library, which I think is the cruelest kind of torture. What am I supposed to do if I have to sit in my room for hours and hours? I can't get pregnant at the library, I tell her, but it doesn't matter. Amá says I can clean, do my homework, and if she's feeling generous, she says she'll let me watch telenovelas with them, but I'd rather poke my eyes out like Oedipus than sit through an episode of that garbage. The acting on those shows is forced and stiff, and the characters are always slapping each other dramatically. The plotlines are always the same, too—a poor woman overcomes adversity and marries a rich asshole and they live happily ever after. All the upper-class people are white, and the servants are dark like me.

I've always had trouble being happy, but now it feels impossible. Everyone in my family tells me what a difficult baby I was compared to Olga. When I was little, anything would set me off—a dirty look, a dropped cookie, a canceled outing. I remember I once sobbed because I saw a three-legged dog. I don't know why I've always been like this, why the smallest things make me ache inside. There's a poem I read once, titled "The World Is Too Much with Us," and I guess that is the best way to describe the feeling—the world is too much with me.

It's not like my parents are happy, either. All they do is work. They never go out anywhere, and when they're home, they hardly even talk to each other. I don't understand why everyone just complains about who I am. What am I supposed to do? Say I'm sorry? I'm sorry I can't be normal? I'm sorry I'm such a bad daughter? I'm sorry I hate the life that I have to live?

There are times I feel completely alone, like no one in the world can possibly understand me. Sometimes Amá stares at me like I'm some sort of mutant that slithered out of her body.

Lorena listens, which I appreciate, but she doesn't really get it. She's practically a science genius, but she doesn't care about literature or art. I don't think anyone likes what I like. Sometimes I feel so lonely and hopeless that I don't know what to do. Usually, I just bottle up all of my feelings and wait until my parents go to sleep so I can cry, which I know is totally pathetic. If I can't wait, I do it in the shower. It builds and builds all day, tightening my throat and chest, and sometimes I feel it in my face. When I finally let it out, it cascades out of me.

On top of everything, I haven't been able to sleep. Even if I'm completely exhausted, even if my body is screaming and begging that it needs to rest, some nights I just stare at my ceiling for hours and hours. I look at the clock, and it's almost time for me to get ready for school. I hear the world go to sleep and wake up: the slowing of traffic, birds chirping, cars starting, my parents making coffee. I've tried everything, too—counting sheep, counting kittens, drinking hot milk, listening to relaxing music—but nothing helps. The times I do sleep, I have nightmares about people trying to murder me in an upside-down house or something equally weird. At least I haven't had any more dreams about Olga.

In the mornings, I'm a shred of a person. There are days I feel like I'm being held together by string. Other times I feel entirely unstitched or unhinged. I can barely keep my head up, let alone get good grades so I can get the hell out of here and go to college. I have only a year and a half left, but it feels eternal. It feels *infernal*.

Today my Honors English class, the only class I enjoy, feels like a never-ending burden. Mr. Ingman is going over

Huckleberry Finn, which I've already read three times, but I can't pay attention. I look out the window, at two squirrels chasing each other in a tree, and think about our upcoming field trip to Warren Dunes. Sometimes nature makes me feel better, more human, like I'm connected to everything and everyone. Other times I want to lie under a tree and dissolve into the earth forever.

Mr. Ingman asks the class about the symbolism of the Mississippi River, and though I know it inside and out, and no one else wants to answer, I don't even bother raising my hand because I'm afraid that if I open my mouth, I'll start crying like a loser and won't be able to stop.

After class, Mr. Ingman calls me over to his desk.

"Is everything okay, Julia?"

I nod.

"Are you sure?" He crosses his arms. Ever since I told him my sister died, he looks as if he's trying to stare into my soul or something.

"I'm fine," I mumble. *Please don't cry. Please don't cry. Please don't cry.*

"You don't seem fine. You look really upset. I know you love *Huck Finn* because we've talked about it many times," he says. Sometimes I stay after school to talk to Mr. Ingman about books and college. He even lets me borrow some from his personal collection and gives me a list of schools he thinks I should apply to, which is why he's my favorite teacher. "You haven't said anything sarcastic in a few weeks now, which is what's worried me the most, to be perfectly honest." Mr. Ingman's smile is nice. I bet he was hot twenty years ago. I just wish he wouldn't wear so many dad sweaters.

"I guess you're right." I try to laugh politely, but the laugh doesn't come out. "It's just that I'm on my period, and it feels like someone is stabbing me in the uterus." I grimace and make a stabbing motion with my hand. A few years ago, I learned you can get away with nearly anything if you mention menstruation to your male teachers.

Mr. Ingman looks uncomfortable, but it's clear he's not going to let me go. "Is something happening at home? How's your family doing since. . . you know, your sister and everything?"

"We're okay, I guess. It comes in waves for me. Lots of waves. Big, big waves. And I guess I have this feeling, you know? That I'm missing something, that there's something I should know, but I can't figure it out." My voice cracks.

"Like what?"

I'm not about to tell Mr. Ingman about the underwear and hotel key, so I just shrug and say, "I don't really know. Something's just off."

"I'm sorry. It must be so hard." He crosses his arms and looks down.

"It's impossible . . . and sometimes I think it's my fault. Like, what if I would have done something differently that day? Would she still be alive?"

"You can't think of it that way."

"Why not?"

"Because it's not your fault. You didn't want your sister to die. Things like this just happen in life. Shit's fucked up sometimes." Mr. Ingman looks embarrassed for swearing, but doesn't apologize. "My mother died when I was ten. Heart attack. Just collapsed at work one day. I had been awful to her that morning. I threw a tantrum about my lunch and told her I hated her, and then she died. Just like that."

"Whoa. I'm sorry." I'm stunned. I don't know why, but I always assumed that Mr. Ingman had an easy life. I imagined him growing up with a tree house or some shit. "Does it go away, that feeling?"

"It gets easier, but I still think about her every day." Mr. Ingman sighs and looks out the window. I get a whiff of his aftershave. Something about that smell—the smell of man—is comforting.

• • •

When I get home, Apá is on the couch, soaking his feet in his tub. Because he works all day packaging candy, he always has problems with his body—cuts, back pains, glue burns, and swollen legs, just to name a few. Some days he works twelve hours and comes back home looking like someone beat him with a bat. A few times a week, they force him to work the night shift, too. Apá doesn't say much, but he always tells me, "Don't work like a donkey like me. Be a secretary and work in a nice office with air-conditioning." I never tell him I'd rather clean toilets than be some man's assistant. Fetching coffee and being bossed around by a jerk in a suit? No thanks. Once, I told Apá that I wanted to be a writer, but all he said was that I had to make enough money so I didn't have to live in an apartment full of roaches. I never brought it up again.

I plop down on the couch before I go to my room and start my homework. Apá is watching *Primer Impacto,* that horrible tabloid news show that covers the most bizarre stories—Siamese twins, exorcisms, child abuse, hauntings, disfigured people. I don't know why people watch that stuff. When the segment on the cockroach-eating baby begins, I go into the kitchen for a glass of water. Amá is hunched over the sink, scrubbing pans. I wonder what it's like to clean houses all day and then come home and keep cleaning. I hate seeing her this way because it makes me feel so guilty—guilty for existing, guilty that she has to work like that for us.

"How was school?" Amá asks, and kisses me on the cheek.

Even when I'm punished and I'm convinced she doesn't love me anymore, she still kisses me on the cheek.

"It was okay."

"You look sick. Have you been eating junk at school?"

"No."

"Are you lying to me?" Amá always asks so many questions. I feel perpetually interrogated.

"I swear to God, I just ate a sandwich."

"I don't like the color on your face." Amá gets closer. She smells like dish soap.

"What color?"

"You look yellow."

"I'm brown, definitely not yellow," I say, staring at my arm.

"Well, you don't look right. I might have to take you to the doctor. You can't have a quinceañera looking like that, you know? You have to be pretty for your family. What will your sister think when she looks down on you from heaven?" The thought of Olga sitting in a cloud in the sky watching me is so stupid it almost makes me laugh. Does Amá actually believe she can see us?

"Is there something you're not telling me?" she says, feeling my forehead.

"I said no! Jesus Christ, leave me alone," I snap, which surprises both of us.

"You're going to be sorry when I'm not around, you'll see." Amá turns back to the sink. She is always going on and on about how she'll be dead one day. Do all mothers do that? It used to make me feel bad, but now it just gets on my nerves.

Suddenly, I feel something gurgle inside me—a warm, stretching pain—but it's not my stomach. When I go to the bathroom, I see a smear of reddish brown on my underwear. My period is a week early, but that's what I get forlying.

TEN

Winter is finally over. Christmas and New Year's came and went like a slow and anguishing blur. We spent the holidays at tío Bigotes's house with the rest of the family. Though my aunts and uncles tried to make it festive with loud music and a giant feast of tamales and roasted goat, Olga's absence floated silently around us. No one mentioned her, probably so Amá wouldn't cry—which she did anyway when we got home—but we could all feel it.

Every spring the teachers organize an outdoor field trip for each class. They've been doing it ever since Olga was in high school, maybe even before. I bet they feel sorry for us because we live in the city and never get to go anywhere. The only animals we see are pigeons and rats, which are essentially the same thing. Nancy from chemistry class told me she had never been outside of Chicago until two years ago, when she went to Wisconsin. I don't even know how that's possible.

I guess these trips are a way of giving us poor kids a taste of nature. Last year they took us to Starved Rock State Park, which was beautiful. I spent the entire time alone writing in my notebook next to a waterfall. Some people made out in a cave all day. Another group just sat around looking at their phones. What a waste. I don't understand how people can ignore beauty like that. I saw rabbits, beavers, toads, and all sorts of colorful birds. I saw a freaking eagle, which I wasn't even sure actually existed. I started to wish that I could live alone in a cabin by myself, like Henry David Thoreau, but I'd probably start to get restless after a few days.

This year after a never-ending bus ride, we finally arrive at the dunes. The sun is shining, and though it's chilly, it's beginning to look and feel like spring. The trees are growing leaves again, and some flowers are beginning to sprout. Not bad for April.

Ms. López and Mr. Ingman tell us we have to meet near the bus at 2 p.m.

"Under no circumstances will you leave the park. Do you understand?" Ms. López says, with her hands on her hips, trying to look tough but failing, because she's probably not even five feet tall.

As soon as we all mumble yes, Ms. López goes back to flirting with Mr. Ingman. I heard her laughing at all of his stupid jokes throughout the entire bus ride. I know both of them are divorced, and the way she looks at him makes me wonder if they're boning.

Lorena, Juanga, and I wander around the forest until it's time for lunch. I still haven't been able to shake him. He and Lorena are inseparable. I thought his charm would have worn off by now, but, no. The whole time he complains that he doesn't have any cell phone reception. I try to block him out and focus on the buds on the trees, the smell of leaves, and the sounds of birds, but he's so annoying that it's almost impossible. I have to put up with him because I'm going to ask him to help me get in touch with Jazmyn through his friend Maribel. I keep wondering who Olga told Jazmyn about when she ran into her at the mall a few years ago. I mean, it's hard to believe that she could have been talking about Pedro. How could anyone be excited about *him*?

"Ugh, I hate nature," Juanga says.

"How can you *hate* nature?" I grow more exasperated by him by the minute.

"I just do. It's boring."

"So what do you like to do for fun? What is your idea of beauty?"

"Shopping, partying, and. . . fucking," he laughs.

"That's all you like? Do you have any sort of inner life? Do you even know what that is?"

Lorena glares at me. "God, Julia. Shut up already, okay?"

"I'm sorry, but I don't understand how a person can say they hate nature. It's like saying you hate happiness or laughter. Or fun. I don't get how someone could be so freaking vapid."

"I don't know what that word means, but just stop."

Juanga looks like he wants to say something, but instead, he walks a few feet away from us and looks down toward the lake.

"Okay, okay. I'm done." I lift my hand to show that I giveup.

We climb to the top of the highest dune when it's time for lunch. The view is incredible. The waves are splashing, and the white dunes against the blue sky are unreal. I had no idea something so beautiful was close to Chicago. Lorena sets the blanket down for us. Amá had to be all Mexican about it and pack me cold cheese-and-bean burritos. God forbid I eat a regular sandwich.

Before we even start eating, Juanga, who is clearly obsessed with all things penile, starts talking about different shapes he's seen in his life. The craziest one, he says, was long and pointy, which seems like something out of a horror movie.

"That sounds terrifying," I say. "I would have run out of the room screaming, worried for my life."

"It was ugly," Juanga says, closing his eyes, then taking a small bite of his smelly tuna sandwich. "But it felt likeheaven."

I shudder.

"This one over here used to think that penises had hair on them. Not just the balls—the actual penis." Lorena points at me and laughs.

"What?" Juanga nearly chokes on his food. "How is that possible?"

"I had never seen one, so I assumed," I say, looking down at my cold burrito. "I mean, women have hair down there, so it made sense to me." I don't tell him I still haven't seen one in real life.

"Yeah, I had to be the one to break it down for her," Lorena says, and Juanga laughs so hard, he almost spits out his Coke. "She's a virgin, you know?"

Juanga's stunned. I had no idea that a fifteen-year-old virgin would be such an oddity. It's as if Lorena just told him I had a sixth toe or something. She lost her virginity when she was fourteen and thinks she's some sort of sexpert now.

"So what?" I glower at her. I can't believe she's embarrassing me in front of this idiot. I feel the burritos hardening into cement in my stomach.

"I'm just saying that for all the shit you talked about your sister being such a saint, you're really not that much different.

You're always so scared of your mother."

"Are you serious? Are you really talking about my sister right now?"

"Well, it's true, isn't it?" Lorena is defensive, all of a sudden. We've argued about stupid stuff a million times over the years, but this feels different. We've never done it in front of other people like this.

"And who is there for me to have sex with? Please, tell me. Am I supposed to just bang any loser I see?"

"That's not what I'm saying." Lorena looks frustrated.

"Then what are you trying to say?"

"Sometimes you're kinda stuck-up. I mean, I guess I shouldn't blame you. That's how your mom is." Lorena knows this is a low blow, and looks nervous right after she says it. Being compared to my mother makes me want to punch Lorena right in the mouth, but I do my best to control myself.

"So I'm stuck-up because I don't want to have sex with anyone? Am I hearing that correctly?"

"No, it's not even about that. That's not what I'm saying. Sometimes it's like you think you're too good for everything. You're too hard on people." Lorena doesn't make eye contact.

"That's because I *am* too good for everything! You think this is what I want? This sucks. This sucks so hard, I can't take it sometimes." I swing my arms, gesturing toward I don't know what. I'm so angry my ears feel as if they're on fire. "Just because you have sex with everything with a penis attached to it doesn't mean you're better thanme."

Lorena looks hurt. Juanga pretends to be distracted by his

phone, but I'm sure he's enjoying every second of it.

"Forget it. Sometimes I just can't talk to you," Lorena says.

I throw the rest of my sad burrito into my backpack and run down the dune, nearly slipping on my way down. I'm sure Juanga would love to see me topple over and break my neck in front of everybody.

When I get to the bottom, I kick the sand out of sheer frustration, and thanks to a gust of wind, some of it flies right into my eyes. I'm so pissed at Lorena, and I've had it up to my armpits with Juanga. Now I can't even ask him for Maribel's number. I don't even want to look at either one of them. I walk farther away from everyone and decide to make sand angels to see if that will calm me down. I close my eyes. I've always loved the feeling of sand against my skin. We rarely went to the lake when I was a kid, even though it was close. They were some of the only times I've ever seen Apá happy. He built sand castles with us, and swam and swam until it got dark. He said it reminded him of swimming in Los Ojos when he was young.

When I open my eyes, I see Pasqual standing over me. I nearly jump at the sight of his brown, pocked face.

"What the hell, man! What are you doing?"

"Watching you, duh."

"Yeah, I see that, you weirdo," I say, getting up and dusting the sand off my clothes.

"Your sister is dead."

"No shit. How do you know?"

"Everyone knows. Do you miss her?"

Pasqual looks like a nerd, but he's not even smart, which is always disappointing. It surprises me every single time he opens his mouth in class. His clothes are so dorky they're borderline offensive. He smells like basement and wears video game T-shirts, which he sometimes pairs with socks and sandals. Even his name is uncool—Pasqual is the name of an old Mexican man who sits on a dusty porch muttering about his lost chickens.

"Of course I miss her. She was my sister." I don't know why I bother replying. I should probably just tell him to eat a bag of wieners.

"Must be really hard."

I nod.

"Was she pretty like you?"

"Ew. Don't even. Geez." I wrap my jacket around me. A seagull squawks above us. I hate those things. They always look like they're up to no good.

"You don't even know you're pretty. That's sad."

"Shut up. Leave me alone." I walk toward the lake.

"You shouldn't hate yourself so much. Everyone is messed up, even when it doesn't seem like it."

The wind is starting to provoke the water, and a big beefy cloud drifts toward us. I can see the faint and hazy Chicago skyline across the lake. It'll probably rain soon, which will make this day even worse. Pasqual walks toward me, looking up at the sky with his mouth wide open, as if he's never seen it before.

"You don't know what you're talking about," I say.

"I do. And you know I do." Pasqual puts his hands in his

pockets and walks away.

I sit down and pull out *The Stranger* by Albert Camus. I try to read, but I'm distracted because I'm still seething about my fight with Lorena. I just stare at the water and count the waves. When I reach 176, I hear someone yell behind me.

It's Mr. Ingman. "Hey!" he says, and sits down next to me. "What are you reading now?"

I hold it up for him to see.

"So, a light beach read?" Mr. Ingman chuckles.

I nod. "I guess so."

"What do you think of it?"

"It's like nothing means anything. Nothing has a real purpose. I guess that's how I feel a lot of the time. Sometimes I really don't see the point in anything."

"Existential despair, huh?"

"Yes, exactly." I smile.

"I really want to know that you're okay. You keeptellingme you're fine, but I'm worried about you." Mr. Ingmanscoops sand with his hands and tries to form a pyramid.

"I don't know what okay means anymore. I don't know what normal is." What I don't tell him is that I can hardly get out of bed most mornings, that simply getting through the day feels like a monumental task.

"I think you should talk to someone. You can always talk to me, but I think you need a professional. I can try to find you a free program."

"That's very nice of you, but no thanks. I'm fine. Seriously." I'm a terrible liar, and I hope he doesn't notice.

"Okay. I'm going to trust you here. Please don't let me down."

"I won't." I force a smile. "I promise."

ELEVEN

We're barely halfway through the second semester of junior year, and all I can think about is getting the hell out of here and going to college. I feel as smothered and restless as ever. It's like I'm a wound-up toy with nowhere to move.

I keep looking for the key to Olga's room every time I'm alone in the apartment, which is rare these days. Either Amá or Apá is always home. It's as if they don't trust me to be by myself. Whenever they run out for a quick errand, though, I hunt for the key. I've even risked stumbling upon sex stuff in their room by searching all of their drawers. I found a key in a jewelry box once, but it didn't fit. I've also thought about removing the lock with tools, but I'm afraid they'll catch me in the act.

Meanwhile, I don't know what else to do to find out more about my sister. Angie isn't going to tell me anything, that's for sure. I think she might hate me, and I'm not even sure why. Olga didn't have many other friends, except some from high school I haven't seen in a long time. I also keep worrying that if Amá goes into her room and goes through her boxes, she's going to find her underwear and keel over. I didn't have a chance to take them out the day she caught me in there.

All I can come up with so far is: 1) Go to Olga's work; 2) Get her transcripts from community college; or 3) Swallow my pride and ask Juanga to get me Jazmyn's phone number from Maribel.

The more I think about it, the stranger it seems that Olga went to this school for years and never seemed close to getting a degree. What was she even studying? The few times I asked her she said business blah-blah, and since that is something I know absolutely nothing about and have no interest in, I never probed any further. I guess that's typical of me.

After school, I take the train to the college on the south side of the city. The building is so dreary and sterile that it almost looks like a prison. The outside is made of concrete, and the windows are only small, tinted slits. Amá is crazy if she thinks I'm going to go to a school like this. There are students all over the hallways, yelling and playing loud music on their phones. How can anyone learn anything in this place? This is not the kind of future I imagine for myself.

Before I approach the Records and Registration desk, I practice my script in my head. I know that they might not want to release her records, just like at the hotel, but maybe if they feel sorry for me, they'll give in. I have to emphasize how Olga is dead and how distraught I am. Maybe I should make myself cry.

"Hello, my name is Julia Reyes, and my sister came to school here," I tell the middle-aged woman at the desk. "I was hoping you could give me her transcripts. She's dead."

"Who was her emergency contact?" She sounds as if my request were causing her bodily harm. Her expression is so sour I bet her mother might not even love her.

"I don't know. My mom, I guess."

"What was her name? What years did she attend? And how

long ago did she die?" She types something into the computer.

"Olga Reyes. She attended school here from 2009 to 2013. She died in September."

The woman knits her bushy eyebrows. "What years did you say?"

"From 2009 to 2013," I repeat.

"Hmmm." She looks at the screen again and purses her lips. "Are you sure?"

"Yes, I'm sure. Why? Is it showing something different?"

"I can't give you that information."

"Why not? How are you going to say that and then not tell me why?" My ears grow hot.

"We are not allowed to release any records until one year after the student's death. At that time, the college will use its own discretion in deciding whether, and under what conditions, a student's information will be released to survivors or third parties." The woman sounds like a machine regurgitating information. I just told her my sister is dead, and she acts like a goddamn robot.

"You can't make any exceptions? I mean, she's dead. Please. You won't be violating her privacy. She's not going to come back from the grave and file a complaint. I really, really need this information. I don't think you understand how important it is. I'm very upset about my sister's death and would really appreciate your help. Please, just give me more information." I try to be as patient and polite as possible, even though I hate this woman.

"That's the school policy. No exceptions. You can come back

in September and see if the office will release the information then. Until that time, there is nothing I can do. Now please move along. There are people waiting behind you." The woman purses her thin lips and motions with her hand for me to get going.

I feel the anger rippling throughout my entire body. I know that I have an awful temper that is often impossible to control, but this woman is something special. *Relax*, I tell myself. *Get ahold of yourself, Julia.* I wish Lorena were here. She would probably know what to do.

"Do you have a soul? I mean, are you such a miserable sack of crap that you lack any kind of compassion? I guess I'd be upset, too, if I had a face like yours."

"Young lady, if you don't leave right now, I'm going to call security. I'm not joking." Her face is bright red now.

“Oh, go to hell,” I say, and turn around. The woman behind me gasps as if it were the most scandalous thing she’s ever heard in her whole entire life.

TWELVE

The quinceañera hangs over me like the blade of a guillotine. Okay, maybe that's a little dramatic, but I'm dreading it. Amá is making me take waltz classes with all my chambelanes, and I keep getting all the steps wrong. At first, I refused to do it, but then she said she wouldn't let me out of the house unless I did. What kind of quinceañera doesn't have a dance? What kind of daughter would refuse this tradition? I got so tired of her threats and complaints that I sucked it up and gave in.

I've been to many quinceañeras, and they're all the same—gross dresses, bland food, and odious music. My cousin Yvette played nothing but reggaeton at her party and then did a choreographed dance in an outrageous sequined outfit. I almost died of embarrassment for her.

I typically sneak a book inside and hide it under the table and pretend that no one can see me reading, but this time I can't because I'll be the star of this disaster. I keep thinking of ways to get the party canceled—shave my head and eyebrows, get a face tattoo, break my own legs, give myself the flu by licking a pole on the bus—but the truth is that Amá would probably wheel me in on my deathbed. There is no escaping this. I understand that this isn't necessarily meant as a punishment for me. Even though Amá doesn't understand me at all, I know she's not doing it to make me miserable. I'm not that naive. I know she feels guilty for not giving Olga a party because we were too broke at the time, but why should I have to suffer because of it?

I kept asking Amá where she was going to find the money to pay for it, but she insisted it was none of my business. A few weeks ago, though, I overheard her and Apá talking, and it turns out that Olga had accumulated a few thousand dollars in life insurance while she was working at the doctor's office. She also had some money in her savings account. Amá got the checks in the mail a few months after Olga died. Why couldn't they put that in a college fund or at least buy an air conditioner so we don't melt in the summer? Why couldn't they find a better apartment than this roach-infested dump?

On Sunday morning, Amá makes me help her with the party favors. We sit at the kitchen table covered with tulle, figurines, ribbon, and candied almonds. I don't know who would want such a gaudy souvenir. The candy is hardly even edible. What a giant waste of money, time, and resources.

I look closely at the porcelain quinceañeras and realize that they're all blond and their skin is literally white. They almost look like zombies.

"They didn't have brown ones?" I ask, holding one of the figurines up to the light. "This doesn't look like me at all."

"That's all they had," Amá says.

I want to throw them onto the floor and stomp on them, crushing their stupid little faces, but I do my best to keep calm because I know it's important to Amá.

"Where did you get these?"

"La garra. Now stop asking so many questions and get to work."

I should have figured. Everything from my party seems to come from the flea market.

After hours of gluing, stuffing, and tying, we hear the doorbell ring.

"Probably Jehovah's Witnesses," Amá says. "Tell them to stop bothering us. We're Catholic. I've told them hundreds of times."

But it's Lorena, wearing bright pink leggings and a furry white hoodie.

"What do you want?"

"I'm sorry I was being such a bitch," she says, looking down at my bunny slippers. "I can't stand this anymore. I hate it that we're not talking."

I cross my arms. "Whatever."

"Look, I said I'm sorry. What else do you want?"

“Why did you have to say all those things about me? Do you really think I’m stuck-up because I don’t want to have sex with any of the guys at school?”

“No, of course not. I was just being stupid, but sometimes you *are* too judgmental. I get frustrated with you.” I don’t even know if I can argue with that. I do dislike most people and most things, which is something Lorena doesn’t understand. “Aren’t *you* sorry? You were a bitch, too.”

“Yeah, I guess I’m sorry, but I hate Juanga and I don’t want to hang out with him anymore.”

“Are you a homophobe or something?”

“Seriously? How many times have we gone to the Pride Parade? Who introduced you to *Rocky Horror Picture Show*? And the *L Word*? Get out of my face with that.”

"Okay, okay. Sometimes Juanga can be a little bit of a sangrón."

Sangrón. That's exactly right. The word is usually used to describe someone who rubs you the wrong way, a jerk, or a douche. I think it means someone's blood is too heavy, or maybe it's that they have too much blood.

"A little bit?"

"All right, all right. You've made your point. Juanga says that you intimidate him, though. Just try to be nice, okay? He's really fucked up right now."

"What do you mean?"

"His dad. . . he beats him up. You know, because he's gay."

"What? Are you serious?"

"Yeah, he calls him a joto and tells him he's going to burn in hell. They're some weird religion. I forgot what it's called . . ." Lorena taps her chin with her forefinger. "Well, whatever, they even tried performing an exorcism on him. Or some shit like that. That's why he's always running away."

"Oh my God, really?" Now I feel guilty.

"It's okay. Just try to be nice from now on. Now get out of those stupid slippers, and let's get some pizza. I'll pay."

Though we can go anywhere to get a slice, we take the train all the way to the North Side because we're always looking for excuses to get out of our neighborhood. Life is much too boring otherwise.

I order three slices—two for me and one for Lorena.

"Two? Seriously?" Lorena raises her eyebrows.

"I can eat three but didn't want to embarrass you."

We sit at the only table available, next to an unattractive family. The three little kids are yelling and squirming all over the seats, and their sad, sloppy parents just ignore them.

"I never want to get married," I tell Lorena. "Look at that guy. He's wearing sweatpants with elastic on the ankles. Jesus. It's making me lose my appetite."

"I don't want to get married, either. My mom and José Luis are such idiots," Lorena says, putting down her pizza. I've never heard her talk about her mother that way.

"Gimme juice! Gimme juice!" the toddler next to us screams, his little red face smeared with grease and tomato sauce.

"Oh my God," I mouth to Lorena. She just shakes her head.

I'm still hungry when I finish both slices, but I tell my stomach to shut the hell up.

As we sit in silence, I feel sadness spreading inside me. I never know what to do when this happens. I try to convince myself that everything is okay, but I can't. It must show on my face because Lorena asks me what's wrong.

"Do you ever hate your life? Because I do. Like, all the time. I know it's messed up, but sometimes I wish I were dead, too. Why does everything have to be so hard? Why does everything have to hurt so much?" My throat aches like I'm about to cry, which startles me. I close my eyes for a second.

"Jesus, Julia. What the fuck? How can you say that?" Lorena slaps me on the arm. She looks angry.

"I don't know." I rub my eyes. "Sometimes I wonder if I'll make it to college. I mean, I can't take this anymore. It's not like my life was great before, but then Olga dies and everything turns to complete crap. Why, though? I don't understand. Nothing ever makes sense. I never get what I want."

"You're so close, Julia. You're almost out of here. You know you're smart. You're not going to live like this forever."

"Yeah, I guess," I say, though I don't entirely believe her.

"Please don't ever say anything stupid like that again, okay? Promise?"

"Okay, I'm fine." I take a sip of my water. I know I should change the subject. "So, I tried getting Olga's transcripts the other day."

"Where?"

"The community college."

"For what, though?"

"Because I've been realizing how weird it was that she never seemed close to getting her associate's degree. There's something that isn't right. I don't know what it is, but I have this feeling that won't go away. It's driving me crazy."

"You're always so paranoid. Just because you found some underwear doesn't mean anything. I told you already, all girls wear thongs. Well, except you."

"Yeah, because they're stupid and uncomfortable." I pause. "And what about the hotel key?"

"She could have found it at work and used it as a bookmark or something."

"Unlikely. I hadn't seen her read a book in years. And it was in an envelope."

"I think your imagination is messing with you. Some people are ordinary. I doubt your sister was living some interesting life. The girl was sweet and all, but she wasn't exactly fascinating. She never even went out. You need to stop worrying so much about Olga. I'm sorry, but she's gone and there's nothing you can do about that. You need to focus on your own life now."

Even though Lorena is right, I already know I'm not going to listen to her. "Can you ask Juanga to get Jazmyn's number from Maribel? You know, Olga's friend from the masquerade. I keep thinking she might know something."

Lorena rolls her eyes. “How’s she going to help you figure anything out?” The toddler next to us starts screaming again, and his parents don’t bother to shut him up.

“I don’t know. Maybe Olga said something to her. She probably doesn’t know anything, but I have to at least try. Promise you’ll ask?”

“Fine.” Lorena sighs. “But I really don’t see the point.”

As I walk home from Lorena’s, I notice the house on the end of her block is covered with red and black graffiti so scraggly and lazily painted, it pisses me off. If they’re going to ruin someone else’s property, they should at least try to make it beautiful. What did they paint that with—their butts?

When I cross the street on the next block, a car pulls up next to me. The driver lowers the window.

"Hey, girl."

Sometimes I yell things back when guys try to talk to me, but I know I probably shouldn't, because what if they come out of their cars and kick my ass?

"I said hi. Didn't you hear me?" the driver barks. "I have something to show you. You know, 'cause you have nice tits."

I don't even know how he can make that sort of assessment with my jacket and scarf.

"Yeah, didn't you hear him, bitch?" The passenger has joined in now. Wonderful.

I'm sweating even though it's so chilly I can see my breath. It's technically spring, but winter still has us in its clutches.

Typical Chicago. The icy dampness in my armpits reminds me of the time in health class we learned that sweat from stress smells worse than the kind your body produces when you exercise. It's because of some sort of hormone. I can picture the stink lines hovering above me right now. I look around, in case there's anyone nearby, but I only see a couple of kids playing catch down the street. The car follows me as I walk.

Halfway down the block, an old man comes out of his house. I stop in front of him, not knowing what to say, the words all coiled inside my mouth. What can this frail viejito do to help me?

"What's wrong, mija? Are you okay? You look like you saw El Cucuy." His sunken eyes look worried, and I have a sudden urge to press myself against his withered, little body and bury my face in his shoulder. Maybe it's because I never knew either of my grandfathers.

When I was a kid, I assumed that El Cucuy was a hideous monster that hid under the stairs, not an actual person. I thought he was a creature covered in matted fur, his face grotesque and contorted, with giant fangs and bloody eyes. I was wrong. If only terror could be that simple.

I point to the car, which has now made a full stop. The men stare at us, and I notice the driver has a neck tattoo, but I can't tell what it says. I think it might be a woman's name. How romantic.

"What do you want with this young lady?" the old man yells, shaking his fist. He must be at least eighty. A light wind could probably knock him down and shatter his bones.

"You got this old dude to protect you, bitch? I could kill you both." The driver laughs. "Don't worry, I'll find you again."

The car speeds away.

"Are you okay?" the old man asks.

I nod.

"Do you need to call your parents? Or the police?"

"No, I'm fine. I'm only a few blocks away."

"I'm not letting you walk alone," he says, shaking his head.

I wish he wouldn't, because if Amá sees us, it will be difficult to explain. But how can I argue with him? Maybe he saved my life. At the very least, he probably saved me from having to see that guy's penis.

We walk in silence until we get to my building. "Here it is," I say. "May God repay you." Though I don't believe in anything,

I know it's important to sound religious when talking to old people. It feels wrong not to pretend after he protected me from those dirtbags.

"May God protect you," he says, making the sign of the cross the way my grandma does when we leave Mexico. She calls it la bendición.

On Monday, I get Maribel's number from Juanga so I can call her for Jazmyn's number. What I like about Maribel is that she doesn't even bother asking why I need it. In fact, she says it's none of her business, which is perfect, because I don't feel like explaining. I can't stand nosy people. I wish everyone would leave me alone. I guess it's ironic that I'm all up in Olga's business now, but she's dead, so maybe it shouldn't count. Everything about Maribel conveys confidence and independence, like she's constantly giving the world the finger. I've never met anyone like her.

"Honey, I hope you find what you're looking for," she says in her gravelly voice, and hangs up.

I get inside my closet and dial Jazmyn's number. It rings and rings, and then it goes to her voice mail. I don't want to be annoying, but I feel like I have to talk to her, and I'm tired of waiting. I dial again. Maybe she thinks I'm a telemarketer. Right when I'm about to hang up, she answers.

"Hi, Jazmyn, this is, uh, Julia, Olga's sister." I don't know why I'm so nervous.

"Oh, hi. . . . How did you get my number?" She doesn't sound annoyed, just surprised. I can hear a dog barking in the background. She tells it to shut up.

"Through Maribel."

"Huh. Okay, so what's up? What can I do for you?"

I realize I probably should've been nicer when I saw her at the masquerade. I just didn't feel like explaining about my sister. That's not really the kind of news I'm eager to deliver, especially during a party. Plus, I was drunk. Plus, Jazmyn has a very irritating personality. I never liked her, and apparently, neither did Amá. She never knew when to shut up, always going on and on about pointless things. "Yeah, so I was wondering if you could tell me more about what Olga said when you saw her? Do you remember what year it was?"

“That was a long time ago. I don’t remember. Why do you want to know anyway?” Jazmyn sounds suspicious.

“Because, well. . .” How do I explain this to Jazmyn without telling her what I found? It’s none of her damn business, after all. “There are some things I’m trying to piece together, and I’m hoping something Olga said will help me.”

“I don’t get it. How?”

“Can you just please help me? I mean, my sister is dead.” Jazmyn is trying my patience once again. I hear Amá walk past my room. I hope she doesn’t come in here and ask me why I’m sitting in my closet.

“I don’t remember exactly when. It was, like, four years ago, I think,” Jazmyn says.

“Before or after graduation?”

"I really don't remember."

"So you don't remember the month or anything?"

Jazmyn sighs. "No."

"Was it hot or cold?"

"It was spring, I think.. . . Or was it summer? Hmm."

"What was she wearing?"

"I don't remember."

Jesus, Jazmyn is useless. "What did she tell you about the guy she was in love with? Did she tell you his name?"

"Maybe, but it was so long ago. I don't know." The dog barks again. Someone slams a door.

"Was it Pedro? She dated him senior year."

"Look, Julia. I'm telling you, I don't remember. I wish I could help you, but I can't."

"Did she say anything else? Like, where she met him or. . . or. . . anything, really."

"All she said was that she was in love and that he was amazing, and she kept telling me how happy she was. That's all I remember."

I know this isn't Jazmyn's fault, but I'm still frustrated.

"That's it?"

"Yes, that's it. Wait, she did say something about how he had a good job or something. I think. . . unless I'm not remembering it right."

"What kind of job?" Pedro worked at Little Caesars, so it can't be him. I don't think there is a person on this planet who would want to make those loathsome pizzas.

"I don't remember. I'm sorry. Like I said, it was a long time ago."

“Are you absolutely sure?”

“Positive. I wish I could help you more.”

“All right, well, thank you anyway, I guess. If you think of anything else, can you please call me back at this number? Really, it’s important.”

“Sure. Take care.”

I lean back into my clothes and take some deep breaths. Why does it always feel like life is a stupid puzzle I’ll never figure out?

THIRTEEN

With these majestic violins, you'd think we were in some castle on the English moor instead of a dingy church basement in Chicago. If I'm going to be forced to dance, I want to do it to the Smiths or Siouxsie and the Banshees, but Amá refused, of course. What would the family think? And why do I have to always listen to Satan music?

I feel like a fat sausage in this tight and tacky dress covered in frills, ruffles, and sequins. I can hardly breathe in my girdle, which I bet is rearranging my internal organs. *Girdle:* such an ugly word, a word as gross as what it does. Amá even chose the worst color imaginable for my skin—peach. It's as if she did it on purpose.

I'm the bad daughter who didn't deserve a quinceañera, but my parents wanted to throw a party for my dead sister. It didn't matter that the last things in the world I wanted were to pile my hair into a bunch of stiff curls on top of my head, wear this disgusting dress, and pretend to be happy in front of the whole family right before my sixteenth birthday. What a joke.

Thousands of dollars down the toilet, and here I am, dancing to this awful waltz with all of my boy cousins, some of whom I hardly know, most of whom don't even like me. It took weeks to learn the dance, and now I'm forgetting all the steps. I'm not graceful or smooth like I'm supposed to be, and Junior, my chambelán de honor, looks angry when he spins me around and

I lose my rhythm. Pablo sighs and shakes his head. I try forcing a smile to ease the tension, but it seems as if they all want to kill me right now.

Finally, the dance is over and everyone claps. I bet they just feel sorry for me because I ruined the whole thing.

Now I have to sit in a chair someone has placed in the middle of the dance floor. It's time to give my doll away to my little cousin and change into a pair of heels, which is ridiculous, because I haven't played with dolls since I was seven and I'll never wear high heels again in my life.

My parents approach me with a pair of shiny white shoes on a satin pillow. They slip off my flat Mary Janes and replace them with the new heels. I want to crawl into a hole and die, but I make myself smile, and everyone claps.

Then my cousin Pilar brings me a doll, and I walk over to my baby cousin Gabby, who is wearing the same exact peach dress as I am and is spinning in circles all around the dance floor. I guess the idea is that she's supposed to be me as a little girl. More clapping!

The DJ asks for a moment of silence for Olga, and Amá clasps her hands together and begins to cry. Apá looks down at the floor. I just stand there like a stump of a person.

Gabby runs to her mom, and I wobble over to Apá for the father-daughter dance. I don't understand why we have to do this, pretend I'm Daddy's little girl when he hasn't paid attention to me in years. He doesn't know anything about me. If you ask him what my favorite band or food is, he couldn't tell you. I can smell the beer wafting from his clothes and skin. Standing so close to him makes me uncomfortable. I don't remember the last time he's touched me. As he twirls me around the dance floor, everyone is smiling like crazy, as if this were the most precious thing they've ever seen. Some of my tías are crying, which probably has little to do with me and everything to do with Olga.

"Are you enjoying your party?" Apá asks.

"Yes," I lie.

"Good."

Finally, the song winds down and the show is over. According to this tradition, I'm a woman now. I'm available to men. I can wear makeup and high heels. I can dance! But if this is what it means to be a woman, maybe I don't want to be one.

I sit down and wipe the sweat from my face with a napkin. I'm sweating so hard I think I can smell my own crotch beneath all the layers of fabric. I bet my makeup has melted off.

I decided to invite Juanga to my party in my attempt to be less of an asshole. His parents kicked him out again, and he's been staying on his cousin's couch. My life is shitty, but at least I have a home, I guess. It makes me wonder how Amá would react if I were gay. Maybe in some sort of weird way, she would be relieved, since she's so afraid ofmen.

Juanga is wearing a suit one size too big and a skinny purple tie. He runs to me and kisses both cheeks. He says that's how they do it in Europe.

"Oh my God, that dress is a monstrosity, but you still look beautiful," he says. "Right, Lorena? That face. I mean, wow.

Who did your makeup?"

"My cousin Vanessa. My mom said I couldn't be trusted to do it myself."

Lorena laughs. "Yeah, the makeup is bomb, but the dress . . ."

"I know," I say. "I can't stand to look at myself."

I ask Lorena to help me with my dress while I pee. She smells sweet like perfume and sweat. Her makeup is smeared under her eyes, and her giant orange-blond curls are starting to fall flat.

My dress drags on the wet and dirty floor of the handicapped stall. I ask Lorena to unzip me for a second because it's been smashing my stomach and boobs all day, and I can't take it anymore. Amá insisted it had to fit this way because otherwise it would be "indecent." I try loosening my girdle, but I'm completely strapped in with a series of hooks and buttons. Can this be considered child abuse?

Tía Milagros comes into the bathroom as we exit the stall. I don't know how it's possible for a person to look worse when they dress up, but she's managed to do it. Her green dress is short and exposes the varicose veins crisscrossing up her legs. I try not to roll my eyes, but it's become a reflex whenever I see her.

"Ay, Julia. What a nice party. I bet Olga is so happy for you right now." She sighs.

"Olga is dead." I know I should probably shut up, but I'm tired of everyone pretending Olga is an angel looking over us.

Tía Milagros shakes her head as she looks at herself in the mirror. "Que malcriada. What happened to you? You weren't always so angry, so . . . I don't know . . ."

"What? I wasn't always so what, tía?" I feel the loud music vibrating all of my insides like jelly.

Lorena's eyes open wide, and she sucks in a big gulp of air. She knows I'm about to pop off.

"I don't know, never mind." Tía Milagros shakes her head and applies another coat of her light orange lipstick in the mirror.

"Just say it," I insist. "What is so terrible about me? Why does everyone treat me like I'm a disappointment? Who are you to judge me, huh? Tell me. Like you're so great—all bitter because your husband left your ass years ago. Get over it already."

Tía Milagros's eyes glisten. She presses her mouth shut as if to keep herself from saying anything else.

"Holy shit, Julia," Lorena whispers as tía Milagros storms out of the bathroom.

• • •

Lorena makes me dance with her cousin Danny, who I've never seen before. I don't even know how he got in because he wasn't invited. Before I can protest, Lorena pushes me right into him on the dance floor.

Danny is not my type at all—shaved head, shiny shirt, snakeskin boots, and a gold chain that looks like a rosary. Plus, he smells like vinegar. That's the opposite of what I like, and Lorena knows it. She's always making fun of me for liking dorky white guys in the movies we watch, and tries to set me up with dudes I would never in a million years touch with a latex glove. Danny doesn't say much, and neither do I.

I can barely keep up with the fast cumbia. As Danny spins and jerks me around, I can feel Amá's eyes hooked to my back. According to this party, I can dance with boys now, but she doesn't seem happy about this.

I keep thinking of tía Milagros the rest of the night. She had it coming, but I know I'm screwed. Gossiping is her favorite pastime. If she had a dating profile, it would probably read something like: "My hobbies include knitting, cooking, teasing my bangs, talking shit, and collecting polyester dresses that look terrible on my body."

Toward the end of the night, Angie comes in with a giant yellow gift bag. She looks so much better than the last time I saw her. Her curly hair is in a loose bun, and her green eyes are outlined with dark eyeliner. Her blue wrap dress hugs her body perfectly.

I pretend I don't see her, but she walks toward me anyway.

"Happy birthday. Congratulations," she says, handing me the bag.

"It's not my birthday, and I'm practically sixteen."

"Oh yeah. Then why. . ." Angie scrunches her face.

I don't feel like explaining. "Why are you here?" I know that's rude, but I'm still angry.

"Your mom invited me."

"Yeah, I guess the party is more for Olga than it is for me."

"What do you mean?" My little cousin Gabby runs between us.

"Forget it."

"Well, I just wanted to say congrats."

"How nice of you! I'm so delighted." I'm not entirely sure if Angie knows I'm being sarcastic.

"No problem." Angie looks at the door like she wants to leave.

"Did Olga have a boyfriend?" I say before she walks away. "Or girlfriend?"

"What?"

"You heard me. Why did you say that thing about her love life the last time I saw you? Did she?"

"First of all, I didn't say anything about Olga having a love life; you put those words in my mouth. Second of all, you're her sister. Don't you think you would know? How would she be able to keep that from your family? You really think Olga would be able to have some sort of secret relationship without your mother finding out? You know better than anyone that you can't get anything past your mom."

"What do you mean by that? Why would you say 'secret relationship'? That's really freaking suspicious."

Angie sighs.

"There's something you're not telling me. I know it. That's why you're acting so weird."

"Calm down, Julia."

One of the things I hate most in life is people telling me to calm down, as if I'm some out-of-control lunatic who isn't entitled to have feelings.

"Don't talk to me like that. Just get out of my face. Just. . . just leave, okay?"

Angie walks away, and I grip the bag until my knuckles turn

white. I remind myself to breathe. When I turn around, she's hugging Amá. She's probably telling her that she stopped by only to drop off the gift, that she has another obligation.

After the music stops and people start gathering the leftovers, I see tía Milagros talking to my parents. Apá furrows his brow and shakes his head. Amá covers her mouth with her hand. I sit at an empty table and eat the rest of my cake. It's peach, the same color as my dress, and so sweet, it makes me sick, but I keep shoveling it into my mouth anyway. Maybe I can poison myself with sugar.

We ride home in a thick fog of silence. The apartment smells funky because we forgot to take out the garbage before we left.

Apá flicks on the light, and the roaches scurry in all directions, looking for dark corners to hide in. We do the cockroach dance, which consists of stomping all over the kitchen floor, because they have a party whenever we're not home. This time I have to lift my dress and kill them with my new white shoes.

When we're done, Amá sweeps them up and flushes them down the toilet, in case some of them still have babies inside them. Usually, she mops the floor with bleach or Pine-Sol, but it doesn't seem like she's going to do that tonight.

Amá comes back from the bathroom, and they both turn toward me.

"Your aunt told me what you said to her in the bathroom." She comes closer. "All this money we spend on your party, and you act like this and embarrass us?"

"It was her fault," I say, looking away. "She never knows when to shut her mouth."

"Is this how we raised you, cabrona? To disrespect your elders? Who do you think you are?" Apá yells suddenly. This is probably the most he's said to me in years.

"Julia, I didn't raise my children to be disrespectful. Why are you like this? What have I done to deserve this?" Amá keeps using the plural, even though I'm the only one left. She turns to Apá. "Rafael, I don't know what to do with your daughter anymore," which is what she says when she's mad at me. Suddenly, I no longer belong to her.

Apá doesn't say anything, as if he's so angry that words are useless to him.

Amá sighs and wrings her hands. “Maybe Bigotes is right. Maybe this country is ruining you.”

“Like living in Mexico would fix anything,” I say. “My life sucks, but it would suck even harder in Mexico, and you know it.”

I wonder if Amá is going to cry, hit me, or both, because she looks like I annihilated her. And it startles me.

Amá just shakes her head. “You know, Julia, maybe if you knew how to behave yourself, to keep your mouth shut, your sister would still be alive. Have you ever thought about that?” She finally says it. She says what her big, sad eyes were telling me all along.

After summer break

FOURTEEN

I meet Mr. Ingman after school every Thursday so he can help me prepare for the ACTs and apply to colleges. He insists, even though he isn't my teacher anymore now that I'm a senior. I told him that my counselor was already helping me, but he said she didn't know her ass from her elbow. (His exact words.) He's one of the smartest people I've ever known, so I would be stupid to refuse. And after spending the entire summer cleaning houses with Amá, I'm almost happy to be back in school, working my brain instead of my hands.

My grades last year were okay. I managed to pull them up at the end and mostly got B's, but I'm still worried about getting into the colleges I want. This semester I'm determined to kick some serious ass, though. *I'm back with a vengeance, bitches!* I'm applying to three schools in New York, two in Boston, and one in Chicago. Mr. Ingman helped me pick out diverse schools with good English programs. Even though I don't want to stay here, he says I have to apply to at least one school in the state, just in case. But I know I have to go far away. I love my parents, of course, and I feel guilty for wanting to leave them, but living here would be too hard. I need to grow and explore, and they won't let me. I feel like I'm being kept under a magnifying glass.

Mr. Ingman is showing me all the ins and outs of college applications, which I appreciate, because I have no idea what I'm doing. Some of the schools charge up to ninety dollars, and since I'm what they like to call "low income," Mr. Ingman is teaching me how to apply for waivers.

Though I had to fork over most of what I made working with Amá, I was able to save $274, which should at least cover my flight if I end up choosing a school on the East Coast. I've been in desperate need of a new pair of shoes, but I refuse to touch any of that money.

According to Mr. Ingman, I have to emphasize the fact that my parents are still undocumented. "Admission committees love that stuff," he insists.

"But it's a secret," I say. "My parents told us we weren't supposed to tell anyone. What if I send in my application, and then the school calls immigration and my parents get deported? Then what?"

"No one is going to deport them. That would be impossible."

"But they're illegal," I whisper.

"Undocumented," Mr. Ingman corrects me.

"My family call themselves ilegales or mojados. No one says *undocumented*. They don't know about being politically correct."

"It's a very stigmatizing word. I don't like it. Same with *illegal aliens*. That's even more repugnant." Mr. Ingman shudders as if the words feel venomous inside his body.

"Fine, *undocumented*." I finally give in.

I grew up learning to be afraid of la migra and listened to my parents and family members go on and on about papeles. For a long time, I didn't understand what was so important about these pieces of paper, but I eventually figured it out. My parents could have been sent back to Mexico at any moment, leaving me and Olga here to fend for ourselves. We probably would have ended up with one of our aunts with papers, like some of the kids at school, or we would have gone back to Mexico with our parents. I remember the raids in Apá's factory when I was little. La migra shipped mojados back by the busload, separating families forever. It must have been some sort of miracle that these sweeps were never during his shift. Although Apá is only physically present most of the time, like some sort of household fixture, I can't imagine what it would be like to live without him.

Like my parents, I've always been suspicious of white people, because they're the ones who call immigration, who are rude to you at stores and restaurants, who follow you when you're shopping, but I think Mr. Ingman is different. No other teacher has ever been this interested in me.

"Okay, how do you know for sure that they won't get deported?" I insist one last time.

"Please, Julia. Trust me. I've helped dozens of students like you get into college. We're in Chicago, not Arizona. That doesn't really happen here. Not like that. No one is going to read your essay and track your parents down. Plus, have I ever lied to you?"

"Not that I know of."

Mr. Ingman nods. "Fair enough. But I wouldn't lead you astray. I really want you to go to school."

"Why, though? I don't get it. Why do you care so much?"

"You were one of the best students I've ever had, and I want to see you do well. You have to get the hell out of this neighborhood. You have to go to school. You can become something great. I see it in you. You're a fantastic writer."

No one has ever said anything like this.

"Come on. Get writing. I don't have all evening," Mr. Ingman says, looking at his watch. "You need to jot down some ideas, at the very least."

I stare at the giant world map, not knowing where to begin. What makes me interesting? What makes me who I am? What story does the world need to know?

In 1991, my parents—Amparo Montenegro and Rafael Reyes—got married and left their hometown of Los Ojos, Chihuahua, in search of a better life. My sister, Olga, was born later that year. All they wanted was the American dream, but things didn't work out that way for them. Amá cleans houses, and Apá works in a candy factory. Life for us was already difficult, and then last year my sister was run over by a truck.

We have a half day, so I take the train to the used bookstore in Wicker Park after school. I've saved a total of seventeen dollars from my lunch money in the last few weeks and should be able to buy two books. My stomach felt like it was eating itself those times I had nothing but a scoop of lumpy mashed potatoes, but it was worth it. If—*when*—Ibecome rich, I want a library so big that I'll need a ladder to reach all my books. I want first editions, too. I want ancient tomes that I have to handle with forceps and rubber gloves.

I go to the poetry section first to see if they have any

Adrienne Rich books. I read one of her poems in English class last week, and I haven't been able to get it out of my head. It just repeats and repeats. Sometimes I'm washing my hands or brushing my teeth, and there it is, just bouncing in my brain: "I came to explore the wreck./The words are purposes./The words are maps." I'm so excited to find one of her books for only six dollars.

I love the smell of old bookstores—paper, knowledge, and probably mildew. I hate the cliché that you shouldn't judge a book by its cover, because covers say so much about what's inside. Take *The Great Gatsby*, for instance—the woman's melancholic face against the city lights in the distance is the perfect representation of the quiet misery of that era. Covers matter. Those who don't think so are full of crap. I mean, I wear band

T-shirts for a reason. Lorena wears leopard-print spandex for a reason.

I fantasize about what the books I'll write one day will look like. I want colorful artwork on the covers, like a Jackson Pollock or Jean-Michel Basquiat painting. Or maybe I can use a haunting photograph by Francesca Woodman. There's one of her crawling on the floor in front of a mirror that would be perfect.

I see an older edition of *Leaves of Grass* and hold it up to my face. It smells amazing, and it's only six dollars.

I walk up to the third floor and find a table near the critical theory section. It's crammed, but there's one free chair left. After a few minutes, the woman next to me leaves, and a guy approaches and asks if he could sit down. He is tall, with shaggy brown hair, and is wearing a flannel shirt and tight, dark jeans. He's cute.

"Sure," I say, and bury my head in my book.

"That's one of my favorites," he says.

Something between a croak and a squeak comes out of my mouth. I'm horrified. "What?" I finally manage to say. "Are you talking to me?"

"Uh-huh. *Leaves of Grass*. But that's probably not worth saying. Whoever doesn't like Walt Whitman is probably dead inside."

I can't believe this. Is this guy really talking to me about poetry right now? "I would have to agree. He is, indeed, amaster."

He nods. "So, what's your favorite book?"

"I don't know. I mean, how do you decide? I love so many. . . . *The Awakening? One Hundred Years of Solitude? The Great Gatsby? Catcher in the Rye? The Heart Is a Lonely Hunter? The Bluest Eye?* Poetry or prose? If poetry, then maybe Emily Dickinson . . . or wait, maybe. . . Fuck, I don't know." I'm not sure why the question fills me with panic.

"I love *The Catcher in the Rye* and *The Great Gatsby.* Haven't read *One Hundred Years* yet. Don't you think it'sironic that after the *Gatsby* movie, people started throwing 1920s parties? It's so stupid, romanticizing that time."

I laugh. "People really threw parties? Like, flappers and shit?"

"Yeah, some of my mom's friends did it. I was, like, wow, you totally missed the point of the book."

"I doubt a person like me would've been allowed into those

kinds of parties in the 1920s. Maybe I'd be in the kitchen or cleaning the bathrooms," I joke.

He laughs. "Exactly. Like it was such a magical time. It probably was for, what, ten people?"

"What about you? What's your favorite book?"

"*A Clockwork Orange.*"

"I tried reading it once, but it made no damn sense. And the movie was so violent." I shudder.

"Could be you're not giving it a chance. It's a critique, you know?"

"Yeah, I guess. Maybe I should read it again." The truth is I'll never read it again because the book got on my nerves, but I want to keep the conversation going.

"What's your name, anyway?"

"Um. Julia?" I don't know why my answer comes out sounding like a question, as if I don't know my own name.

"I'm Connor," he says, and shakes my hand. His eyes are brown and intense, like he's trying to figure something out.

"It's nice to meet you," I say. I'm so nervous, I can hardly look at him. This is new and hazy territory for me. Guys never talk to me, unless you count the creeps on the street who whistle and say gross things about my body.

The two of us sit there in awkward silence for several seconds. I look at a stack of books on the table and try to think of something witty, but my mind is blank.

"Do you ever smell books?" I finally say.

"What do you mean?"

"I mean, literally. Don't you like the way they smell? They're all so different. I once found one that smelled like cinnamon. I wonder if they kept it in a pantry. I always wonder about those kinds of things. Sometimes you can tell that they were kept in a basement because they have that dampness, you know?" Crap, I can't believe that just came out of my mouth. He's going to think I'm a complete weirdo.

"So, you're a book sniffer, is that what you're telling me?" Connor pretends to be serious, as if I just told him I was a meth addict. He exhales loudly. "Wow."

I let out a yelp and cover my mouth. The other people at the table glare at us. I can't stop laughing.

"Maybe you should go. Looks like you're having trouble controlling yourself." He turns to the others at the table and shakes his head. "Sorry, guys. I think she's having an episode."

That makes me laugh even harder. I gather my things, and Connor follows me downstairs.

After I buy my books, we both walk outside. The sun is bright and makes me squint.

“Are you okay now?” Connor puts his hand on my shoulder.

“It was your fault! You started it.” I pretend to be mad.

“If that’s what you want to tell yourself.” He shrugs. “How about some coffee? Or some warm milk to calm you down?”

“I don’t know. . . .” I hesitate, even though I already know I’m going to say yes.

“Come on. It’s the least I can do after all the trouble I’ve caused you.”

“Fine,” I say. “I guess you do owe me.”

• • •

Connor takes me to a coffee shop bustling with hipsters and their expensive computers and gadgets. I imagine a giant spotlight on me as I enter, emphasizing my ancient jeans, torn sneakers, and greasy hair. I wish I could go back in time and take a shower and put on better clothes. But how would I have known this was going to happen? I was planning on being invisible today.

We settle into a small table in the corner, near a man with a stupidly big mustache. How can a person walk around like that and expect to be taken seriously? The hideous thing almost reaches his ears.

I keep wondering if this is a date because, technically, I've never been on one before. The closest I ever came was that time at the lake with Ramiro, Carlos's cousin, who treated me like I was some sort of cheap prize. If Connor tries to kiss me, then, definitely, it's a date. Otherwise, I'll have to ask Lorena. She knows about these kinds of things.

"So, tell me about yourself, Julia."

"What do you want to know?"

"Where you're from, what you like, what your favorite color is. You know, boring stuff like that."

"I'm from Chicago. I like books, pizza, and David Bowie. My favorite color is red. Your turn."

"But where are you *from* from?"

"I'm *from* from Chicago. I just told you."

"No, what I mean is . . . Forget it." Connor looks embarrassed.

"You mean you want to know my ethnicity. What kind of brown I am."

"Yeah, I guess." Connor smiles apologetically.

"I'm Mexican. You could've just asked, you know?" I can't help but smirk. "I prefer it when people are straightforward."

"Yeah, I see your point. Sorry."

"Don't worry about it. It's cool. What about you, though? Where are you from? What are you into?"

"Umm. . . Evanston, burgers, and drums."

"But where are you *from* from?"

Connor laughs. "I'm a typical American mutt—German, Irish, Italian, and—"

"Wait, wait! Let me guess. Your great-grandmother was a Cherokee princess."

"No, I was going to say Spanish."

"Ah yes, our conquerors. And your favorite color?"

"Yellow."

"Yellow? Gross, man."

"Whoa. Tell me how you really feel." He laughs. "Yellow like the sun. You can't tell me you hate the sun."

"Of course not, I'm not a monster." A man with a neck beard sits down next to the mustache guy. What a perfect pair.

"If you are, you're the cutest monster I've ever seen."

I don't know what to say, so I take a big gulp of coffee that burns my mouth and throat. Smooth. "Have you ever read 'The Yellow Wallpaper'? Ever hear of yellow fever? Jaundice? Yellow can be bad news, is all I'm saying."

Connor's eyes crinkle when he smiles, which I think is kind of charming. "Tell me more. Any other strong opinions on colors? Shapes? Patterns? I have a feeling you're a very interesting person."

"Me?"

"No, that mustachioed dude over there," he says, pointing.

The man looks over at us, outraged, which makes me laugh so hard, I nearly spit out my coffee. "I think paisley is detestable and should be banned until the end of time. Same goes for pastel-colored clothing. Oh, and khakis are repugnant." I close my eyes and stick out my tongue to show my disgust.

The moment seems almost surreal. I picture myself watching us from another table. I've never been in a coffee shop like this, and no one ever wants to get to know me. The only other person besides Lorena who cares about what I think is Mr. Ingman, and he's paid to be interested in my opinions. Sometimes I'm convinced the world wants me to shut up, that I'm better off folding myself into a million pieces.

"You're funny," Connor says, but doesn't laugh.

"My sister died last year." I don't mean to say that. It just comes out.

"Oh my God, I'm so sorry." He takes my hand, and I almost recoil. It feels warm and moist. I don't remember the last time I've been touched like this. "Were you two close?"

"Well. . . no. Not really. I don't know. I don't think I really knew her. We were really different, and now that she's dead, it's like I want to get to know her. It's weird. A little late for that, I guess."

"It's never too late. Don't say that."

I'm not sure why I'm telling him all of this. He probably doesn't even care, but I can't stop myself. Maybe I shouldn't drink so much coffee because it always makes me nervous and talkative.

"I went through her room once and found a few things. Then my mother locked the door, and I haven't been able to get in since. I don't know what else to do. I need to keep looking, but it seems pointless sometimes. She has this laptop, but I don't have her password. First, I have to find a way to get back into her room, though."

"I actually know a lot about computers. Don't tell anyone, but my friends and I have hacked into a few things. Okay, *a lot* of things. If you're able to get it, I can probably unlock it for you."

"Are you serious?"

Connor smiles and squeezes my hand. "Totally, absolutely, completely serious."

Connor and I walk around for hours and hours. We go into neighborhoods I didn't even know existed, looping and zigzagging with no real destination. We end up in some of the same places without realizing how we got there. I'm smiling so much my cheeks hurt. When we get tired, Connor buys us donuts, and we sit on the swings of a giant park even though it's chilly. It smells like wood chips and wet leaves. We talk about our plans for college, books, and our favorite bands. Finally, someone who likes David Bowie. Someone who reads!

At the train station, he kisses me on the cheek and tells me he wants to see me again soon. This is definitely a date. It's such a beautiful day, I bet all the birds are doing it.

Today I meet Connor on Devon Avenue after successfully lying to Amá about a homework assignment that supposedly requires me to go to the Cultural Center downtown. As always, she's suspicious, but I'm able to convince her after some coaxing and whining. It takes me two buses and one train to get there, which is a pain in the ass, especially because it's cold and on the verge of snowing, but I'm glad to see another part of the city. I'm in awe of all the beautiful and bright saris glittering in the store windows. I wonder how much they cost because they look cool as hell. The day is gloomy, and I'm glad to see sparkles and loud colors.

My legs feel rubbery as I walk toward the restaurant and see Connor standing outside with his hands in his pockets. Is that what love feels like? I don't know.

"Why, hello there, Madame Reyes," he says, and gives a little wave.

When I get nervous, sometimes I clown around because I'm not sure what else to do. I curtsy and give him my hand like some pretentious aristocrat, which makes him laugh.

"It's nice to see you," he says.

"It's nice to see you, too." I suddenly feel so shy that I can't even look at him.

"This is the best Indian restaurant in the city, in my opinion," Connor says as we sit down. "Super-cheap, too."

I hope he's paying, because when I look at the menu, even though it's "super-cheap," I still can't afford it.

"You know, I've never had Indian food," I say as I scan the lunch specials.

Connor puts his hands on the table and looks straight at me. "Never? Are you serious? How is that possible?"

"I didn't even know this neighborhood existed, to be honest."

"Well, that is a very sad story," Connor says, and pretends to look devastated.

The air is heavy with spices I can't identify. A musical is playing on the TV near the register. A tall man sings mournfully as he chases a beautiful woman down a mountain. I think it's meant to be romantic, but it seems pretty rapey to me.

The food is so good I can't believe it. "Where have you been all my life?" I say to my plate, and scoop another generous helping. There is so much going on—cheese, spices, peas, and God knows what else—and it tastes like a foreign paradise.

"It seems you like the food more than you like me," Connor teases. "I'm starting to get jealous. Maybe I should leave you two alone."

I don't know what to say to that, so I just smile and continue to stuff my face until I'm too full to move.

Connor wants to go back to the used bookstore where we met because he's looking for a novel by a Japanese author I've never heard of, so we take the train south together. After finding his book, we sit on a bench at the park down the street. I zone out, staring at the trees for a while, and when I turn back toward him, his face is right next to mine. He leans in for a kiss.

My heart is beating so hard I wonder if Connor can feel it. He puts his hands through my hair and holds my neck as if kissing me were some sort of emergency. This is nothing like the time with Ramiro. Connor is gentle with his tongue, and something about the way he touches me makes me feel so wanted.

After a while, we finally stop kissing and sit there in awkward silence until we see a woman walking a hairless cat in a puffy jacket. We just look at each other and lose it. I laugh so hard I think I might bust a gut.

FIFTEEN

I always catch myself staring at the door, like a dope, waiting for Olga to come home. People said it would get better with time, but that's not exactly true. There are moments I miss her just as much as I did when she first died. I know we weren't that close, but now that she's gone, I feel like I'm missing an organ. I still have dreams about her, too. Sometimes they're harmless, like the two of us in the car or at the kitchen table, eating breakfast, but every once and a while, she appears covered in blood, her body twisted and crushed, and I wake up screaming.

Amá still cries a lot. I can hear her in the bathroom sometimes. I think she covers her mouth with a towel to muffle her sobs. Her eyes are always red, too. I wish I knew how to help, but I feel useless, as always. Apá is as silent as ever. He could be dying inside, and no one would even know.

I've gone back to Olga's school three times now, but each time I saw the same bitter-looking woman, and walked right back out. She would probably remember me and call security for real this time. I've also called the Continental five more times, hoping to get a worker who'll bend the rules, but they keep saying they're not allowed to give any information about their guests, even if they're dead. If only I could get Olga's laptop from her room so Connor can unlock it.

Dead. Dead. Dead. Always dead ends. Story of my life.

I remember the stupidest things now, too, small details about me and Olga I never even thought about before. Like the other day, I was waiting in line at the grocery store and remembered the time I got a paper cut on a *Sesame Street* book when I was four, and became so afraid of it that I refused to touch it again. Olga knew how much I loved the book, so she read it to me over and over. I'm sure she memorized it. Then yesterday I was walking home from school and thought of the night at Mamá Jacinta's house when our cousin Valeria told us about La Llorona, the ghost woman who wails through the streets because she drowned her own children. I couldn't sleep for days, convinced that every squeak or rustle meant that La Llorona was coming to drag me by the hair and kill me in the river. Olga stayed with me every night until I got over my susto. This morning, as I was brushing my teeth, I remembered when we bought a bag of chocolates and hid it in her room. We'd eat one in secret every day after school, as if the candy were some sort of high-stakes contraband. That was probably the most disobedient thing Olga ever did when we were kids.

When I get these flashbacks, I feel like someone scooped my soul out and trampled it on the dirty ground. Everything was so much easier when we were little. What I thought was hard at the time, now seems easy in comparison.

Happiness is a dandelion wisp floating through the air that I can't catch. No matter how hard I try, no matter how fast I run, I just can't reach it. Even when I think I grasp it, I open my hand and it's empty.

Every once in a while, I do have moments of joy, though, like when I get to see Connor. He calls me almost every night, and we talk until my ear gets hot. What I like most about him is that he makes me laugh harder than anyone I've ever known. The other day he cracked me up with a story about him and his best friend arguing over some sports team. They got so angry that they ended up throwing hot dogs at each other. And because they were still hungry and didn't want to waste food, they picked the hot dogs off the grass and ate them right before a flock of seagulls usurped them. I laughed so much I snorted, which made us both laugh even harder.

Each time I'm on my phone, Amá just happens to walk by my room. It's hard to really talk when someone is always hovering over you. Although Amá doesn't understand English that well, I'm still afraid of what she'll hear. She must already know that I'm talking to a guy.

The idea of college also cheers me up when I feel shitty. Thank God I skipped a grade, or else I'd be stuck here for another year. The only people I'll miss are Lorena, Mr. Ingman, and Connor. Juanga has grown on me, too. I just wish he and Lorena would stop drinking and smoking weed all the time. Sometimes they act kind of erratic, which scares me a little, like the time they were convinced we should crash a party even though the host threatened to kill Juanga over his ex-boyfriend last year. With a knife and everything. I was able to persuade them it was a horrible idea, and we went to the movies instead. Lorena smuggled a bottle of Jack Daniel's in her purse, and she and Juanga polished it off, drank it as if it were water and they were dying of thirst in the desert. I only drank a few sips, told them it tasted like violence, and they looked at me like I was out of my damn mind. And weed makes me paranoid, like something terrible is about to happen, so I stopped smoking it. Real life is scary enough, thank you.

Lorena insists we go sledding because, according to her, winter is boring as fuck, and she's going to lose her mind if she's sequestered in her apartment any longer. I'm getting stir-crazy, too. It happens every single year. It doesn't matter that I've lived in Chicago forever; the winters here are always a kick in the teeth.

I've never been sledding in my life. I've heard of it, have seen it on TV, but my parents have never taken me, just like we've never been to Disney World or watched *The Sound of Music*. I assumed it was just something white people did.

"Where are we going to get the money for sleds?" I ask Lorena as she fiddles with my makeup on my dresser. "And how did you even think of this anyway?"

Lorena shrugs. "I dunno, saw it in a movie. We don't need to buy real sleds, dummy. All we need is pieces of plastic to slide on." She blows into her hands and rubs them together. It's cold as hell in here because Amá always keeps the heat down in the winter to save money. I usually walk around the apartment wrapped in a blanket and wearing a hat, looking like a fool.

"And where are we gonna find that?" I'm usually up for an adventure, and I'm bored, too, but the idea of being all wet and cold is not at all enticing.

"I don't know, but it can't be that hard." Lorena puts on a coat of my lip gloss.

I think about spending the entire weekend indoors, and suddenly sledding doesn't seem so unpleasant. "I guess that sounds kind of fun."

After a trip to the hardware store, Lorena, Juanga, and I are at the top of the hill at Palmisano Park, in Bridgeport, holding cheap plastic mats. The man who helped us seemed confused about our purchase but wasn't interested enough to ask. He just scowled and sent us to the register.

There are no real hills in Chicago, but the park used to be a quarry, so it has a decent slope. There is a circle of white Buddha heads half buried in the snow and a perfect view of the skyline at the top of the hill. I can't believe I'd never been here before.

Sometimes it feels like I've been living in a dark hole. There's probably so much of the city I've never seen.

Unlike us, several families are using legit sleds, and two little kids are rolling down the hill in their snowsuits, squealing the whole way.

"See, it's not just for white people," Lorena says, with a smug smile.

"Well, color me embarrassed!" I say dramatically, and put my hands on my cheeks in fake surprise.

Lorena laughs. "Shut up."

"I hope this works," I say to Lorena. "There's nothing to grip on to."

"Jesus, just hold on to the sides. Shouldn't you be more positive now that you're in love and all that?"

I can't help but grin. "First of all, I'm feeling fine at this particular moment, if you must know, and second of all, I'm *not* in love," I say. But maybe I am. When I think of kissing Connor, I get a little short of breath and my insides feel hot.

Lorena shrugs. "Whatever you say."

"This is definitely a first for me. The sportiest thing I've ever done is run after the bus," Juanga says as he ties his shoelace.

"I don't think this qualifies as a sport," I reply. "It's not like we're going to be panting or anything."

"What is it, then?"

"I don't know, to be honest. An activity?" The glare of the snow makes me squint. "Ah, whatever, it doesn't matter."

"Okay, let's do this." Juanga smiles, positions his mat, and sits down. He is not dressed right for the weather—an old leather jacket, thin black gloves, jeans, and battered gray gym shoes. He's not even wearing a hat or scarf, so his face is bright red. Sometimes the way he dresses makes me wonder about his mother.

The three of us get in a line and push off at the count of three. The whole way down, we scream and laugh like crazies. When we get to the bottom of the hill, we just lie on the snow, giggling. I look up at a scrawny tree, the branches covered in frost, and am stunned by how beautiful it is.

"Oh my God, Lorena, you are a genius," Juanga says. "Entertainment for under eight dollars. I never thought being outside in the cold could be fun. At first, I was all, like, this bitch is crazy, but, nah, this is cool."

"What did I tell you?" Lorena raises her eyebrow at me.

"You were right. I'm sorry I doubted you. This is fun, much

better than being inside the apartment, listening to my mother complain about how lazy I am."

Juanga and Lorena get up and dust the snow off their clothes, but I lie there for a few seconds, listening to the church bells in the distance.

When Connor asks to visit me, I make up some dumb excuse and hope he never brings it up again. He says he's curious about the south side of the city, and I tell him there's not much to see. It's not that I'm ashamed of where I'm from, but we have such different lives. How do you explain to someone that you're poor? I think he knows, but it's different if he sees it for himself. I avoid it by asking him to meet somewhere in between.

After school, Connor and I meet in Uptown, at his favorite thrift store. His face is flushed from the cold, and he looks cute in his big, puffy jacket and purple stocking hat.

Though I love looking at old and used things, I kind of hate thrift stores because they make me feel itchy and remind me that I have no money. For Connor it seems like a fun adventure, probably because he's never had to shop there. Amá, Olga, and I used to go to the one in our neighborhood on Mondays because it was half off. How sad is that? A sale at a freaking thrift store.

"Oh my God, look at this," Connor says, and holds up an embroidered sweater with three cats on it, something an old lady would wear. "This is amazing. It's so ugly, I kind of want to buy it."

I smile. "Yeah, it's pretty hideous, like, disrespectful to the senses. Where would you wear that, though?"

"Anywhere. I'd wear this to school, the grocery store, to a bar mitzvah, I don't care."

I have six dollars to my name, and he's gonna buy something as a joke. I know it's not his fault, but I can't help feeling a little annoyed. I try not to show it, though, because I don't want to hurt his feelings. "I think you should do it. You will be the belle of the ball." I twirl in the aisle like some sort of princess.

I need new pants, but it's impossible to buy them at a thrift store since I can't try them on. Pants rarely fit right because of my thick legs and round butt. Instead, I look for dresses that stretch and forgive, but find nothing.

I always wonder who wore these clothes before they ended up here, why and how they got discarded. Sometimes I see stains and I try to guess where they came from—coffee, mustard, blood, red wine, grass—and create a story in my head, like the time I found an old wedding dress with mud stains at the fringes. I imagined rain began to pour in the middle of the outdoor ceremony, and that instead of cursing the sky for bad luck, the bride and groom held hands and ran for cover under a tree, the guests and wedding party all laughing about their wet clothes, ruined hairstyles, and dripping makeup.

Everything is picked over, and I start to lose my patience. My eyes itch, and I imagine bedbugs latching on to my clothes. I want to leave, but Connor looks like he's having so much fun. He walks toward me smiling and holding a framed painting of an old-timey clown on a unicycle.

"Man, they have the coolest shit here. This is ridiculous," he says, and laughs.

"Do you mind if we leave? I don't really like this." I scratch my neck.

"What do you mean, you don't like it? What's wrong? You said you wanted to come with me."

"Yeah, I know, but I want to go now. Is that okay? I'm sorry." All of a sudden I'm sad, and I'm not even sure why. I'm always excited to see Connor, but there's a heaviness that has set inside me that I don't understand.

"What's wrong?" Connor looks hurt and stares at the clown picture.

"Nothing, I swear. I'm okay. I'm just tired, really." So far, it's been nothing but giggles and kisses, and it would be so typical of me to ruin it.

"All right, let's go then." Connor puts his items on a shelf and walks toward the door.

I catch up to him and touch his arm. "No, wait. Buy your cat sweater and your clown thing. You wanted them. I'm sorry I'm being weird."

"Okay, I guess. But are you all right?"

I'm afraid to tell him exactly how I feel—how one second I'm okay and the next I'm sad for no good reason. I don't want to scare him away. "I just keep thinking about bedbugs, and it's freaking me out a little. And maybe I'm getting my period."

"Ah, I see. Well, let's get you some chocolate, and then I will inspect you for vermin." Connor says, and pretends to pick a bug out of my hair.

"Oh my God, that's so gross." I bat his hand away. "And how do you know chocolate will make me feel better?"

Connor shrugs. "Works for my mom."

"I guess it works for me, too, so, yes, I will accept your offer." I take his hand and lead him to the register. "Hurry up, before I really get stabby."

We can't find any bakeries, so we settle for a nearby grocery store, one of those fancy ones where a bag of organic apples costs more than our rent. Connor and I walk up and down the aisles for a while. I think we're both trying to stretch our time together as much as we can.

"Once, when I was a kid—I think I was about nine—Iwas with my mom at a grocery store," I tell him when we pass the cleaning supplies. "I got bored, so wandered off and got a bunch of embarrassing things and put them in strangers' carts when they weren't looking."

"Like what?"

"Like constipation pills, adult diapers, ointments. A bunch of butt-related stuff, now that I think about it."

Connor covers his face as he laughs. "What did they do?"

"I watched some of them when they got to the checkout line. Most of them were confused. One lady kept trying to explain to the cashier that she didn't put the items in her cart. She was really pissed off. I laughed so hard. Does that make me a bad person?"

Connor turns to face me and takes my hand. "I didn't want to tell you this, but"—he sighs—"you're the worst person I've ever met in my life, hands down."

"Wow, that's impressive. I'm kind of proud of myself."

Connor nods solemnly. "And somehow I still like you."

"I wish I could say the same about you," I joke.

Connor laughs.

When we get to the candy aisle, he places his hands on my shoulders and looks into my eyes. I'm almost startled by it. I wonder if he's going to kiss me. My hands get shaky.

"Okay, Ms. Reyes, pick whichever chocolate suits your fancy," he says.

"Even some fair-trade, sustainable, locally-grown-by-a-community-of-gnomes kind of shit?" I ramble. "Because that's the only kind I'll tolerate. I have very high standards."

"Anything." Connor smiles. "Artisanal and pesticide-free, if that's what you want."

"You know how to treat a lady," I say, and kiss him on the cheek. "A real gentleman."

Connor tells me his parents are out of town on a business trip this week and his brother won't be visiting from Purdue this weekend, so he wants me to come over on Saturday afternoon. Everyone's parents in my neighborhood work in factories, so the idea of a "business trip" is foreign to me, but I don't ask any questions so he doesn't think I'm stupid. I'm shocked that his parents trust him to stay home alone.

Amá and Apá have never left us by ourselves or let us sleep anywhere else. Not in a million years, not even with our cousins. The only other place we've ever stayed in is Mamá Jacinta's house when we went to Mexico. I think Amá has always been afraid that we'd get molested or have sex. She doesn't even like it when people kiss on TV, and if two characters are about to get it on—forget about it—she shuts it off and runs out of the room, muttering about cochinadas.

White people are different, I guess. Nancy from algebra went out with a white guy from Oak Park once, and she said that his parents let her sleep over.

I wonder if Connor expects us to have sex. I think about it all the time, but now that it's a real possibility, the idea of it scares me. What does it mean to be ready? How do you know for sure? I mean, I like him, and when we make out, it's obvious my body wants it, but what will it mean? Would he see me differently once he's gotten what he's wanted? At the same time, I want it, too, and if he judges me for doing the same exact thing he's doing, then that's bullshit. I lie on my bed thinking and worrying until I can't stand it anymore.

I need Lorena's advice, but I have to make sure Amá doesn't hear. She's sitting on the couch, knitting a blanket, so I get inside my closet and close the door. I barely fit, with all the boxes of useless crap and old clothes, but it's the most private place in the house.

Lorena says I have to shave my pussy before I go.

"But I don't know how. Why do women always have to do such unpleasant things? Heels, thongs, shaving, plucking, bleaching. It's really not fair." I like makeup and dresses, and I will shave my legs and armpits, but everything else is such an ordeal.

Lorena sighs. "You have to, or else he's going to get grossed out."

"Why did we evolve with hair down there if we didn't need it? Isn't there a reason for it?"

"Jesus, Julia. Why did you call me for advice if you weren't going to listen?"

I guess Lorena has a point. "Okay, so tell me how."

"What do you mean how? You just do it."

"The whole thing?"

"Yes, stupid."

"What if I cut myself?"

"You won't. Just do it slow."

"It hurts, right? Not the shaving but the. . . *you know.* Ugh. I'm freaking out."

Lorena is silent for a few seconds. "At first it does, but then it gets better."

I tell Amá I'm going downtown to an art gallery. I make something up about a new exhibit featuring female artists from Latin America. Sometimes I'm impressed by my own lies, but I can see the suspicion radiating from her eyes.

"Amá, I'm so *bored.* Please."

"Why don't you clean, then? There's plenty to do at home," she says. "Olga never wanted to go anywhere. Work, school, home. That's it."

After I whine about my need for cultural enrichment and go on and on about how this neighborhood is going to suffocate me—both emotionally and intellectually—she finally lets me go. "You better not be lying. You know I always find out." She points her spatula at me and turns back to the flautas frying on the stove.

I walk to the pharmacy to get condoms first. I don't know if he's supposed to have them or what, but I don't want to take any chances. Will he think I'm a slut, though? Or what if a nosy neighbor sees me buy them? What then? I guess either scenario is better than ending up pregnant or infected with a deadly STD.

I have to take three trains to get to Evanston. The houses are massive, and the streets are lined with looming trees. Bushes and hedges are trimmed with a precision that seems almost silly. I figured Connor's family had money, but I wasn't prepared for this.

I'm supposed to walk east from the station once I get there—toward the lake—but I still get lost for almost twenty minutes, going in circles and ending up in a cul-de-sac. I've never been very good with directions.

Finally, I find his block, so I pull out my pocket mirror to make sure I look okay. My eyeliner isn't smudged, and my lip gloss is still intact. Thank God the gigantic pimple on my cheek is gone. I iced it for days, but it was super-stubborn, with roots so deep, they felt like they reached my skull. I was starting to think I'd take it to the grave. I almost named it; Ursula and Brumhilda were my top two choices.

Connor's house has a giant wraparound porch and enormous

windows. It's as big as our entire apartment building. Part of me wonders if I should go back home. I feel nervous and start tugging at my hair. My crotch is beginning to itch like crazy, too. I shouldn't have listened to Lorena. Maybe she doesn't know everything about sex.

When Connor answers the door, I feel a surge of anxiety. He's wearing a Foo Fighters T-shirt, pajama pants, and a pair of moccasins—total suburban white boy—but he's so hot, I'd like him even if he wore a tattered garbage sack.

"You smell like Mexican food," he says as he hugs me. "Like fried tortillas or something. You're making me hungry."

I laugh, even though I'm mortified.

Connor gives me a tour of the house, which is two stories high, not including his giant bedroom in the attic. I try to play it cool and act unimpressed, but the only fancy houses I've ever seen in real life are the ones I've cleaned with Amá. Every room is expertly decorated and looks like it belongs on TV. The kitchen is the size of our apartment, and fancy copper pots and pans hang over two stoves (two!). They even have a fireplace and a giant black piano in the living room. These people must be rich as fuck.

The mantle is covered with photos. There's one of who I assume is Connor's mom, laughing on a swing. They have the same light brown hair and crinkly eyes.

"You and your mom are identical." I turn to him and smile.

"Yeah, that's what everybody says. I think I look more like my dad, though. Jeremy is the male version of my mom, basically her with short hair."

"Is this your dad?" I pick up a frame of a tall man wearing a baseball cap in front of a stadium.

"No, that's Bruce, my stepdad. I haven't seen my dad in five years. He lives in Germany now."

"Oh, I didn't know." Connor's never said much about his family. "What does he do there?"

"He's an engineer. Lives in Munich."

"When did they get divorced?"

"I was six, and then Bruce married my mom when I was nine."

"What's he like?"

"He's pretty conservative, watches Fox News and shit like that. We don't agree on a lot of things, but he's been more of a dad than my real dad, that's for sure."

I see a photograph on the mantle of Bruce holding a rifle in front of a giant dead animal. I can't tell what it is exactly, but it looks majestic. Its long horns are twisted and beautiful.

"What is it? The animal, I mean."

"Spiral-horned antelope."

I can see Connor is embarrassed, so I don't ask him more.

The Thai food he's ordered is supposed to arrive in an hour. We watch music videos on his laptop while we wait.

"You're so pretty," he says as he searches for a video.

"Thanks." I feel my face flush.

"No, seriously. I really like you."

I don't know what to say, so I just look at my dry hands—one of my knuckles is cracked and bleeding from the cold.

"I like you, too, even though you're wearing those pants,"

I tease.

"What's wrong with my pants?"

"Where do I begin?" I giggle.

"You're horrible, you know that?" Connor says, trying not to smile.

"I know. We already established that."

We both laugh, then get quiet.

Connor puts down the laptop and kisses me, and though we've kissed many times before, my hands and legs begin to shake. I hope he doesn't notice. We kiss and kiss for so long that my jaw aches. Then he lies on top of me and slips his cold hand under my shirt. After a few minutes, he tries to pull down my jeans, but I have to take my shoes off first. This is the part I was most afraid of. Every time I take my shoes off in someone's house, I remember the time in kindergarten, a roach crawled out of my sneaker. Though it's happened to me only once, I still worry about it every single time. What if there's a roach nestled in there somewhere, ready to ruin me?

"Wait," I say.

"What's wrong?" Connor cocks his head to the side. He seems concerned.

"Well . . . it's just that . . ." My eyes dart around the room. I'm too nervous to look at him.

"Oh shit, you've never done this before, huh? Are you sure you want to?" He holds my face in his hands and looks straight into my eyes.

"Yeah, I'm sure." I nod.

Connor looks skeptical.

"Don't you feel special? Since you'll be the first? You can strut around wearing a crown, throw some confetti or something."

Connor smiles. "So you're absolutely, one hundred percent positive? I don't want to do it if you're not ready. There's no rush, you know."

"Yes. Really. Now shut up and kiss me." I laugh and pull him closer.

After we kiss for a while, Connor pulls a condom out from under a couch cushion. I guess he was prepared. I look away as he puts it on.

My body tightens, bracing itself—it hurts more than I imagined, but I pretend it doesn't.

"Is that okay?" he whispers.

"Yeah."

I'm not sure what to do. Am I supposed to say something or move a certain way? I hold my breath for a long time, my mouth against his neck. Then I wrap my legs around him, grip his back, and inhale. I don't know how to describe his smell exactly—clean and sweaty at the same time—but I like it.

Connor kisses my face and then bites my lip, which surprises me. I can't help but gasp.

"Sorry," he says, his voice raspy.

Though it hurts, kissing and touching him feel amazing. At the same time, I keep thinking I'm doing something dirty. So many feelings all jumbled together. There's also this sensation building, like I have to pee or something. I've never experienced anything like that before. It's not bad, just intense.

Once Connor is finished, he kisses my forehead and sighs. I

rush to put on my clothes. I'm suddenly so embarrassed, I can't even look at him. I know that sex isn't evil, that it's a normal part of being a functioning mammal, so why do I feel like I've done something wrong? Lorena is always going on and on about how great it is to come, but I don't think I did. At least there isn't any blood. I was afraid of that.

Connor grins at me, which makes me feel shy.

"What?" I laugh and turn away.

"Nothing. I'm just looking at you. Is that okay?"

"Absolutely not," I kid with him.

"Fine," Connor says, and covers his eyes with his hands. "What do you want to do now? Watch a movie?"

"I'll only stay if you change those pants." I make a disapproving face.

Connor laughs and reaches his hand toward me, and when I get closer, he pulls me onto his lap. I wrap my arms around him and bury my face in his shoulder.

My parents aren't home when I get back, thank God. I bet Amá could read it on my face. She claims she can tell a woman is pregnant just by looking at her eyes, so maybe she'll be able to see that my hymen is gone now.

I'm starving, even though I scarfed down all of my pad Thai, but there is nothing to eat. Maybe sex counts as exercise because I'm also tired as hell, like I just ran laps or something. I ravage the pantry and fridge, but we don't even have tortillas—nothing except condiments, eggs, and one sad pickle floating in a jar.

The freezer is just as disappointing. All I find are a bag of corn and a box of waffles so old I think they've been there since before Olga died. They're freezer-burned, of course, so I'll have to smother them with syrup. When I throw the box away, I notice something's still inside. I pull out a small, knotted plastic bag full of two gold chains, three rings, and one key. Olga's key. This has to be Olga's key.

I suddenly remember the time I was five and saw Amá put her jewelry in the freezer. When I asked her why, she said it was in case we were ever robbed. Even then I wondered why anyone would ever want to break into our apartment. We've never had anything worth stealing. Months and months of secretly searching the entire apartment, and I never once thought of looking in there.

I have to make sure the key works. And it does.

• • •

That night I wait until my parents fall asleep and go back into Olga's room. It's completely covered in dust, so I know Amá hasn't been in here. I write my name on the dresser with my finger, then wipe it away. It's eerie, like going back in time or something. I take the laptop, underwear, lingerie, and the hotel key to hide in my room, in case Amá ever decides to come in here. I'll make an extra copy of the key after school tomorrow.

Amá is crying on the couch with three cardboard boxes in front of her when I get home. At first I don't understand, and I ask her what's wrong. I assume it has something to do with Olga, but she doesn't reply. Then I see one of my old shirts peeking out of a box, a faded red-and-blue button-down from the thrift store I was always too embarrassed to wear.

Fuck. Shit. Fuck. My life is over. I'm basically a living corpse.

"What are you doing? Why are all these boxes here?" I feel light-headed.

Amá just shakes her head.

"Why did you go through my things? Why would you do that to me? Why can't you ever leave me alone?" I tug at my hair with both hands. I feel like I can't breathe.

"This is my house, and I will do whatever I want. I was going to donate these clothes to kids in Mexico, and look what I find." She opens one of the boxes and pulls out Olga's underwear and lingerie, the hotel key, and my box of condoms. "What is this?"

She didn't find the laptop because it's still in my backpack. I carried it around all day in case I was able to see Connor after school.

How do I explain that the underwear, lingerie, and key are my sister's? How do I explain that I bought the box of condoms because I had sex and was terrified to get pregnant? How do I tell Amá that both of her daughters are and were probably impure?

"They're not mine." My body tenses as if a wire were running through it.

"Why are you always lying to me, Julia? What have I ever done to deserve this? I always knew you would do something like this. Ever since you were little, you've given me so much trouble, even before you were born." Her voice cracks at the end of the sentence. Tears are streaming down her face, and her hands are shaking. She's referring to the complications she had when she gave birth to me, as if it were my fault I almost died and took her with me.

I don't say anything. I just stare at a crack in the wall shaped like a letter Y.

"What must your sister think of you right now? What a disgrace." Amá looks away, disgusted.

"They're not mine," I say over and over, my body trembling. "They're not mine. They're not mine. They're not mine."

Amá has taken away my phone, so I call Connor every day after school from what I believe is the only remaining pay phone in the city. I have to go five blocks out of the way and use up a lot of quarters, but it's worth it. Sometimes I call him from Lorena's phone. We haven't been able to see each other in three weeks now, which sucks for both of us. Mostly, I tell him how miserable I am, and he tells me everything is going to be okay. He's offered to come meet me after school, even if it means seeing me for only twenty minutes, which is sweet, but if Amá saw me with him, I'd be in even deeper shit. This is getting so frustrating. I should have known that everything would fall apart. It's as if, when I was born, someone decided that I was not allowed to be happy.

Connor is always a good listener, but today he feels distant, as if he were on the other side of the world and we're talking through two paper cups connected by a string, like in cartoons.

When I tell him how horrible my day was, he pauses for such

a long time, I think maybe the call has cut off. Then I hear him exhale.

"Julia, I don't know how to help you."

My heart becomes heavy. "What do you mean?"

"I care about you and everything, but it's too much, don't you think?"

"What's too much?"

"I don't even get to see you anymore. All we ever do is talk on the phone, and you're always crying. I don't know what to do. It's every single day. It's just a lot for me. I really like you, but. . . how can we do this? I want you to be my girlfriend, but I need to actually *see* you. You understand that, don't you?"

I begin to cry. A woman passes by and asks if I'm okay. I nod and wave her away. "I want to see you, too, but I can't. I don't know what to do. I feel like I'm suffocating. I can't stand living like this anymore. Fuck, why does everything have to be so impossible all the time?" I kick the pay phone so hard it rattles.

"I just don't know how to help you, especially when I can't actually be there. When will I see you again? Do you have any idea? You can't be grounded forever, right?"

I hear the ice crunch under my feet. I hate that noise. I can always feel it in my teeth. "I. . . I. . ." I take a deep breath and try to say something else, but nothing comes out.

"You mean a lot to me, I swear. Please believe that."

"I don't know when things will get better," I finally say. "All I know is that I feel like shit, like no one in the world understands anything about me."

"I understand. I'm trying to, at least."

"How could you? Do you have any idea what my life is like? What it's like to be me? To have your sister die? To live in a shitty neighborhood? To be scrutinized all the fucking time?"

"I guess I don't," Connor says quietly.

"No one does." I say it so loudly that I surprise myself. I'm having trouble breathing at a normal pace.

"I'm not sure what you want me to do. Have you thought about talking to someone, like a therapist or a counselor? What about that teacher you're always talking about?"

"All I do is fuck up. No one cares about who I really am."

"Stop, just stop, okay? That's not true at—"

"No one cares. No one cares. No one cares," I yell, and hang up the phone.

SIXTEEN

I can't leave the apartment again because Amá decided to ransack my room to make sure I didn't have anything else that might be considered scandalous or immoral. At first all she found were an old clove cigarette and a pair of shorts she didn't like. But then she tried reading my journals, even though she doesn't understand English. Unfortunately, she does recognize bad words, so she ripped out all the pages that contained *fuck, bitch, shit,* and even *sex,* which were incredibly common, of course. I screamed and begged for her to leave my journals alone, but she went through them anyway and left me with only a dozen pages or so. I was hysterical and tried to swipe them from her hands, but Apá held me back. I cried on the floor in the fetal position for hours after. I couldn't find the motivation to get up, not even when a roach crawled near my head. Life without writing doesn't feel worth living to me. I don't know how I'm going to make it to graduation because I feel like a husk of a person these days. Some of the poems Amá destroyed I had worked on for years, and now they're gone. Poof. Just like that. I'll never see them again. The one thing I loved most in life has been taken away from me. What the hell do I do now? I'm still lugging Olga's laptop in my backpack, so she doesn't know I have it, but that doesn't even seem to matter much anymore.

I don't know if I'll see Connor again. It's been three weeks since our last phone call, and it feels like a lifetime. I miss him so much I can hardly stand it. I've almost called him many times, but when I get to the pay phone, I tense up and turn around. I have no idea what to say. I'm almost positive that I'll just end up crying again because things are even shittier now. Besides, it's obvious he doesn't want to be with me. Why would anyone want to put up with all my problems?

Christmas vacation was almost as bad as last year's. I don't know if it's worse to spend all day in my room, or struggle through my classes and be forced to speak to other human beings. Sometimes I can't make it through the day without losing it, so I have to take crying breaks in the bathroom, which makes me feel extra pathetic. Lorena keeps asking me if I'm okay and if she could do something to help me, and I say I'm fine, although I'm so far from *fine* that I don't even remember what it is anymore. I feel like my heart is covered with spines.

Mr. Ingman keeps wondering why I've been missing our after-school college sessions. He's excited that I got a 29 on my ACT. If I didn't feel like absolute garbage, I would probably be excited, too. I try to avoid him, and when I do run into him, I tell him that I have to work with my mom in the evenings. My history teacher, Mr. Nguyen, often asks how I'm feeling. He looks worried, but what can I tell him? How can I begin to explain? I just keep relying on the trusty old period card.

In English class today, we discussed one of my favorite Emily Dickinson poems, and it felt as if something were splintering inside me. When we got to the part about the bees, my eyes ached from holding back tears.

Instead of walking home after school today, I take the bus downtown. I'm not even sure where I'll go or what I'll do—I have no money or destination—but I can't bear another evening locked up in my room. I don't care about the repercussions. I give up.

I finally decide on Millennium Park because it's the closest thing I can get to nature and because it's free. It's still freezing, so of course no one is around, only a few annoying tourists who, for some stupid reason, thought it was a good idea to come to Chicago in the winter. The cold here feels barbaric, inhumane. Why would anyone want to come to a place like this?

The snow is pretty when it falls, but it hasn't snowed in about a week. All that's left now is slushy and gray, or yellow from all the dog pee. I wish winter would pack its bags and get the hell out already.

The amphitheater is completely deserted, so it's almost peaceful. The silver architecture looks kind of ridiculous to me, like a spaceship and spiderweb fused together, but everyone always takes pictures of it like it's some sort of masterpiece. I smile when I remember the time Lorena and I came to a summer concert here. We didn't even like the music—some kind of folk band from Serbia or some shit—but it felt great to be outside under the moon and three sad city stars. I thought maybe Connor and I would come here in the summer, too.

I walk toward the ice-skating rink as the sky begins to darken. I wish I had a few dollars for a cup of hot chocolate, but I barely have enough to get back on the bus. I'm tired of being broke. I'm tired of feeling like the rest of the world always gets to decide what I can do. I know I should go back home, but I can't seem to move. I can't keep going like this anymore. What is the point of living if I can't ever get what I want? This doesn't feel like a life; it feels like a never-ending punishment. My body shivers, and the thoughts in my head become hot, confusing swirls. I can't seem to breathe right.

"Go home, go home, go home," I tell myself, but I just stand there, watching a blond boy with ruddy cheeks skate in a tiny circle until his mother yells that it's time for them to leave.

SEVENTEEN

I wake up in a hospital bed, with Amá peering over me. I have a headache so deep it feels like someone pummeled my brain with a meat tenderizer. For a few seconds, I'm confused about what I'm doing there, but then I look at my wrists and remember what I did last night.

"Mija," Amá whispers and touches my forehead. Her fingers are cold and damp. She looks terrified. Apá stands near the door, looking at the floor. I don't know if it's because he's ashamed, sad, or both.

I don't know what to say. How could I possibly explain this? I begin to cry, which gets Amá started, too. I've never been very good at life, but, man, was this a stupid thing todo.

A short man in his twenties and an older lady with light brown hair and green eyes come in and stand at the foot of my bed. Even with her clipboard and white coat, she looks like she should be in *Vogue* or something.

"Hi, Julia. My name is Dr. Cooke, and this is our interpreter, Tomás. He's going to tell your parents what we're saying. Do you remember me from last night?"

I nod.

"How are you feeling?"

"I'm okay. I have a headache, but that's it." I wipe my eyes with my gown. "Can I get out of here now? Please?"

"No, not yet. Sorry. We're going to have to keep you for a bit just to make sure you're okay. Maybe we can let you out tomorrow morning."

I feel a little disoriented by all the translating. My head keeps throbbing. Too many people are talking at once. I guess they didn't trust me to interpret for my parents. I don't blame them.

"I swear to God, I'm fine. I'm not going to do it again. I realize how dumb this was. I don't even know why I did it." Of course I know why I did it, but I don't think that's going to help my case.

Dr. Cooke smiles apologetically. "This is really serious, Julia. And we have to figure out a way to help you."

"It's not going to be like *One Flew Over the Cuckoo's Nest,* is it? Because I'll bust out of here, in that case, just like Chief. I'm not joking. I will lift a drinking fountain or sink or whatever with my bare hands, and break a window and run off into a field, and no one will ever see me again. The end." I rub my temples with my fingers. "Why does my head hurt so much? Did you give me a lobotomy?"

Tomás doesn't know how to translate what I said, so he just looks at us perplexed.

Dr. Cooke smiles again. "You haven't lost your sense of humor. That's a good sign."

"Look, I know what I did was crazy. I won't do it again. I swear to God."

Dr. Cooke turns to my parents. "We're going to conduct some more evaluations to make sure she's all right. And we'll figure out a plan from there. We'll see if we can release her tomorrow."

Amá nods and says, "Thank you." Apá exhales loudly and doesn't say anything.

"The nurse will let you know when to come down to my office. Shouldn't be more than an hour," Dr. Cooke says to me as she and Tomás walk out the door.

The office is so full of plants that it's as if I'm in a tiny jungle. It smells faintly of perfume, which is like a mix of fresh laundry, pear, and spring rain. I'm surprised by Dr. Cooke's paintings, though; judging from her elegant style, I thought she'd have better taste in art. Some of them appear to have been created to soothe crazy people, especially the one of the giraffe drinking from a pond.

"How are you feeling?" She smiles, but not in a way that shows she feels sorry for me. It's real and kind of gentle.

"I'm okay."

"So, what brings you here? What's going on?"

"I just got a little overwhelmed, that's all." I stare at a framed picture of a little girl on her desk. I wonder if it's her daughter.

"How long have you been depressed?" Dr. Cooke crosses her legs. She's wearing a tight red dress and black high-heeled boots that look like beautiful torture. Her hair is in a perfect bun, and her earrings are sparkly and elegant. I imagine she's a rich lady who shops downtown, drinks a glass of wine after work, and gets manicures on the regular.

"Man. . . I don't know. A pretty long time. It's hard to pinpoint exactly when, but it got much worse after Olga died. I know that for sure."

"How long have you thought about hurting yourself?"

"Well, it's not like I planned it or anything. I just kinda lost it last night." I remember Apá pounding at my door and feel ashamed. "I didn't really want to die."

"Are you sure?" Dr. Cooke raises her right eyebrow.

I sigh. "Mostly, I think. Yeah." I get a flashback of my blood on my old green sheets.

"Where do you think it's coming from, that sense of desperation? What triggered it exactly? Did something happen?"

"I don't know how to explain it. Yesterday it just all added up. I couldn't take it anymore. I got home last night and was shaky and hungry and sad, and all I wanted was a stupid peanut butter and jelly sandwich, so I looked in the fridge, and the only things we had were a container full of beans and a half gallon of milk. I said to myself, 'Man, fuck this shit.' I know that sounds stupid, but it just really pissed me off, you know? Then I couldn't stop crying."

"That doesn't sound stupid to me." Dr. Cooke looks concerned and writes down some notes. "What's stupid about it?"

"I don't know," I say. "Like, why does everything hurt all the time? Even the dumbest things. Is that normal?"

"Sometimes little things are symbols or triggers for much bigger issues in our lives. Think about why that particular moment caused you so much distress."

I sit there looking at the floor. I don't know what to say. There's a black stain on the corner of her rug that looks like a paw print. It's so quiet I can't stand it. She can probably hear my stomach growling.

"Take your time," she finally says. "There is no rush. What's important is to reflect in a way that makes sense to you."

I nod and look out the window for a long time. The view is super-depressing—a snowy parking lot. The clouds have blotted out any trace of sunshine. A woman almost slips on a patch of ice.

I take a deep breath. "It's, like, how can I explain? First, my sister dies, which has been a living hell. And. . . there's just so much I want to do, but I can't. The life I want seems impossible, and it just gets so. . . frustrating."

"What is it that you want?"

I sigh. "A million things."

"Tell me about them." Dr. Cooke adjusts the hem of her red dress. I wonder if it's exhausting to look so perfect.

I pause again to gather my thoughts. The question overwhelms me, and I'm not sure why.

"I want to be a writer," I finally say. "I want to be independent. I want to have my own life. I want to hang out with my friends without being interrogated. I want privacy. I just want to breathe, you know?"

Dr. Cooke nods. "I understand. So how are you going to make that happen? What exactly is stopping you?" She asks in a way that's not judgmental or anything but really trying to understand. Hardly anyone talks to me like this.

"I want to move away, go to college. I don't want to live in Chicago. I don't feel like I can grow here. My parents want me to be a person I don't want to be. I love my mom, but she drives me crazy. I understand that she's upset about my sister—we all are—but I feel so suffocated. I'm nothing like Olga, and I never will be. There's nothing I can do to change that." I stare at the ceiling, wondering what life will be like when I go back home.

"Do you think you'd ever hurt yourself again?"

"No. Never," I say, which is not exactly true. How could I ever be sure? But I tell her what she wants to hear. "Can we talk about my mother again? Can we go back to that?"

Dr. Cooke nods. "Go ahead."

"It's like she never trusts me. For example, she is always, always opening the door without asking or knocking, and when I tell her I need privacy, she laughs. I mean, why would you laugh at that? And that's just one example. I can go on forever."

"What about your dad? What's he like?"

I sigh. "My dad. . . he's just there."

"What do you mean?" Dr. Cooke looks confused.

"I mean, he's *physically* there, but he never says much. He hardly even talks to me. It's as if I don't exist. Or sometimes I think he wishes he didn't exist. It's weird, though. It wasn't always that bad. He used to carry me and tell me stories about Mexico when I was a kid. He was always kind of distant, but when I was about twelve or thirteen, he really started ignoring me." I'm surprised at how much it bothers me to say it out loud.

"What's significant about that particular time in your life?"

I shrug. "No idea."

Dr. Cooke writes something in her notebook. "Do you think something happened to make him this way?"

"I don't know. He never talks about anything."

"Tell me what his life is like."

"He works at a candy factory all day, then comes home, watches TV, and eventually goes to sleep. Seems pretty sad to me."

"Why is that?" Dr. Cooke uncrosses her legs and leans toward me again. She looks very serious.

"Because there should be more to life than that. Life is passing him by, and he doesn't even know it. Or doesn't care. I don't know which one is worse." I blink back tears.

"And he and your mother immigrated here, correct? What country did they come from? When was that?"

"Mexico. In 1991. My sister was born later that year."

"Have you ever thought about how it might feel for him to leave his family and come to live in the United States? I imagine that could have been traumatic for him. Well, for both of them."

"I guess I never really thought about it before." I wipe my eyes with the back of my hand. The tears are relentless now. "This is embarrassing."

"The crying?"

I nod.

"You're entitled to your emotions. There shouldn't be any shame in that." Dr. Cooke hands me a box of tissues. "This is the place to let it all out."

"It just makes me feel stupid," I say. "And weak."

She shakes her head. "But you're neither one of those things."

Dr. Cooke says I can leave tomorrow if my parents agree to a short outpatient program for fucked-up kids like me. I'll have to miss a week of school because I'll be there from 9 a.m. to 4 p.m., but I'll be able to make up part of the work while I'm in there. And it's certainly better than being locked up in a hospital. Because of my insurance through the state, the cost will be minimal, she says. According to her, it's set up for poor people like me. Actually, she didn't use the word *poor,* she said *low-income,* but it's the same thing. I guess it just sounds more polite.

She also wants to see me every week for therapy, and says I need to take medication to balance out my brain. It turns out I suffer from severe depression and anxiety, which have to be treated right away, or else I can end up here again. I've had it for a long time, but it obviously got much worse after Olga died. Something in my head isn't wired right. I'm not surprised—I always knew something was wrong; I just didn't know what it was, that it had an official name.

I stare out the window of my room, watching the city lights when the nurse taps me on the shoulder. It's time for my pills. I have to take them in front of her and then open my mouth wide so she can see that I really swallowed them. Dr. Cooke says that it will take several weeks to feel the full effect. My emotions are all over the place right now. One minute I feel like eating a torta; the next minute I want to cry until my eyes dry up.

Suddenly, right when I'm about to turn away from the window to go to sleep, I see Lorena and Juanga standing on the corner across the street. At first I can't believe it's them, but when I get a better look, I recognize Lorena's crazy hair and skinny legs. They start waving and yelling like crazy, but I can't hear what they're saying. I have no idea how they found out where I was. Lorena is wearing a puffy pink coat and is breathing into her hands. Juanga does a ridiculous dance that involves shaking his butt and flapping his arms like a chicken.

I imitate the dance as best as I can, which makes them both laugh. I wave and smile. This goes on for a few minutes until the cold ushers them away.

Our apartment is tense and silent, as if everything is holding its breath. Sometimes I'm convinced I hear the roaches scurrying. I think my parents are terrified of me. Apá is his usual mute self, and Amá looks at me as if she can't figure out how I once resided inside her uterus. I feel guilty for making them feel this way. I didn't mean to hurt them.

That night, after talking to Lorena on the phone for nearly two hours, I unlock Olga's door and crawl into her bed. It's one of the only things that can make me feel better. Not even food comforts me right now, which is kind of alarming. And I can hardly read or write because nothing will stay inside my brain.

I miss Connor, but I'm afraid to call him. I dialed his number a few times but hung up before it rang. It's not like I can see him right now anyway, which was the problem in the first place. I would never in a million years invite him over to our apartment (for *so* many reasons), and I know there's no way for me to get to Evanston without freaking my parents out. But maybe I should risk it to get Olga's laptop to him. What if he's my only hope for getting it unlocked? Who am I kidding, though? My parents would likely call the police if I left the house. And what would I say to Connor? If I told him about what happened, he'd get all weirded out. Even if I tried to keep it a secret, I would probably blurt it out because I can't seem to keep anything to myself. I don't want him to think I'm crazy, because that would definitely scare him away, and I wouldn't even blame him.

For a second, I think I can still smell Olga in the sheets, but it's probably all in my head.

EIGHTEEN

During movement therapy, Ashley, the young therapist with the asexual mom haircut, tells us to say what we feel and bounce the foam ball however we want. "The ball is an expression of our feelings," she says.

I go first. "I feel snacky." I drop the ball softly.

"Thank you, Julia, but that's not really a feeling," Ashley says, as gently as she can.

"It is to me. I'm overcome with a desire for snacks."

"Okay, snacky it is, then."

Now it's Erin's turn. Erin was molested by her dad and speaks very slowly. Everything she says seems like a drawn-out question.

“How do you feel today, Erin?” Ashley asks, in her best therapist voice. Sometimes she sounds as if she’s talking to a baby or puppy that’s about to die. Erin looks around the room and then looks at the ball for what feels like aneternity.

I want to scream at her to hurry up, but I just look out the window instead.

“I feel. . . confused?” she finally says, and flings the ball toward the windows.

Tasha takes the ball from the floor and says, “I feel like my veins are full of sand.”

That makes me wince. Tasha is always saying horribly beautiful things like that. Sometimes I want to write them down. She’s anorexic and probably doesn’t weigh more than ninety pounds. Her wrists look fragile and breakable, and her long, skinny braids seem too heavy for her small body. Although she's emaciated, I can see that she's beautiful. Her eyelashes are stupidly long, and she has the kind of mouth that begs for bright red lipstick.

Luis is next. He's here because his stepdad beat him with cords and hangers when he was a kid. He says one time he even put a gun in his mouth. Luis cuts himself now, and his pink scars crisscross down his arms and onto his hands. I've never seen skin like his. It's as if he's covered with a made-up language. I feel sorry for him, but he scares me. And it makes me uncomfortable that I can see the outline of his junk through his sweatpants. Someone should talk to him about it. How are we supposed to get better when we're subjected to such a vulgar display?

I'm afraid of what Luis is going to say because he has a demented look in his eyes. After a few seconds, he says he feels "sexy" and laughs like a maniac. He bounces the ball so hard it almost hits the ceiling.

Next is Josh. He tried to kill himself with some of his mother's pills, but his pink-haired girlfriend (he's mentioned her hair three times now) found him and called 911. Josh's face is red and shiny with acne. His skin is so terrible that my own skin almost hurts when I look at him. How his pink-haired girlfriend was about to kiss him is a mystery to me. Josh looks as if someone set fire to his face, and it remained blistered and full of pus. His eyes are nice, though. Sometimes, for a second, especially in the sunlight, they pierce through, and you almost forget about the lumpy redness on his face. Maybe that's what his girlfriend saw.

Josh seems to have fed off Luis because he says he feels "aroused." He laughs so hard, one of the whiteheads on his cheek splits and begins to bleed, but no one tells him. Josh and Luis just laugh like buffoons until Ashley says it's time for our break.

Josh, Luis, and I stand at the window and watch a blond woman in a bright green dress and pointy black heels hurry down the street.

Josh says she's a hooker on the way to work.

"Why does she have to be a hooker?" I ask.

"Look at the way she walks. She wants to get boned," Luis says.

"You're gross. Why would you talk about a woman like that?"

Luis pretends he doesn't hear me.

Next, we see a black guy in a leather jacket and baseball cap walking into a diner.

"He's dealing drugs," Luis says. "Crack, for sure."

I turn to Tasha to see if she's heard them, but she's sitting across the room with a magazine on her lap and staring off into space. Sometimes I want to talk to her, but she's as quiet as a sealed jar of air.

"So you guys are sexist *and* racist? How charming." I glare at them.

Erin comes over smoothing her short dark hair. "What's up? What are you guys talking about?"

"Julia here is killing our vibe." Luis points his thumb toward me.

"Oh, shut up, Luis. Stop being a dirtbag."

"Fuck, man. Stop being so uptight. We're just joking. Geez." Luis pokes my shoulder and walks away before I have a chance to respond.

When I head over to the water fountain, Antwon, the new kid with a wispy Afro, comes up to me and asks me to be his girlfriend. He just got here an hour ago, and he's already trying to get a date in a part-time nut house—it's almost funny. "Are you serious?" I ask him. "Is this really happening?" I look around and pretend to address a crowd of people.

"Come on, girl. Let me take you to the movies when we get outta here," he says, picking at his hair with a giant comb.

"First of all, you're, like, what, thirteen? Second of all, I don't want a boyfriend. Don't you see that I just tried to kill myself?" I say, showing him my wrists.

"But I'll take care of you," he says, swatting my hands. "I'll borrow my grandma's car and pick you up. I'll take you to the movies."

"Antwon, you're a child, which means you don't have a license, which means that you can't drive. And I don't need to be taken care of. I can take care of myself."

Antwon shakes his head. I walk back to our next session before he can say anything else.

Every day is the same: movement therapy, homework, lunch, group therapy, art therapy, individual therapy, then "closing circle." During our breaks, we can read, play games, or listen to music. We're always fighting over what kind of music to play. The other day Luis and Josh wanted to listen to heavy metal, and I said I'd rather eat a rat sandwich. I like aggressive music, but heavy metal makes me feel like I'm locked in a box draped with chains. No way.

Sometimes I look out the window and zone out until our break ends. Today Tasha walks over and stands next to me.

"Hey," she says in a whisper. I've never seen her speak to anyone outside of therapy. Everything about her is so quiet, as if she's trying to erase herself from the world. She only speaks when she has to. In group therapy, Tasha told us that for one week straight all she ate was grapefruit. If I went that long without eating real food, I'd probably end up stabbing someone. She said this so softly that I had to crane my neck toward her and really listen. I wonder what it's like to be so delicate, to look at a plate of food and feel like it's your enemy.

"Hi." I smile. "What's up?"

"I'm sick of this place already."

"Yeah, me too." I write my name on the glass with my knuckle. "How long will you be here?"

"I don't know. They won't say. It depends on my progress." She twirls one of her braids around her finger. "What about you?"

"Five days total, if everything goes well. I think I just need to avoid having another meltdown. Then I have to go to therapy, which is not so bad, I guess."

Tasha pauses and looks at my wrists. "Did you really want to die?"

I'm not sure what to say. How do I answer that? I'm glad I'm not dead, but living. . . living feels terrible.

"At the moment, maybe I did, but now. . . no, not really." I don't look at her when I say it. I stare at the droplets of rain beginning to fall against the window.

After dinner, Amá looks at Apá, and then they both turn to me. "Mija, we think you should go to Mexico and spend some time with Mamá Jacinta."

"What? Are you crazy? What about my therapy?"

"After you finish the program."

"What about Dr. Cooke? When am I going to see her again?"

"You have an appointment this week, and then you can see her when you come back," Apá says.

This makes no damn sense to me. Some people think that shipping their children back to the motherland when they get out of control will solve everything. It's happened to some of the kids from my school, mostly gangbangers and girls who are ripe for pregnancy. Usually, they come back exactly the same. Or worse. Maybe parents think their kids have lost their values, that they've become too Americanized. So is Mexico supposed to teach me not to have sex? Is it supposed to teach me not to kill myself?

"What if I don't get to graduate on time because I missed too many days of school?"

Amá sighs. "It won't be for that long."

"I'm not going," I say. "Absolutely not. I need more time at home to recover," I add, trying to lay the guilt on thick.

Amá and Apá exchange glances. I bet they have no idea what to do with me. They look desperate.

"That's the point. It'll do you good. You'll feel better." Amá folds and refolds her napkin.

"How?"

"Your grandmother will teach you things. You'll get to relax." Amá tries to smile.

"Like what? Cooking? You think that's going to make me feel better?"

"You used to love going to Mexico when you were little. You always seemed so happy. You never wanted to come back. Don't you remember?"

That's true, but I don't admit it. I liked to stay up late with our cousins. I loved the smell of the dirt roads after it rained, and the spicy tamarind candy from the corner store. But going there as a teenager? What the hell am I going to do? Make tortillas all day?

"And you'll get some fresh air and ride horses. Mamá said you loved that. Doesn't that sound nice?" Amá hasn't been this friendly in years.

"I don't care about horses." I can hear the neighbors screaming at each other downstairs.

Amá sighs and looks at the ceiling. "Ay, Dios, dame paciencia."

"What about college? What if I miss too many classes and I have to go to summer school? What if all the places I applied to reject me because I missed so much of my last semester?"

"You can go to community college, just like your sister."

"She didn't even graduate. What was the point of her going to school if all she was going to be was a receptionist?"

"What's wrong with being a receptionist? It's a lot better than breaking your back cleaning houses. At least you get air-conditioning. At least you get to sit down. What I wouldn't give for a job like that." Amá looks pissed.

I cross my arms over my chest. "Okay, being a receptionist would be my dream come true. There is nothing I'd rather do than answer phones."

On my last morning of the program, I walk toward Tasha, who's playing solitaire in the corner.

"Can I sit here?" I ask as I pull out a chair.

She shrugs. “Sure.”

“So, do you feel any better?”

“Sometimes. It’s tiring to answer the same kinds of questions over and over. I get sick of talking about my cousin, about food, about my mom.” Tasha’s voice is almost above a whisper today.

“Yeah, I know what you mean. Like, how many times are they going to ask me to explain why I hurt myself? I keep telling them that I’m not going to do it again, but they don’t believe me.”

Tasha nods.

“You know, I’m not sure how all of this group therapy is supposed to help. Listening to other people’s problems doesn’t exactly make me feel good.”

“Sometimes it’s nice to know you’re not alone.” Tasha lays down the queen of diamonds. “Like you’re not the only one who feels like complete shit all the time."

"Do you think the feeling will ever go away? Do you think it's possible that we can be normal people who can be consistently happy?"

Tasha pauses for a long time. "I don't know if I'll ever be a normal person. I'm not even sure what that is. Sometimes I feel happy for, like, a second, but then it goes away."

"I guess the same goes for me. I just can't convince myself to feel good, like my body won't allow it or something. Instead, it gives me the finger."

"We're probably lacking serotonin." Tasha picks at a scab on her arm. "Your brain forgets how to produce it, so you have to teach it how to do it again. I read that in an article. Or something like that."

"My parents are sending me to Mexico after I'm finished here." I sigh.

"Mexico? Damn, you're lucky. I've never even been out of Illinois."

"I don't want to go. I'm not sure how that's supposed to help anything. I think they're just afraid of me."

"I guess you won't know until you do. I know I'd be excited to get the hell out of here."

As I stand near the door, waiting for my parents to pick me up, Erin hugs me and says she's going to miss me. Tasha mouths, "Goodbye," and waves to me from a distance. Josh gives me a high-five and tells me I'll be a famous writer one day. Luis screams, "Good luck!" then runs away giggling. Antwon won't look at me. Even when I call his name, he just looks at the floor.

It's cold and sunny when I walk outside. The wind feels nice on my face. After being stuck inside the stuffy hospital all day, it seems beautiful, even the muddy gray parking lot. The snow is beginning to melt, and I think I can almost smell spring.

After five days of talking about my feelings, making terrible art about my feelings, moving my body to the rhythm of my feelings, it's time to go back to school. People keep staring at me like I'm a quadriplegic or something. When someone asks me where I've been these last few days, I say, "Europe," even though gossip travels fast and they can probably see how I obsessively cover my wrists with my sleeves and bracelets. Some ding-dongs believe me, though, and when that happens, I keep the lie going, spinning it until I run out of ideas: I backpacked through France, Germany, and Spain with my rich aunt from Barcelona. Then we jumped on a ferry to Scandinavia and took a tour of the fjords. Then someone robbed us and took our passports. Then we were forced to be part of an international heist. I almost died in a police chase. Luckily, I survived to tell the tale!

Juanga gives me a hug when he sees me in the hall. "I'm so sorry. Are you okay?" He has a faded black eye and smells like weed, cologne, and dirty laundry. I want to ask him about it, but I'm afraid to.

"I'm all right. The happy pills should be kicking in soon."

"Did you like my dance?" Juanga smiles.

"It was lovely. It moved me to tears." I bring my hands to my chest and grimace.

"Please don't ever do that again. You know you can always talk to me and Lorena, right?"

"Yeah, I know. Thanks."

"Stop trying to die, okay?" He shoves me playfully, then puts his hand on his hip.

Something about how he says it makes me crack up. "I'm so bad at suicide," I tell him between bursts of laughter. "I win at being the worst at killing myself. I'm a champion, an American hero. USA! USA! USA!"

That gets Juanga going. "Girl, you are crazy." We laugh so hard, people stop and gawk at us, but we ignore them. Juanga leans against the locker and slaps it with his hand, all dramatic about it. Every time we try to stop, we look at each other and start all over again until the bell rings.

When I see Lorena at lunch, her eyes well up. Although we talked on the phone, it feels like I haven't seen her in centuries.

"Stop. Don't. I'm okay," I whisper. "We already talked about this."

Lorena takes a deep breath and wipes her eyes with the neck of her faded purple sweater. "Why didn't you tell me? How could you do something like that?"

I just close my eyes and shake my head, because if I open my mouth, I know what will happen, and I'm so tired of having an audience.

• • •

Dr. Cooke is wearing a scarlet sweater dress, a chunky orange necklace, and brown cowboy boots. I bet her outfit cost more than our car, but I don't think she's the kind of person to show off about her money or make you feel bad for being poor. I'm not envious, either. What I feel is more like awe.

I mostly want to complain about going to Mexico, but Dr. Cooke wants to talk about dating and sex again.

"There's not really much to tell. I've technically never had a boyfriend. I thought Connor was going to be, but obviously that didn't work out."

"Why didn't it?"

"He said he couldn't handle not seeing me, that he wanted me to be his girlfriend, but we had to be able to see each other. And how was I supposed to see him when I'm basically living in a prison?" We've already talked about this—the phone call—but I think she's digging for something else.

"Do you think that's reasonable?" Dr. Cooke asks. "That he felt he needed more from you?"

I shrug. "I guess."

"Why didn't you let him finish? You assumed he was breaking up with you without giving him a chance to express how he felt. Do you think it's possible that you were projecting a lot of your frustrations onto him?"

"But I knew it was coming. Why would he want to be with me? I'm too much to handle, story of my stupid life."

Dr. Cooke lets it go for now, but I already know her style. She'll return to it. "Okay, let's talk again about the day you hurt yourself, what led to it."

"After my mom found the condoms and underwear, it's like my whole life crumbled. I was already depressed, looking back on it—definitely—but when she got mad at me like that, I just felt so terrible. She hardly spoke to me and didn't let me leave the apartment for weeks. She already blamed me for Olga, and then when all that happened, it's like she really, *really* hated me. I can't ever be the person she wants me to be. And I was sad about Connor, because being with him made me feel good. He made me laugh, and for the first time ever, I felt like someone could really *see* me, you know?"

Dr. Cooke nods and brushes some hair from her face. "That sounds very painful. But why didn't you explain to her that the underwear wasn't yours, that it was your sister's?"

"Because she probably wouldn't believe me, and if she did, I think it would destroy her, in a way. The thing is that Olga was perfect to her. How could I tell her that she wasn't?"

"Have you ever talked about sex, you and your mother?"

"No. Well, not directly. She just makes comments sometimes. Basically, she makes it sound as if it were the most evil thing a person could do if they aren't married."

"And what do you think about it?"

"I don't see what the big deal is, and yet I feel guilty. I have these two competing feelings, you know? Like, logically, I think it's okay, but it still makes me feel like I've committed a crime or something, like everyone will know and pelt me with stones."

"Sex is a normal part of the human experience, but unfortunately many people attach a great deal of shame to it." Dr. Cooke crosses her legs. Maybe I should get a pair of cowboy boots, too. You could probably hurt someone with those fuckers.

"Yeah, my mom thinks it's the devil's work. You know, I just. . . I just feel like it's unfair, that my whole life is unfair, like I was born into the wrong place and family. I never belong anywhere. My parents don't understand anything about me. And my sister is gone. Sometimes I watch those stupid TV shows, you know? The ones where mothers and daughters talk about feelings and fathers take their kids to play baseball or get ice cream or some shit like that, and I wish it were me. It's so stupid, I know, to want your life to be a sitcom." I'm crying again.

"That doesn't seem stupid to me. You deserve all of those things."

After my parents go to sleep, I go through Olga's room to see if I can find any other clues. Even if I did call Connor now, it would be impossible for him to unlock the laptop because I'm leaving for Mexico tomorrow. I start wondering if maybe she wrote the password somewhere. I mean, I'm constantly forgetting my email password, so I have it written down in a notebook. Maybe Olga also had a crappy memory. I search through all her notebooks and scraps in her junk drawer again—nothing even remotely interesting. What if I'm wrong about my sister? What if she was the sweet, boring Olga I always knew her to be? What if I just want to think there was something below the surface? What if, in my own messed-up way, I want her to be less than perfect, so I didn't feel like such a fuck-up? Finally, when I flip through her old planner for the second time, I find a folded receipt with some numbers and letters circled. I don't know why, but something about that makes my brain itch. I enter them into the laptop. Nothing. I enter them again. Nothing. I enter them for the third time, and they work. I can't believe they work.

Olga didn't have much on her hard drive, just some boring pictures of her and Angie, and old papers from her Intro to

Business class. Luckily, I'm able to connect to the neighbor's Wi-Fi, and Olga's email password is the same as her laptop password. There are hundreds of spam emails from many different companies. I guess the spam bots don't know when someone has died. It seems so disrespectful to advertise to the dead. *50% OFF STOREWIDE!! BUY ONE GET ONE FREE SHOE SALE!!! VITAMINS FOR THE PERFECT BIKINI BODY.* I scroll and scroll forever to find anything that isn't an advertisement.

Finally, there it is. What I've been looking for all along:

Chicago65870@bmail.com
7:32 a.m. (September 6, 2013)

Why are you being like this? I'm giving you as much as I can. Don't you see that? You know I love you, so why are you always making me feel so guilty?

Holy crap, what in the world was my sister doing? Obviously, she had a boyfriend, but who was he? I jump to the oldest ones to read them in order, which takes me forever because there are hundreds. My heart pounds.

Chicago65870@bmail.com
1:03 a.m. (September 21, 2009)

I can't stop thinking about you.

---

losojos@bmail.com
1:45 a.m. (September 21, 2009)

Me neither. When can I see you again? Do you know how hard it is to see you every day at work? I don't know how to pretend. My heart races every time you're near me.

Chicago65870@bmail.com
10:00 p.m. (November 14, 2009)

Meet me at the diner tomorrow for lunch. Sit in the back so no one sees you. Wear the red shirt I like.

losojos@bmail.com
8:52 p.m. (January 14, 2010)

When are you going to tell her? I'm tired of waiting. You promised. I can't keep doing this forever. I love you, but you're tearing me apart. You're killing me.

Chicago65870@bmail.com
12:21 a.m. (January 28, 2010)

Soon. I told you already. You don't know how complicated it is. I have to think about my kids. I don't want to hurt them. You know how much I love you. Can't you see that? Can't you understand that? Please stop being so selfish. I'll see you tomorrow at the C. 6 p.m.

---

losojos@bmail.com
8:52 p.m. (January 29, 2010)

What do you mean *selfish*? All I do is wait for you. I don't know if I can do this anymore. This is destroying me. I can't eat. I can't sleep. All I do is think of the day we finally get to be together. Don't you care?

Then the Internet cuts out. It feels like getting to the end of a book only to discover that the last page has been torn in half.

Dull, dutiful Olga was sexing a married man. This explains almost everything—her faraway look, the hotel key, the underwear, the reason she never graduated from community college. She was with him when she was supposed to be in class. This guy strung her along for years. How could she be so stupid to believe he was actually going to leave his wife for her? I've read enough books and watched enough movies to know that never, ever happens. Who was he? How old was he? How can I find out more about him? The emails are so secretive, as if they were both terrified to ever get caught. From what I can gather, he worked in her office, was married, and had children, but I probably still have dozens and dozens of emails to get through.

How could I have been so dumb not to notice anything? But then again, how would anyone have known? Olga kept this sealed up and buried like an ancient tomb. My whole life I've been considered the bad daughter, while my sister was secretly living another life, the kind of life that would shatter Amá into tiny pieces. I don't want to be mad at Olga because she's dead, but I am.

"Goddamn it, Olga," I mutter under my breath.

There's no way Mamá Jacinta's house will have the Internet, so there's no point in trying to smuggle the laptop to Los Ojos. The safest place to keep it is in Olga's room, since I'm nearly certain Amá never comes in here. And if she did find it, she wouldn't know what to do with it. I remember that my cousin Pilar said there were new cybercafes in town. The computers are supposedly old as hell, but still, maybe I can read the rest of the emails once I get there. I put the receipt inside my journal.

NINETEEN

I reek by the time I land in Mexico, aggressively so. Thanks to severe thunderstorms, I spent the whole flight gripping my seat, worrying that I was going to plummet to my death. First I want to die and then I don't. Life is weird like that. I look at my armpits, and they are drenched. Not exactly a "fresh start" for me here. I search for my water bottle in my bag and discover it's spilled all over my things. I probably didn't screw the cap on right. I don't know why, but I *always* do that. I can be so careless. As I sift through my stuff to see the damage, I remember Olga's receipt. I open my journal, and there it is, wet and smeared, of course. I can only make out some of the numbers and letters, and what scares me the most is that I don't remember if I disabled her password. That is so typical of me, always making things harder for myself. Como me gusta la mala vida. Fuck. What am I going to do now?

Tío Chucho picks me up from the airport in the rusted and battered pickup he's had since I was a kid. His hair is gray and wild, but his mustache is still black and neatly trimmed. Tío has silver-capped, poor-people teeth and looks much older than the last time I saw him. When he hugs me, I can smell the sweat and dirt in his clothes. Amá said tío hasn't been the same since his wife died. I was little, so I don't remember when it happened, but I can sense a brokenness about him that I think will never,

ever go away. I suppose that's why he's never remarried. He and his wife only had one child—my cousin Andrés—who I'm guessing is about twenty now.

Los Ojos is nearly four hours away, deep in the mountains, in the middle of nowhere. Once we get on the road, tío Chucho asks me about school because he's heard I'm having a hard time. I wonder how much he knows. He seems to think Amá sent me here because I was getting bad grades. I'm not going to correct him.

"It's okay. I just want to go to college already."

"Good! That is what I want to hear, mija. Don't work like a donkey, like the rest of your family." He shows me his callused hands, then looks at mine. "Look at you! You have rich-lady hands."

Why is everyone in my family always talking about donkeys? I look down at my hands and realize he's right. They are smooth and soft, not at all like my parents', which are always chapped and worn. My hands look like they've never had to work hard, and I'd like to keep them that way.

"I want to be a writer," I tell tío Chucho.

"A writer? For what? You know they don't make any money, right? You want to be poor your whole life?"

I roll my eyes. "I'm not going to be poor."

"Just make sure you work in a nice office. Remember, don't work like a—"

"A donkey," I say, before he can finish.

Tío Chucho laughs. "Of course. You already know."

I nod. Everyone always tells me to work in an office, which

shows they don't know me at all. That's why I never talk about what I want to do with my life.

"I'm so sorry about Olga," tío finally says. "What a shame. She was such a good girl. We all loved her so much. Ay, mi pobre hermana, la inocente."

I wince. He didn't really know Olga. No one did.

The day is bright with a few fat clouds scattered throughout the sky. The Sierra Madre mountains are so stark and impossibly tall that they fill me with an inexplicable panic. After studying them for a few seconds, I have to look away.

"I miss her, but it's better now," I finally tell tío Chucho. "Time heals, etcetera." That's not true, and he knows it better than anyone, but that's just what I say to make people feel better.

Tío sighs. "You know we couldn't go to the funeral because we couldn't get visas, and then the money, of course. Que lástima. We were all very sad. We wanted to be there for the family."

"I understand," I say. I don't want to talk about my sister anymore, so I pretend to fall asleep until I do.

I wake up with drool trickling down my chin. I must have slept almost four hours because we're already pulling up to Mamá Jacinta's house. The land is dry and dusty, and my mouth is sour with thirst.

Mamá Jacinta runs to the pickup with her arms outstretched and tears in her eyes. She hugs me, and covers my face with kisses. She's just as warm and soft as I remember, but her cropped hair is now entirely gray.

"Mija, mija, you are so beautiful," she says over and over. I start crying, too.

There's a crowd of people behind her—aunts, uncles, cousins, and people I either don't know or don't remember. My cousin Valeria, who is only a few years older than I am, has three kids now, and they all look like eaglets. Tía Fermina and tía Estela look almost exactly the same since the last time I was here. The Montenegro women don't age much, apparently. Their husbands, tío Raul and tío Leonel, stand next to them, both wearing cowboy hats.

Tía Fermina and tía Estela hug me for a long time and call me mija, niña hermosa, chiquita. It makes me feel like I'm two years old, but I have to admit I enjoy it.

According to Mamá Jacinta, everyone is related to me somehow. I just nod, smile, and kiss everyone on the cheek like I'm supposed to.

The house is a brighter shade of pink than the last time I was there, and some of the adobe is cracked. The concrete additions look harsh against the softer colors of the original house, but that's how most homes look in Los Ojos—aclumsy mix of old and new.

The cobblestone streets have been paved, which is disappointing because I always loved the smell of mud when it rained, and the bakery across the street has burned down, so I won't get to wake up to the scent of baking bread in the mornings. A lot has changed in the last few years.

I'm rushed to the kitchen for dinner after I greet everyone.

Mexican ladies are always trying to feed you, whether you like it or not. As much as I get sick of eating Mexican food every single day of my life, if heaven existed, I know it would smell like fried tortillas. Mamá Jacinta gives me a giant plate of beans, rice, and shredded beef tostadas covered with sour cream, lettuce, and chopped tomatoes. "You're too skinny," she tells me. "By the time you leave, your mother won't even recognize you, you'll see."

No one has ever called me skinny. I've lost a few pounds because the medication has made my appetite weird lately—one day I want to eat the whole world, and the next day everything grosses me out—but I'm not even close to being thin.

I finish the whole plate and then ask for seconds, which pleases Mamá Jacinta. I also drink an entire bottle of Coca-Cola, which I normally don't even like, but it tastes so much better here. Tía Fermina and tía Estela sit across from me and tell me how much they've missed me, and the rest of the family crowds around me and asks a million questions: *How is your mother? How is your father? How cold does it get in Chicago? Why haven't you visited us in so long? When are you going to come back? What's your favorite color? Can you teach me English?* I feel like a celebrity. My family back home never treats me this way because I'm the designated pariah. Here, they even laugh at all my dumb jokes, every single one. Maybe Amá was right for once. Maybe this is what I needed.

Mamá Jacinta teaches me how to make the menudo they sell near the town square. Unlike the porquería of other cities and states, her version is made with meat, leg bones, and maíz. That's it. No chile rojo to hide the dirty tripe. First, Mamá has to track down a butcher who's just slaughtered a cow, then she and tío Chucho pick up the buckets of dirty cow stomach and take them to a woman they've hired to wash it. Mamá Jacinta says this poor woman is even more jodida than she is, and I believe her. I don't know what I would do if my job was to literally wash shit. Mamá Jacinta says that she used to clean the meat in the river, but it became so polluted that she had to start washing it in an outdoor sink. Thank God, because yesterday I saw stray dogs splashing in that filmy water, what's left of it anyway.

Once the meat is thoroughly de-shitted, it's rubbed with calcium oxide and left for a while. When the calcium oxide has softened the delicate inner skin, it's peeled off slowly and carefully. Then it's washed again and again until it gleams white as fresh snow.

The piece of tripe that comes from the butt has a beautiful honeycomb pattern. This is called las casitas. The thinner tripe with horizontal grooves has thick seams called callo. All the pieces are cut into slivers, and the slivers are cut into squares. The nerves are tough and slippery and resist the knife. The raw meat has a strong animal smell, and as you slice and slice, the tissue inevitably gets under your nails, and the scent lingers on your hands for hours.

The leg bones, the tripe, and the white maíz are cooked in a giant pot all night on low heat. The texture of the meat can be shocking to the average American tongue, but I like it. The pieces are soft and chewy, and the surface of the soup glitters with yellow globs of delicious fat. It's topped with lime juice, white onion, and dry oregano.

When we're finished slicing, Mamá Jacinta gives me a bowl of yesterday's menudo and a cup of té de manzanilla. She says it's good for nerves.

"Why do you think I'm nervous?"

"You're not?"

"It's more complicated than that."

"Why don't you tell me about it?"

"Thank you, but I don't really feel like it." I look down into my empty bowl. A fly lands on a tiny piece of meat. I wave it away.

"Are you afraid I'll tell your mother?"

"Well. . . yeah."

"Whatever you say stays here with me. I know you and your mother don't get along, but you're more alike than you think," she says, stirring in the honey.

"I seriously doubt that."

"You know, she was always the rebellious one. She was the first one in the family to move to the other side. But you knew that, didn't you? I told her not to go, but she said she wanted to live in Chicago, where she could work and have her own house."

"Rebellious? Amá?" My mind can't process that. My mother is the most rigid person I know.

"She never listened to me, always did what she wanted. You shouldn't be so hard on her, mija. She's been through so much."

"Like what?" I know my sister died, and that's been a living nightmare for everyone, but is there something else I don't know? Something begins howling outside.

"Oh my God, what is that?"

"Oh. The cats. They are very. . . amorous right now. Even during the day." Mamá Jacinta smiles.

"Gross."

"And they're two boy cats. Can you believe that?"

"Gay cats?" I gasp and slap the table. I've never heard of such a thing.

Mamá Jacinta chuckles.

"Okay, back to the story, Mamá. What else happened? Is there more?"

She shakes her head, her pale face suddenly pulled into a deep frown. The menudo gurgles in my stomach. The animal taste crawls up my throat.

"They got robbed when they crossed the border," she says, wiping her hands on her apron and looking toward the door. "Yes, they lost all their money. Didn't your mother ever tell you that?"

"Yeah, she said it was the worst days of her life, but that was before Olga died."

Mamá Jacinta rubs her temples, as if this conversation were giving her a headache. "Ay, mi pobre hija. She's had such bad luck in this life. I hope God has mercy on her from now on. She's suffered too much."

I don't know what to say, so I drink the rest of my lukewarm tea and watch one of the cats pace back and forth outside.

TWENTY

When I look in the faded mirrors in Mamá Jacinta's house, sometimes I think I almost look like my sister, which means I kind of look like my mother, especially when I take off my glasses. Now that I lost a little bit of weight, I can see the faint suggestion of cheekbones. I guess our noses were similar, too—rounded and slightly turned up at the tip. I used to think Olga and I didn't look like sisters, but I was wrong.

There are black-and-white pictures of my great-grandparents in several rooms of the house. They look serious in each one, as if they're ready to stab the photographer. Maybe it wasn't customary to smile for portraits back then. I know people used to believe photographs would steal their souls, which makes sense to me.

I never paid attention to Amá's old bedroom when I was a kid. She and tía Estela used to share a cramped, dusty room all the way in the back of the house. They even had to sleep in the same lumpy bed, which has never been replaced. I can't imagine having to sleep next to my sister my whole life. We've always been poor, and I've never had much privacy, but at least I've always had my own room. When my grandfather was alive, he kept making additions whenever they had more children, but he was never able to keep up. There were eight of them.

I hate when Amá goes through my things, and here I am, doing it to her. I don't find much, though, just a wooden chest with faded flowered dresses and tarnished bracelets. In the corner of the room, I see a framed drawing I never noticed before. It's up high, way past eye level. I take it down and look at it closely. It's Amá wearing a long dress, standing in front of the fountain in the town square. She looks exactly like Olga. Or Olga looked exactly like her. I wonder who drew this.

I find Mamá Jacinta cleaning the kitchen table. "Mamá Jacinta, who drew this picture of Amá?"

"Your father."

"What do you mean, my father? My father doesn't draw."

"Who said he doesn't?"

"I've never heard anything about this." I don't know why, but this almost makes me angry. How didn't I know this about my own dad?

"You didn't know Rafael could draw? He was the town artist. He drew everyone, even the mayor. Haven't you seen that drawing of your tía Fermina hanging in her living room? Your father drew that, too."

Not once in my whole life have I ever seen my dad draw. When I think of Apá, I picture him soaking his feet in front of the TV. "But how could he stop? I mean, if that's what he loved to do, why wouldn't he do it?"

"He probably got too busy with all the responsibilities of being a husband and father. You know how that is. You know how hard he works." Mamá Jacinta takes off her apron and hangs it on a rusty hook near the fridge.

"But he could have made time. If I don't write, I feel like I'm going to die. How could he stop just like that?"

"I don't know, but it's a shame because he was famous around here."

I wonder how much longer until Amá sends for me. Sometimes I lie awake, thinking of what I'll do when I get home. How am I going to find Olga's boyfriend? Or should I call him her "lover"? That word sounds ridiculous, though. I can go to her old office, but I have no idea who he is. Two things are clear, though: he wanted to make sure no one would ever find out, and he's the kind of person who could afford an expensive hotel almost every week. He has to be a doctor.

The nights are usually quiet, except for the meowing cats or the rooster next door that never knows what time it is. I like it when it rains because the soft pitter-patter on the tin roof is soothing, but it never lasts more than a fewminutes.

I twist under the scratchy blankets, thinking about Olga and worrying about what will happen to me if I miss too many days of school. I write notes to myself about what to do when I leave: 1) Read all of Olga's emails; 2) Talk to Mr. Ingman about what to do about my absences; 3) Find a summer job so I can pay for my trip to college. When I'm lucky, I fall asleep before the sun comes up.

My cousin Belén, tía Fermina's youngest daughter, is the town hot girl. She's dark, blue-eyed, and about a foot taller than I am. Her waist is impossibly small, and she loves to show it off in half shirts and skintight dresses. Wherever we go, every living creature eyes her up and down. I swear to God, I even saw a stray dog check her out. She gets marriage proposals when we walk down the street, and all she does is laugh and flip her hair. I feel kind of ugly next to her.

Belén has decided that she's going to show me around and introduce me to anyone we see. She comes over to Mamá Jacinta's house after school and drags me out, though I'd rather stay in the yard reading. My cousin doesn't understand that I can be very awkward and that I don't like talking to strangers. Today we say hello to a pair of twins nicknamed Gorduras and Mantecas—literally, "Fats" and "Lards"—in front of the supermarket. Mexican nicknames are as cruel as they are hilarious.

We usually get ice cream or aguas frescas from the town square and then take a "tour" of Los Ojos, even though I've been here before. When we go up and down the hills, I study all the colorful houses and try to peer inside, since everyone leaves their doors open during the day. Usually, I don't see anything interesting, but yesterday I saw a woman in a towel dancing to Juan Gabriel in her living room. I like taking these walks during dinnertime because of the dinner smells wafting from the houses—toasted chiles, stewed meat, boiled beans.

Belén gossips about everyone in town, even when I have no idea who they are. The latest dirt is that the lady who owns the most popular burger stand is having sex with her second cousin. She also tells me the story of a man named Santos who left Los Ojos many years ago with the dream of becoming a dancer in

Los Angeles. He tried crossing the border several times before he gave up and stayed in Tijuana. The rumor was that he began dressing like a woman and became a prostitute. When he returned to Los Ojos several years later, he was practically a living skeleton. Toward the very end, the sores all over his face and mouth attracted flies. His mother would sit next to him and shoo them away with a rag. Some of the townspeople said that it was his own fault for being gay, for bending over for all of Tijuana. I keep trying to interrupt and explain to Belén that AIDS isn't a gay disease, that anyone can get it, but she doesn't listen. She never seems to listen to anything I say.

I feel a longing in my chest when we pass Apá's abandoned childhood home. Mamá Jacinta points it out every time I'm here. No one has lived there in a long, long time, and it's about to fall apart. All of my father's brothers and sisters are scattered across the United States—Texas, Los Angeles, North Carolina, and Chicago. His parents died right after he and Amá left Los Ojos. My grandfather got a tumor that ate away his lungs, and my grandma followed him a few months later. They say she died of sadness. Can I miss people I've never met? Because I think I do.

Belén tries to get me to talk to boys from her school, but I'm never interested in any of them. Maybe it's because of the medication, but sex—anything related to it—is not really on my mind.

"That's where the narcos beheaded the mayor," Belén says casually, after we pass a group of her friends. She nods toward a depressing park made of metal and concrete.

"What?" I'm not sure if I heard her correctly.

"You didn't know? They used to shoot each other in the streets and blow up houses. It hasn't happened in a while, though. See?" she says, pointing to a charred house in the distance. "A Molotov cocktail."

I shudder as I think of the mayor's head rolling down the concrete and onto the street. Why would Amá send me here?

"Are we safe? Would they murder us, too?" I feel hot and cold at the same time. I jump when I hear a bird squawk.

Belén laughs. "No, tonta. Why would they care about you? Unless you're trafficking drugs and didn't tell me about it."

I shrug, feeling stupid.

"Oh, but never, ever stay out late, especially alone. No one does anymore."

TWENTY-ONE

My cousin Paulina is turning three, so I can't imagine that slaughtering and frying an animal would be very exciting for her, but that's how parties always are. Every milestone or accomplishment leads to alcohol and obscene amounts of fried meat.

That afternoon, Belén, Mamá Jacinta, and I walk over to the venue where the rest of the family has been preparing all morning. When we cross the town square, the Indian ladies, with long black braids that look like rope, try to sell us nopales. Their thick hair reminds me of Amá. Strangers on the street have offered her money in exchange for her shiny braids.

The women sit on the ground, with a large wicker basket full of peeled and sliced cactus in little plastic bags. How poor do you have to be to sell something that's free? I can literally walk up to any nopal in town and cut off a paddle. I see Mamá Jacinta do it all the time. The worst part is not even peeling them; it's getting rid of all the slime.

I've always wondered why the bottoms of tree trunks here were painted white, but I've never asked about it. I stare at the sad, rusted fountain and wonder if they'll ever turn the water back on. A girl, with a baby strapped to her back with an embroidered orange cloth, stands up and puts her hand in front of me. "Por favor, señorita," she pleads. "Una limosna." She looks about thirteen, so small and bony, I can't imagine that baby coming out of her. I pray it's not hers.

"Don't listen to them," Belén says. "They're here begging every day. She should work like everyone else. Typical indias." Belén practically spits out the words. I don't understand why she thinks she's so much better than they are. She's just as dark and wears the same frayed red dress every other day.

"Have you looked at yourself?" I mumble.

"What?"

"Nothing."

I turn back to the baby, who is crying now, his face covered with dirt and snot. I give the girl all the change in my pocket. Belén crosses her arms over her chest and shakes her head.

The party venue is owned by los Garzas, the richest family in Los Ojos. According to Belén, they got rich by selling drugs. When I ask her what kind of drugs, all she says is "the worst kind."

I hear a violent squealing when we approach and look at Mamá Jacinta, my stomach sinking. "They're killing it right now? I thought it would be dead already."

"Sorry, mija. We can take a walk and come back if you want."

"Don't be a baby," Belén says. "You eat meat, don't you?"

"Yeah, but I've never seen my tacos killed before my very eyes."

"Ay, Dios mío, you Americans are so delicate," Belén says.

"Come on, let's go for a walk," Mamá Jacinta says, placing her warm hand on my arm.

"No. It's okay. Let's go."

Tío Chucho and my cousin Andrés drag the writhing pig with a long red rope. Its desperate and brutal cries give me goose bumps. Once they get the poor thing onto a slab of concrete,

Andrés stabs it in the heart.

"Good job, mijo," tío says.

The pig squirms all over the ground, and its squeals become deeper and more anguishing. The blood gushes from its chest. I feel light-headed.

"Are you excited for the chicharrones, prima?" Andrés shouts to me.

"Oh yeah. Delicious. Can't wait," I yell back.

When the pig finally dies, Andrés and tío Chucho hang it by its hind legs and bleed it out into a bucket. Once it's drained, they begin to cut it into pieces. I try not to look, but I can't help it—my eyes are drawn to the blood.

After a while, I can hear the pop and crackle of the frying flesh. I'm sick to my stomach, but my mouth still waters. The human body is so weird sometimes. Once all the meat is cooked, tía Estela brings me a plate of rice, beans, and chicharrones.

"Ándale, mija," she says, and squeezes my shoulder. "You need to put some weight back on." It's funny how in the United States I'm too fat, and in Mexico I'm too skinny. I know tía is worried about me. The Montenegro women are all excellent worriers.

I smile and say, "Thank you," because the rudest thing you can do to a Mexican lady is refuse her food—might as well spit on a picture of La Virgen de Guadalupe or turn the TV off during *Sábado Gigante.*

I take a few chicharrones, put them in a soft tortilla, and drown them in dark red salsa. I eat them without much difficulty, but when I make my next taco, I see a few thick hairs jutting from the skin. I don't want everyone to think I'm a spoiled American princess, so I close my eyes and inhale the taco as quickly as possible. I imagine my face a beautiful shade of putrid green when I'm finished, but I'm proud of my triumph.

The dance floor begins to get crowded once everyone is full of pig meat. The music is tinny and crackly—partly because of the cheap sound system—but I still like it. The accordions sound ridiculously joyful, even when the songs are about death. Tía Fermina and tío Raul dance cheek to cheek. Belén dances with Mamá Jacinta's lanky next-door neighbor. I watch everyone's jumpy little dances as the sun bakes me into a cocoon of laziness. I start to nod off in my chair when Andrés pokes me in the shoulder and tells me we're going to ride horses.

"Come on, prima," he says, pulling me up.

“I’m tired. I don’t feel like it.” I try to slump back down.

“It’ll be good for you.”

“How?”

“Trust me.”

Defeated, I follow Andrés to the field next to the venue, where two black horses are tied to a fence.

“This one is Isabela,” he says, pointing to the smaller one. “And this is Sebastián.” Andrés rubs the horse’s side and smiles.

“Nice to meet you.” I pretend to shake their hooves.

“They’re married, you know.”

“Married! What are you talking about?” Imagining Isabela in a wedding gown makes me laugh so hard I snort. “Did they have a wedding? Did they waltz? Did she throw a bouquet?”

“Obviously, they didn’t have a wedding, tonta, but they’re a real couple." Andrés seems annoyed that I find it so funny, that I'm having a hard time believing in romantic love between two animals.

"Really?"

"When they're separated, Sebastián cries, I swear to God. Big, fat tears!" Andrés looks serious, so I stop laughing. He even crosses himself to make a point.

As Andrés gets the saddles from the shed, I pet Isabela's back and run my fingers through her coarse black mane. Her coat is so dark it's almost blue. Her muscles are tight and shimmer in the sunlight. I don't think I've ever seen something so beautiful in my whole entire life. It's almost bewildering.

I'm surprised by how much I love being on a horse again, to feel its tremendous strength under me. Andrés and I ride toward the river. It's quiet except for the clacking hooves and buzzing insects in the yellowed grass. A flock of gray birds passes over us and settles in a giant tree. "Doves," Andrés says. The river is nearly gone now because of the drought. The only water that remains is brownish green and full of garbage—plastic bags, bottles, wrappers, and even a solitary shoe. I shiver when I remember my dream about Olga as a mermaid; I can still see her glowing face so clearly.

The abandoned train station next to the river is boarded up now, the red paint peeling off in giant strips. The tracks are rusted, and the wood is worn. Andrés says the train has been gone for years now. It used to be bustling with people, but the company was crooked and couldn't sustain itself. I remember Mamá Jacinta bringing me and Olga here when I was little. She bought us tiny wooden boxes of cajeta that was so sweet and sticky, it hurt my teeth for hours. I also know that Papá Feliciano used to take this train to sell pots and pans in other towns. He died before they closed the line. I guess, in a way, it's good that he never saw it shut down. He loved that train.

Big fat flies begin biting Isabela's face and neck when we approach a clearing. She shakes her head to get them off, but it's no use; even if I swat them away, they come right back. My hand is smeared with blood when I rub her where the flies have landed. I kiss the back of her head when Andrés isn't looking.

We ride along the river until the sun dips behind the trees and the crickets begin to sing. A field of corn in the distance looks dry and shriveled, and I wonder what would happen if someone flicked a match at it. I could ride Isabela forever, but

Andrés says we should get back to the party so Mamá Jacinta doesn't worry. When I say goodbye to Isabela, I press my face against her side and run my hand over her back. I think I can hear her heartbeat. Suddenly, I remember the time Olga and I rode our great-uncle's horses the second time we came to Los Ojos. At first, I was too scared, but Olga told me that the horses wouldn't hurt me because they were magical creatures. And I believed her.

Andrés laughs. "What are you doing?"

I smile. "Nothing. Just giving her a hug."

Tío Chucho walks toward me, holding a beer. "Ándale, mija, let's dance." He looks a little wobbly.

"No thanks, tío. I'm not much of a dancer."

"Nonsense!" he says, and leads me to the dance floor. "The Montenegros are the best dancers in Los Ojos!"

The song is about three girls who drive to a carnival and plummet to their deaths when the truck flips over the side of a cliff. I'm not sure why anyone would want to dance to that. Tío Chucho smells like he's sweating beer. His shirt is damp and his skin is sticky, but I keep dancing because I don't want to hurt his feelings. He's having a great time, spinning me around and singing along at the top of his lungs.

After the third song, a group of men wearing black masks and holding rifles walks toward the entrance of the venue. Tío lets go of my hand. His face slackens. "Chingue su madre," he mutters.

"¿Qué, tío? What's happening?"

"Nothing, mija. I'll take care of it," tío says, and walks toward them.

Everyone looks stiff and worried, but no one says a word. It's suddenly a party full of statues. Andrés just keeps blinking. He looks like he might pass out.

Are they soldiers? Are they narcos? I have no idea.

One of the masked men stares at me the entire time, as if he's drilling holes into my body with his eyes.

Tío Chucho pulls an envelope from his pocket and hands it to one of the men, who nods toward Andrés. Tío returns to the party looking pale and terrified. When the man finally turns away from me, I notice a faded Santa Muerte tattoo on his fore-arm.

"What the hell was that?" I whisper to Belén.

"You need to stop asking so many questions," she says, and turns away from me.

TWENTY-TWO

Belén forces me to go to the soccer game, even though I tell her I have a hatred for sports that is located deep inside my entrails. She says it doesn't matter, that's not the point of going. Soccer games are where young people hang out and hook up. There's not much else to do in Los Ojos. Stare at the mountains? Chase chickens? Shoot bottles?

We sit on the top bleachers with Belén's friends, a group of mildly attractive girls who wear way too much makeup. Although they don't say anything petty or snarky, I can tell right away that they're jealous of my cousin. I don't know why I always notice these types of things. There's something about the way their eyes outline her body and settle on her face, a sort of longing. It's not that they *want* her; it's that they want to *be* her.

After Los Tigres score their first goal, a dark guy in a cowboy hat comes toward us with bottles of Coke and plastic bags of pork skins slathered in red salsa. He distributes the drinks and snacks to everyone in our group and squeezes between me and Belén. All the girls laugh as if it were the funniest thing they've ever seen. I can feel the beads of sweat form on my upper lip.

"How are you doing tonight, Señorita Reyes?"

At first, I wonder how he knows my last name or who I am, but then I remember everyone knows everyone's business in Los Ojos. Tío Chucho says you can't even fart without the whole town finding out.

"Medium," I say, looking at the field, trying, for once in my life, to understand a sport.

He laughs. "Why won't you look at me?"

I shrug. I'm mute all of a sudden.

"Don't mind Esteban," Belén says, smirking. "He can be a little pesado sometimes."

I wouldn't call him pesado, but he's definitely assertive. I can't keep myself from staring at his dark and veiny forearms. I imagine how they would feel against my fingertips. I cross my legs so they don't brush against his.

After the game, Belén and her giggling friends flee before I can ask them to wait for me.

"I guess I should walk you home." Esteban smiles. His teeth are bright and perfect.

"Yeah, I guess," I say, remembering what Belén said about walking alone at night. The sky is beginning to purple. I can see the sun and moon at the same time.

Esteban makes me feel as if something were filling my chest with warm syrup, as if all my bones were being slowly removed from my body. For a second, I wonder what Connor might be doing, if he still thinks about me, but I remind myself that things are over between us. I have no idea why, but even though I just met Esteban and know virtually nothing about him, he makes me feel all goopy inside.

A truck blasting a narcocorrido wakes me from my reverie.

When we get to the corner of Mamá Jacinta's block, Esteban takes my hand. "I've liked you since you got here."

"Well, I'd never seen you before, so that's kind of weird." I'm too nervous to look at him. Why do I have to be such an asshole, even when I don't want to be?

"You don't remember seeing me that time you and Belén came into the fruit store? That's where I work."

I knew I had felt someone looking at me that day, but I didn't bother searching for the source. It's funny how your body knows things before you do.

I shake my head. "No, I didn't see you."

Esteban's dark skin glistens under the streetlight. It reminds me of coffee. I want so much to touch his face, but I don't.

We sit in tía Fermina's backyard gnawing on figs we picked from her tree. Tío Raul and tío Leonel are inside watching the news.

The sky is full of stars, and I stare at it in awe for such a long time that everyone notices and laughs at me. How could I forget the nights were like this?

"Poor city girl," tío Chucho says, smiling. "She probably never sees stars in Chicago."

"Not really. Maybe three or four at a time, if I'm lucky," I say, and pick a tiny leaf from my sweater. I look back up and think about how some stars don't even really exist anymore, that seeing them is seeing the past. It's hard for me to wrap my brain around that. What a mind fuck.

The ground feels good under my bare feet. Tía Estela sits behind me in a chair and braids my hair, her fingers cool against the back of my neck. Her hands in my hair are soothing. She's gentle, doesn't yank my hair like Amá used to when

I was a kid.

"Dios mío, mija," tía Estela says as she holds the braid up for everyone to see. "You have so much hair. How do you walk around like this? Doesn't your head feel heavy?"

"Sometimes, when it's wet," I say, and wonder what it would feel like to chop off all of my hair. What would I look like? I've had long hair my entire life. When I was born, my hair was a ridiculous shock of black. Amá said the doctors and nurses had never seen anything like it.

I feel Belén stare at me from across the yard. I think she's used to being the beautiful one and doesn't appreciate the attention I'm receiving. It's both uncomfortable and satisfying at the same time.

"Beautiful hair runs in the family," Mamá Jacinta says. "Though you wouldn't know, looking at mine now." She runs her hands through her short gray hair and smiles.

Tío Chucho grins and shakes his hair as if he were in a shampoo commercial. "It's true. I look like a movie star."

I've eaten so many figs that my stomach hurts, but I can't stop. I love the taste of the sweet flesh, the crunch of tiny seeds between my teeth.

The night is always perfect here—never too cold, the air smelling of dirt and leaves. I think I almost get a whiff of the river, then remember it's practically dried up. A phantom smell, I guess. I can't think of anything more calming than the sound of crickets and the rustle of the fig tree. If tía had a hammock, I would ask to sleep here every single night.

The white and yellow roses planted in old buckets are thriving despite the drought, because tía Fermina cares for them as if they were children. Their persistence makes me feel hopeful.

Andrés gets up from his chair and approaches a cactus in the corner of the yard. I wonder what he's doing, but I don't ask. He presses his finger to the bud and whispers something. After a few seconds, he turns to all of us and says, "This one never bloomed, and the season's almost over." He frowns.

"What kind of flower is that?" I ask.

"Nocturnal cactus flower. Forgot the name, but this one is a flop, I think."

"I've never heard of that. That's . . . that's . . . amazing." I run out of words. A flower that blooms only at night sounds like something out of a fairy tale.

Tía Fermina comes out from the kitchen with a jug of agua de jamaica and pours each of us a glass. "This is good for digestion and high cholesterol. After eating those carnitas tonight, we all need it." Tía Fermina is the oldest and always trying to take care of everybody. It's almost hard to believe that she's Belén's mother, because Belén is kind of selfish, mostly concerned with how pretty she is. The first night I got here, tía Fermina gave me a small cloth bag full of paper worry dolls. She told me that before I go to sleep each night I should tell them all my worries and put them under my pillow. They're supposed to disappear by morning. I never told her it didn't work.

The agua de jamaica is tart, sweet, and refreshing. I pour myself another glass. If the night were made into a drink, it would taste like this.

• • •

Tía Fermina takes me to Delicias, three towns over, to buy some cheese. Supposedly, it's the best in the whole state, and I think I might agree, because it's sharp, creamy, and melts perfectly. It tastes amazing in enchiladas. A cheese worthy of a pilgrimage.

Tía complains about the drought the whole ride over. "It's ruining all the crops," she says. "The cows are emaciated. People don't know what to do anymore." The land is definitely drier than I remember. The trees are yellow and brittle.

Everything in the desert hunkers toward the ground. The huizaches that dot the mountains are short, and the twigs are armed with spines. Everything protects itself with needles here.

Once in a while, a pregnant cloud hovers and teases the land with a trickle of rain.

Tía Fermina is a few years older than Amá, and though they look so much alike—same black hair, light skin, and bright red lips—she's just not as pretty. That doesn't mean she's not attractive, though; tía has a captivating face, like all the Montenegro women. It's just that hardly anyone is as beautiful as Amá. I wonder what it was like for them growing up. Did tía always compare herself to her? Was she jealous? Did she ever wish she had crossed to the other side like her little sister?

We park the truck at the bottom of a hill because it won't fit through the narrow streets. I suddenly have déjà vu; I know I came to this town with Mamá Jacinta once, long ago, but I don't remember why exactly. Did it have something to do with a goat? Or am I making that up? Sometimes my memory feels like a smeared photograph.

"How is your mother?" tía Fermina asks as we pant our way up. "Have you talked to her?"

"She called me yesterday. She sounds okay."

"How was she before? You know, when she lost Olga."

"She couldn't get out of bed. Just when I thought she was doing better, she'd go right back to sleeping for days and days. She hardly ate or drank anything. It scared me. She hasn't done that in a while, though."

A man walks a blindfolded bull across the street. "Buenos días," he says, and tips his hat. That's the thing about Mexico—you have to say hello to people you don't even know.

"My poor sister. And all of us here, useless, unable to help her. Ay, Diosito." Tía Fermina sighs. "Every time I called her, she'd tell me she was fine, but I knew she wasn't. Of course she wasn't. How could she be fine without her daughter? That's the worst thing that could ever happen to you. I can't even fathom it. God forbid." She crosses herself.

"She wasn't fine, and neither was I."

"Ay, mija, I can't imagine what it's like to lose your sister." Tía turns to me and touches my face. "Pobre criatura. And what about you and your mother? I know you two have fought a lot over the years. She's always said you were very terca."

That's how I've been described my whole life—terca, necia, cabezona—all the synonyms for "stubborn" and "difficult." A gust of wind carries the smell of burning garbage toward us.

"Yeah, we don't really understand each other."

"You need to try harder, especially with your sister gone. You're all she has, Julia. She loves you so much. Maybe you don't see that, I don't know. Just please, don't make her life harder. I ask you as your aunt, as your mother's sister, please be good to her." Tía Fermina is out of breath now. She stops and wipes the sweat from her face with her forearm. I don't think Amá told her I tried to kill myself.

"You don't understand, tía. I try. I really do. We're just so different. She thinks I'm wild and crazy, but what I want makes sense to me. I want to be independent. I want to be my own person, with my own life. I want to make my own choices and mistakes. And she wants to know what I'm doing every second of the day. It makes me feel like I'm drowning."

"Ay, mija. There is so much you don't understand."

"Why does everyone say that to me? I know I'm young, but I'm not stupid."

"That's not what I mean. It's that your mother has had such a hard life. You can't even imagine."

"I know. She reminds me of it all the time. She's always telling me how hard she works and that I'm ungrateful."

Tía Fermina doesn't say anything for a long time.

"Tía? Are you okay?"

"I'm only telling you this so you can understand, so you can have more compassion." She looks at the sky. "God, forgive me for doing this."

My muscles tense. I'm suddenly overwhelmed with thirst. "What? What is it? Tell me, tell me now. I want to know now."

Tía finally looks at me. "You know how your parents crossed the border?"

I've heard the story several times. Amá left with Apá against her mother's will. They crossed with a coyote. When they got to Texas, a man stole all their money. They stayed in El Paso with Apá's distant cousin and worked at a restaurant until they were able to save enough money to take the bus to Chicago. It was in the middle of winter, and they didn't have jackets. Amá said she had never felt so cold in her life. She thought her eyes would freeze inside her head. That's all I knew.

"Your mother, el coyote . . ." Tía looks like she's trying to untangle what she needs to say. She begins to cry. "He took her . . ."

"He took her where?" I scream. I don't mean to, but it just comes out that way. "Where did he take her? What did he do?" I squeeze her hand so hard, I think I might break her fingers.

Tía can't get the words out. My brain is pounding. A tattered gray cat darts past us.

"I can't say it. I shouldn't have told you this. God, forgive me." Tía Fermina covers her mouth with her hand. She doesn't have to finish.

"And Apá? Where was he? What did he do?" I can't stop screaming.

"They held him down with a gun. There was nothing he could do." Tía Fermina shakes her head.

"No. No. That can't be true. No. I can't . . ." I sit down on the ground, near a mound of red ants, but I don't care. My body feels like it weighs a thousand pounds. I picture my mother's face streaked with tears and dirt, my father bowing his head in defeat. "And Olga? What about Olga? She was . . . She was . . ." I can't get the words out.

Tía Fermina clasps her hands to her chest and nods. "See, mija, that's why I want you to know. So when you and your mother fight, you can see where she's come from and understand what's happened to her. She doesn't mean to hurt you."

That night, I don't fall asleep until morning. I just lie there thinking about my parents and how little I know them. I wake up at noon, my body aching.

Because I don't have anywhere to go, no real obligations, the days blend together; I can't even tell them apart most of the time. I wake up, eat breakfast, help Mamá Jacinta cook and clean, and then lie around reading and writing. After Belén gets home from school, she and I wander through the town aimlessly, eating all the junk food that will fit inside our bodies. Well, at least when my appetite hasn't disappeared. Sometimes we meet Esteban after he gets out of work. We either sit on a bench or walk around the square until we have to go home. Belén always leaves us alone for a while. She pretends she needs to run an errand, but I know exactly what she's doing.

Esteban has never tried to kiss me, and it's all I can think about. I imagine his thick lips on mine. I picture his hands running through my hair and down my back, his body pressed against me. I never do anything about it, though. I feel as scared and vulnerable as a plucked bird. I know he said he liked me, but what if he didn't really mean it? What if he thinks I'm weird? What if I'm not pretty enough? Besides, how could I, with the whole town watching? I just sit there like a fool, making small talk and boring observations about stray animals, hoping I don't embarrass myself with my limited Spanish vocabulary.

Today Esteban is wearing jeans, a faded Beatles T-shirt, and a straw cowboy hat. I like the combination.

"Where did you get that shirt?"

"My cousin left it at my house, and I kept it," he says, smiling.

"Do you even like the Beatles?"

"Not really."

"You're weird." A mangy stray dog creeps toward us and begins sniffing me.

Esteban seems very amused by this. "Weird, huh?"

"Yeah, everyone likes the Beatles."

"Apparently, that dog likes you." He points his chin toward it.

"He's not my type."

Esteban laughs. "You're silly, you know that? What exactly is your type, then?"

"I prefer them to be better groomed. Not so many fleas."

Esteban smiles and pats my hand. I almost gasp and feel my eyes bug out with surprise. I'm so nervous I can't even move. We sit like that for a few seconds until Belén comes out of the store with the sack of meat we have to take to Mamá Jacinta for dinner. I jump up and leave without looking at Esteban, my heart inside my mouth.

At dusk, Belén, my tías, Mamá Jacinta, and I watch telenovelas. That's what all the women in Los Ojos do at that hour. They're all glued to their televisions. I could probably run around with my hair on fire, and they wouldn't even notice. During the opening credits of *La Casa de Traición*, a horrible show about a rich family with a shameful past, we hear shouting outside.

"¡Hijo de tu pinche madre!" a man yells. "You're going to pay!"

Belén mutes the TV, and we all stare at each other, confused.

I can't understand the rest of the yelling. The only words I can make out are puto and piedras. Someone honks a car horn. Tires screech. A dog barks.

The commotion stops after a few seconds, and just when we think it's over, the gunshots begin. Everyone drops to the floor, even poor Mamá Jacinta. "Again? I thought this had ended," she says. "Why, God, why?" Tía Fermina rubs her back and tries to calm her down, but Mamá Jacinta whimpers and cries. She is distraught beyond consolation. Tía Estela crosses herself over and over.

Everyone crawls toward the back of the house. I'm the last one. I peek out the cracked door before I go. Two dead bodies are lying in the middle of the street.

Tía Fermina says she needs to give me a limpia to get rid of my susto. She says they can't send me home like this after what happened. What would my mother say? My family members claim that "a scare" can kill you. I call that a "heart attack," but whatever. I'll go along with this if it makes everyone feel better.

Tía takes me to the storage room where Mamá Jacinta keeps her extra dry food. There are sacks of flour, beans, and dry corn scattered on the floor. I lie on a small cot, and once I get comfortable, tía Fermina makes little crosses all over my body with an egg, beginning with my head and working her way down to my feet. The cool shell against my skin feels comforting. When I was little, I was confused about the process of this spiritual cleansing. All I knew was that it involved an egg, so I imagined they used a cooked one—likely fried—which left the recipient greasy and smeared with yolk. Boy, was I stupid, but I figured it out when I saw them do it to my cousin Vanessa after she was almost hit by a car. The raw egg traps all the rotten crap clogging up your soul.

Tía Fermina whispers the prayers so faintly I can't understand them. After she makes dozens of crosses all over my body, she says it's time to see inside the egg, to understand what's been stewing inside of me. Tía cracks the egg into a glass of water and holds it up to the light. The water turns thick and cloudy, and when we look closer, we see a dot of dark blood in the center of the yolk.

"Dios mío, mija," tía gasps. "What's going on with you?"

I have to go back home because Mamá Jacinta is afraid the narcos will continue killing each other. After a year and a half of relative peace, Los Ojos has erupted into violence again. She tells me I need to take the bus to the airport because it's much less likely that the narcos will pull us over. It's especially dangerous for tío Chucho to drive, since the cartel has been after Andrés for years.

"Why did tío Chucho give that man an envelope?" I ask Mamá Jacinta before bed. "At Paulina's party."

She sighs. "It's a bribe, so they'll leave Andrés alone. They want him to work for them, and they come around every once in a while. Can you imagine working for those animals? Ni Dios lo mande. Those men have no soul, forcing a man with no money to pay them like that. Your tío is a humble truck driver who does his best to provide for his family, what's left of it. Ay, Dios mío, my little town has turned to garbage." Mamá Jacinta presses her palms to her eyes. “Please stop worrying about what happened, and try to get some rest. You’ll be home soon. I didn’t know this would happen, mija. I’m sorry. I thought the fighting was over. Nothing like this has happened in a long time.” She makes the sign of the cross and gives me a kiss goodnight.

“It’s okay. It’s not your fault,” I say. Part of me wants to tell her I know what happened to Amá. It beats inside me like another heart, but I don’t know if I’ll ever be able to say it out loud.

Esteban says he’ll miss me, and I tell him that he won’t. How could he? He hardly knows me. He just laughs, though. He laughs at nearly everything I say, even when I’m not trying to be funny.

"Maybe I'll see you on the other side," he tells me at the square. "I might be crossing soon. I can't work at the fruit store forever. There's nothing for me here. I'm sick of this place." He looks around, disgusted, and kicks a rock toward the empty fountain.

"Be careful. Please. The border . . . The fucking border." I feel a wildness spreading through me. "It's nothing but a giant wound, a big gash between the two countries. Why does it have to be like that? I don't understand. It's just some random, stupid line. How can anyone tell people where they can and can't go?"

"I don't understand, either." Esteban takes off his cowboy hat and looks toward the mountains. "All I know is that I've had enough of this life."

"It's bullshit, utter bullshit." I clench my fists and close my eyes.

Esteban cradles my face in his hands and pulls me toward him. The whole town will probably find out within the hour, but I don't even care.

I cry quietly on the bus after I say goodbye to my family. I don't look outside, because if I see Mamá Jacinta standing there staring at me, which I'm certain she is, I'll probably start wailing. After she gave me la bendición, she handed me Apá's drawing and said she trusted me to take care of my mother. "You are a beautiful young woman. You will do amazing things. Please just make sure you look after my daughter." I never imagined I would have to protect and care for my mother—I didn't know that was my job—but I said, "Yes, of course." How could I not?

I try to sleep when the bus finally pulls away, but the man in front of me is snoring so loudly he wakes himself up every few minutes. His snores are so deep it sounds as if he's being suffocated by his own flesh. I stare out the window and study the brown and brittle land. The worst drought in ten years, they say. Every few miles, I see a bright desert flower or white crosses with plastic roses on the side of the road. I wonder why so many people die here.

The sun begins to set as we finally approach the city. The colors are so beautiful they're almost violent. I feel a pang in my chest and remember a line from a poem I read a long time ago about terror being the beginning of beauty. Or something like that. I don't quite remember.

There's a dead donkey in a field behind a barbwire fence. Its legs are bent and stiff, and its mouth is open, as if it had been smiling when it died. Two vultures circle above it.

TWENTY-THREE

Amá takes me to a restaurant in Chinatown after she picks me up from the airport. I can hardly believe it because I honestly don't remember the last time we ate at a restaurant together. The tables are sticky, and it smells like old carpet, but I'm glad I'm there with her. Plus, she said her coworker told her it was good. Maybe I shouldn't judge a book by its cover, for once in my life.

We sit by the window because I tell Amá I want to look outside. Chicago is finally beginning to thaw—most of the snow has melted, except for a few dirty patches—and everyone looks brighter, more alive. A red fish with a mean face swims in a tank near the register. Amá laughs when I tell her that I think he's giving us dirty looks.

"Your grandma tells me you helped her so much," Amá says, smiling.

"It was nice. I didn't realize how much I'd missed her."

"See? I told you it would make you feel better."

"Yeah, I guess so. The shooting was scary, though." I take a deep breath.

"I'm so sorry about that, mija. They told me it was calm when I sent you. Nothing like that had happened in over a year. You know I wouldn't have let you go if I had known."

"I'm fine. It's okay. It's not your fault."

"Your teacher called me last week," Amá says, and slurps her tea.

"Which one?"

"Mr. Ingman."

"But he's not even my teacher anymore. Why would he call you? What did he say?"

"He heard you were out of school for a few weeks. He was worried. I told him you were in Mexico because of a family matter, and he said that it was very important that you come back so you can graduate and go to college. He kept telling me you were the best student he's ever had, that you're an amazing writer. I didn't even know. Why didn't you tell me?"

It's always been hard for me to explain these things to Amá. "I tried," I say. "I really did."

"You know, I hardly went to school. I had to drop out to work and help take care of my family when I was only thirteen. I'm ignorant, mija. Can't you see that? There are so many things I don't know. I wish things were different. I know you hate me, but I love you with all my heart. I always have, ever since I knew I was pregnant with you. I just don't want anything to ever happen to you. I worry and worry all the time. It eats away at me like you can't believe. All I do is think of ways to protect you." Amá begins to cry. She dabs her eyes with the corner of her napkin.

"I don't hate you, Amá. I don't hate you at all. Please don't say that." The waitress brings us our food. I love sweet and sour chicken—it normally makes me salivate like a Saint Bernard—but I'm not hungry anymore. Amá, of course, has ordered a plate of steamed vegetables. I look up at the ceiling, trying to keep myself from crying, but it's no use. Everyone can watch us if they want.

"I know I'm not the best mother sometimes. You're just so different, Julia. I've never known how to deal with you, and then after your sister died, I had no idea what I was doing. When I found out you were having sex, I was so scared you'd end up like your cousin Vanessa, alone and with a baby. I don't want you to have that kind of life. I want you to have a good job and get married." Amá takes a deep breath. "I've been talking to the priest lately. He's been helping me understand all of this better." She puts her hand over mine. "I'm sorry. I really am. And . . . and. . . I know what happened to your sister was not your fault. I never should have said that. I'm just trying to put myself back together, but it's so hard, mija."

I can't look at Amá without thinking about the border. I keep picturing her screaming on the ground, Apá with a gun to his head. I don't think I can ever tell her that I know. But how do we live with these secrets locked within us? How do we tie our shoes, brush our hair, drink coffee, wash the dishes, and go to sleep, pretending everything is fine? How do we laugh and feel happiness despite the buried things growing inside? How can we do that day after day?

"I'm sorry, too," I finally say. "I'm sorry I hurt you. I'm sorry I wanted to die."

Amá returns my phone to me when I get home, so I decide to call Connor. Now I miss both him and Esteban. "Love," or whatever—I don't even know what I feel—is confusing. I wonder if it's normal to have feelings for two people.

When I turn the phone on, I see that I have fifteen texts and eleven voice mails, and they're all from Connor. Most of them are the same: "I hope you're okay. I miss you. Please call me back."

I can hardly breathe as I wait for him to pick up the phone. I almost hang up when he answers.

"Oh my God, it's you," he says.

I'm so nervous my voice cracks. "How are you?"

"I called you a million times. Why didn't you ever answer? I was hoping you had your phone back."

"I was in Mexico."

"What? Mexico? What were you doing there?"

"It's kind of a long story. I'll have to explain in person. It's too complicated to tell you over the phone."

"I thought you hated me."

"I don't. Not at all."

"I still want to help you with your sister's laptop, you know?"

"Thank you. I appreciate that, but, well, that's something else I'd rather explain in person."

"Listen, I missed you. I'm sorry about before."

"It's okay. It was mostly my fault. I should have let you finish. I shouldn't have hung up. And I missed you, too. I have so many stories for you. One involves two married horses."

Connor laughs. "That sounds pretty crazy."

"Man, you have no idea. Meet me at the bookstore tomorrow at five-thirty? We can sniff books together." I don't even know if Amá will let me go, but I have to find a way to see Connor again.

When we hang up, I walk to Amá at the kitchen table. She's staring at a pile of bills.

"Amá," I say quietly. "Can I please go out with Lorena tomorrow?" There's no way I'd ever tell her about Connor, so I have no choice but to lie. I hold my breath, waiting for her to say no.

Amá rubs her temples. "Where?"

"I don't know, downtown or something. The park. Somewhere not here. I haven't seen her in a long time."

Amá is silent for a while. She looks like she's thinking hard, holding her fingers to her forehead.

"Ay, Dios," she finally says.

"Please."

"Fine, but you have to be back before it's dark." Amá looks like it pains her to say it.

• • •

Because Amá is making such an effort to be a better mother, I've decided to be a better daughter, so I agree to attend a prayer group at our church that night. It's in the same basement as my quinceañera, and when we walk down the stairs, I get flashbacks of that horrible night. I hope Amá isn't thinking about it, but I'm nearly certain she is. How could she not?

The most exciting thing about the church group is the free coffee and cookies, which I run to immediately. There are few things better than vanilla wafers dunked in milky coffee.

The leader of the group is a middle-aged woman named Adelita. She's wearing a very unfashionable fleece vest, and her hair is cut short like a lot of women's when they get older. (I really don't understand why that's a requirement once you reach middle age.) Adelita begins with an Our Father, then adds her own prayer at the end. "I hope that everyone here finds the love and understanding they're looking for. God lives in each and every one of you," she says.

Adelita tells us about her ten-year-old son, who died after a long, painful battle with leukemia. Even though it's been fifteen years, his death haunts her every day of her life, she says. When she begins describing his amputated leg, a tear trickles down my face against my will.

"Are you okay, mija?" Amá whispers, placing her hand on my knee.

I nod.

Next is a man named Gonzalo, who is wearing blue work pants and a Bugs Bunny T-shirt that's probably from the nineties, which depresses me like few things can. He tells the group that his son is gay and he doesn't know how to forgive him.

"Forgive him for what?" I ask when he's finished.

"Julia, be quiet," Amá says. I'm already embarrassing her, like always.

"It's okay for her to ask questions," says Adelita.

"I just don't understand," I go on. "Being gay isn't a choice. Don't you know that?"

"What do you mean, you don't understand? What he's doing is a sin!" Gonzalo is all worked up now, his fists clenched and his face flushed.

Whatever compassion I had for him and his Bugs Bunny T-shirt has quickly evaporated. "I'm sure that your son would do anything to stop being gay to avoid dealing with you. Besides, didn't Jesus preach that you should love everyone? Isn't that what Christianity is all about? Or did I miss something?"

If I keep going, I think Gonzalo might punch me in the face, so I stop. I can feel Amá's anger quivering beside me, but she doesn't say anything. By the time it's her turn, we've heard about affairs, deaths, abused gay children, bankruptcy, and deportations. My soul is a puddle at my feet.

"As you know, I lost Olga almost two years ago. I think about her always. There's not a moment that passes that I don't feel her absence. She was my companion, my friend. I don't know when I'll feel like myself again. It's like I've been cut in half. And Julia here, my beautiful daughter, I love her so much, but she is so, so different. I know she's a special kind of person. I know she's smart and strong, but we don't always understand each other. Olga, for example, always wanted to be at home with us, loved to be close to her family, and Julia can't ever sit still." Amá blows her nose. "Where I grew up, women were supposed to stay at home and take care of their families. The way women live in this country, having relations with cualquier fulano and living on their own, I just don't understand it. Maybe my morals are too different for this place. I don't know." Amá looks at the crumpled tissue in her hand. She has no idea who Olga was, but how do I tell her that? Do I even have the right?

"That's not how I want to live, Amá." I'm not sure if I'm supposed to speak, but I can't help it. "I'm sorry that I'm not Olga and I never will be. I love you, but I want a different life for myself. I don't want to stay home. I don't even know if I ever want to get married or have kids. I want to go to school. I want to see the world. I want so many things sometimes I can't even stand it. I feel like I'm going to explode."

Amá doesn't say anything. We all sit in silence until Adelita tells us to hold hands for the closing prayer.

Once my parents are asleep, I use my extra key to go back into Olga's room to see if I can finish reading her emails. It turns out I did leave her computer unlocked, which is a huge relief.

The neighbor's Internet is slow, but at least it works. This time I read the newest emails first. I don't have the patience to go in order. Most of the emails are the same—planning when to meet, Olga complaining about his wife, Olga asking when he's going to leave her, him promising that he will. Sometimes he begs for forgiveness, sometimes he doesn't. They repeat with little variation. They never use each other's names or specific locations. I assume what they keep referring to as *the C* is the Continental. From what I can tell, it sounds like his children are probably in high school, which means they are almost Olga's age, and I'm certain he's been married for twenty years, since he tells Olga that over and over, as if somehow that justifies anything.

How could she have put up with it for such a long time? What did she think was really going to happen? This is a side of Olga I never saw: desperate, clingy, and delusional. Here I thought she was virginal, passive, and complacent, letting the world pass her by, when, in fact, she was letting the world pass her by while having sex with an old married dude, hoping he would one day leave his wife. She wasted four whole years with him—from the age of eighteen, when she started working at the office, to the day she died. What was she thinking? No wonder she was static. No wonder she never wanted to leave and go to school. She was waiting, and she would have been waiting forever. Then it strikes me. I think to check the sent box. Maybe she sent an email he never answered.

losojos@bmail.com
5:05 p.m. (September 5, 2013)

The ultrasound was yesterday. Why didn't you show up? I left the picture in your desk, if you even care to look at it.

My dead sister was going to have a baby.

TWENTY-FOUR

I call the hotel where Angie works and hang up when I hear her voice. I'm in front of her building two trains later. The hotel is luxurious and full of men in suits and perfectly groomed women in high heels. Everything is shiny to an oppressive degree; I can practically see my reflection in the marble floor. A middle-aged lady with a pointy nose and expensive trench coat scowls at me when I enter the lobby, like I don't belong there, like my existence offends her sensibilities or something. I smile and wave at her, hoping she can detect my irony.

I wonder how much it would cost to spend the night here. Probably hundreds, maybe thousands.

Angie is at the front desk, which is what I was hoping, wearing a navy blue pantsuit that makes her look ten years older. Her wild hair is drawn into a tight ponytail, and her makeup is muted and faint. Maybe the dress code requires them to look as dull as humanly possible.

Angie, of course, is surprised to see me.

"Oh my God, what are you doing here?" She sets down the phone.

"It's so nice to see you, too, Angie. It's been too long, really."

Angie sighs. "How are you?"

"Oh, I'm just wonderful."

"I can't really talk right now. I'm working, as you can see." She rubs her neck and looks around nervously.

"You don't have time to talk to me about Olga's pregnancy

and married boyfriend?" I smile.

"What?"

"You heard me."

"Let's go get some coffee." Angie grabs her purse and turns to her blond coworker at the end of the counter. "Melissa, I'll be back soon. Taking a quick break."

When we settle in a corner table in the coffee shop across the street, Angie searches inside her purse and puts on another coat of pale lipstick, using her phone as a mirror. She doesn't say anything. She must be waiting for me to go first, so I just sip my coffee and let her squirm for a while.

“So why didn’t you tell me? You knew this whole time,” I finally say. “Why would you do that to me? I’m her fucking sister, Angie.”

“What would anyone gain from that? She’s gone. She’s never coming back. What difference would that have made? Why would your family want to know that about her? It would have devastated them. Maybe you’re too young to understand, Julia, but sometimes people don’t need the truth.”

“Why is everyone always saying that to me? I’m not an imbecile. I have a brain, a pretty good one, too. And they would’ve found out eventually. How was she going to hide a baby coming out of her? ‘Oh, don’t mind this child here. It was a result of immaculate conception.’ Just tell me who he is. I know he worked in her office. You have to tell me. He was a doctor, wasn’t he?”

Angie shakes her head. "Look, I tried to get her to leave him, for years, but she wouldn't. There was no stopping her. She was obsessed. You have no idea. It was obvious he was just using her because he was in a miserable marriage, but she couldn't see that, no matter how many times I tried to explain it to her."

"I was even starting to think that you guys were a couple. I didn't know what to believe."

"Wow. Seriously? Me and your sister?"

"It's not that ridiculous. I knew you were keeping something from me, and you were always together."

Angie looks disgusted.

"When did you find out about the baby?"

"Wait, how do you even know about all of this?" She puts both hands on the table.

"I went through her emails."

"Well, that's kind of messed up."

"More messed up than keeping this secret? Than letting me think I was crazy for sensing something was wrong?"

"Why do you want to know who it is, though? What are you going to do once you find out?"

"Because I deserve to know. Because I, apparently, had no idea who Olga was. I guess none of us did, except for you and that old guy she was banging. Why was she living like that? Why couldn't she just have a normal boyfriend and go to school? I don't get it."

"You know Olga never wanted to leave your parents. She would have done anything for them. She always wanted to be a good daughter."

I wonder what else Angie knows. I try to read it in her face, but I don't know what to make of it.

"They should know about this. It's not fair to me or to them. How am I going to carry this by myself my whole damn life?"

"I'm sorry. I understand that it hurts, believe me, but this isn't about you. This is about protecting those who are still here. Why would you want to cause your family more pain?"

"Because we shouldn't be living lies," I say. "Because they deserve to know. Because I feel like I'm going to explode if I don't say it. It's all I can think about. I'm tired of pretending and letting things blister inside me. Keeping things to myself almost killed me. I don't want to live like that anymore."

"What are you talking about?"

"Forget it." Part of me wonders if Angie is right—who am I to do this to my family?—but I hate this feeling, like the weight of this will make my chest collapse.

Angie wipes the tears from her eyes with her palms. "Some things should never be said out loud, Julia. Can't you see that?"

I take another train to Wicker Park to meet Connor at the bookstore. As soon as he sees me, he hands me an old photography book and asks me what it smells like. I press it against my face. "Hmm . . . A sad man looking out the window as it rains . . . lamenting a time at the train station. Yeah, that's it."

This makes Connor laugh. "Wow, that's specific," he says. "Is he wearing a hat?"

"Uh-huh. Porkpie."

"It's good to see you," he says, and hugs me.

"Lovely to see you, too, sir. I see you have a new hairstyle." Connor's shaggy brown hair is now short and neat. It makes him look older.

He shrugs. "Yeah, I got sick of it one day."

"I like it," I say. "You look distinguished."

We walk through the bookstore as we catch up on the last several weeks. We're laughing and talking so fast that people stare at us as if we're crazy. I tell him about Isabela and Sebastián, the gay cats, the shooting, Apá's drawings, Olga's affair. I'm almost out of breath, trying to cram it all in. I don't tell him about the hospital, though. I'm not ready to talk about it yet.

After the bookstore, we walk to the 606. One of the best decisions the city has ever made was to convert an old rail line into an elevated park. The trail spans two and a half miles—from Wicker Park to Humboldt Park—and it has great views of the skyline and neighborhoods below. Though it's chilly today, there are several people walking and running, some with strollers and dogs. The trees and bushes are mostly bare, but I see a few green blades emerging. Connor and I walk west for a long time without saying anything. As I stare at the graffiti on an abandoned factory with shattered windows, he takes my hand and squeezes it.

"So what else have you been up to?" I ask. "Any new ladies in your life?" I'm not sure why I say this. Sometimes I blurt out stupid things when I get nervous.

Connor shakes his head and laughs, but he doesn't say no. A pulse of jealousy surges through me, even though I try to reason with myself. I had Esteban, after all, and I'd be lying if I said I didn't miss him.

"Have you heard from any colleges yet?" he asks.

"No, not yet. You?"

"I got into Cornell." Connor smiles.

"Holy shit. Congratulations!" I give him a fist bump.

"Yeah, it's my top choice. I'm pretty excited."

"I applied to some schools in New York City, so maybe we'll be in the same state."

"I can visit you. We can go to museums or Central Park or just eat our way through Manhattan. Oh, and we can visit all the landmarks in *The Catcher in the Rye.* That would be fucking cool."

"Let's see if I get in first."

"You will. You know you will." Connor says as a guy with a man bun runs past us.

"Thanks."

The sun is beginning to set. A blaze of orange light outlines a giant cloud. I love dusk; it always astonishes me that something so beautiful happens every single day.

We're quiet for a long time. "So, what now?" I finally say.

"What do you mean?"

"I don't even know." I laugh nervously.

"All I know is that I missed you." Connor smiles and hugs me. "And I'm glad to see you."

"I missed you, too. What's going to happen now, though?"

"We're both going away to college, right? So let's just enjoy this without overthinking it. That's what makes sense to me."

A flock of pigeons flies over us as he takes both of my hands in his.

"You're right," I say, but that's not the answer I wanted to hear.

TWENTY-FIVE

Lorena missed her period this month and is terrified she's pregnant. She took a home-pregnancy test, but it came out all fuzzy, so she made an appointment at a clinic, just to be one hundred percent sure.

I was only away for two weeks, but so much has happened since I left. Lorena thinks she might be knocked up, Juanga found a hot new boyfriend, and Mr. Ingman got engaged to Ms. López. I don't know why it surprises me that the world doesn't stop just because I'm gone.

• • •

On the way to the clinic, the train is so crammed with people that some dude's butt is right next to my face. Lorena's knee keeps jerking up and down. She wants to pretend she isn't nervous, but I notice right away.

"Are you sure you're not going to tell Carlos if it's positive?"

"Why would I do that? He'd just want me to keep it. I know him. He'd get all sentimental about it and cry or some shit. And there's no fuckin' way I'm going to have a baby. I mean, I'm trying to get the hell out of my house and do something with my life, you know? I don't even like kids. They're gross."

"Yeah, I wouldn't have it, either. I see my cousin with her baby, and it seems like the worst thing that could ever happen. I don't think she's even going to finish high school. What kind of job can you get without a diploma?"

"A shitty one." Lorena shakes her head.

"Okay, so say you *are* pregnant, where are you going to get the money? I mean, I know it's expensive."

"José Luis has a stash of money hidden inside one of his boots in his closet. He thinks I don't know about it. Dumb ass."

"But he'd find out. What would you do then?"

"Honestly? I don't care." Lorena looks down at her chipped red nails.

A man sitting across from us takes a fork from his garbage bag and uses it as a microphone. The old lady next to him gets up and moves to another seat when he suddenly starts screaming "Thriller" by Michael Jackson. Everyone in the car looks super-irritated. Lorena and I turn to each other and laugh. Trains are disgusting, but at least they're entertaining.

• • •

The protesters gathered outside scream at us when we approach. They all hold idiotic signs that say things like *Abortion is murder* and *Mommy, why do you want to kill me?* Some of the kids are even holding pictures of bloody fetuses. What the hell is wrong with these people?

“We’ll take care of your baby!” yells a skinny woman with a bowl cut and crooked teeth. “Don’t do it! You’re going to burn in hell!”

“Get out of our faces. I swear to God, lady. Don’t mess with us,” I say.

“Jesus loves your baby!” yells another.

“You don’t even know why we’re here, so why don’t you just

shut up?" My heart is thumping, and my hands feel weak. Who are these people to judge anybody?

"Calm down, Julia. Just forget them."

Twenty minutes later, Lorena comes out the door with a gigantic grin on her face. I stand and drop the book from my lap.

"What? No? Negative?" I whisper.

Lorena shakes her head. She's beaming.

"Oh, thank God." I let out a sigh of relief.

When we get outside, Lorena jumps up and down and gives me a high five. I guess she was trying to contain herself in front of the other girls who may not be as lucky. The protestors look at her as if she were a humongous ogre. I give them a thumbs-up and smile.

"God, that was scary as hell. I feel like we should celebrate or something." Lorena is pacing back and forth on the sidewalk and rubbing her hands together.

"How? We don't have any money. What could we even do? Split a hot dog?"

"Well. . ." Lorena looks guilty.

"What?"

"I already took José Luis's money, just in case."

"You what? Are you serious?"

"I didn't want to take any chances. What if I needed it and then it was gone? Where would I get five hundred dollars? Look, I want to do something fun for once in my life. And I really don't care about José Luis. He can seriously go fuck himself. What have you always wanted to eat?"

"Oh my God, Lorena. You're insane. Are you sure?"

"Trust me. Please. I want to do this." Lorena shakes me by the shoulders. "It'll be fun. When will we have another opportunity like this?"

"Shit, I don't know. What about seafood? That's pretty expensive, isn't it?"

"A toast to you not being pregnant," I say, raising my glass of water. "Now, please use condoms. Promise?"

"Okay, okay. I know. I promise. I learned my lesson. Never again."

We watch boats sail down the Chicago River. It's a perfect day to be near the water and blow a bunch of money on fancy food. When the waitress brings out a basket of bread, we just stare at each other confused until we see the couple next to us dip their bread in olive oil.

"Is that really how you're supposed to eat it? People eat oil like that?" I whisper, and motion toward their table with my head.

Lorena looks perplexed and shrugs.

I pour the oil onto my plate.

"So you and Connor are back together, or what? What's up with that?"

"I mean, not exactly. I don't know what we are. I like him a lot, but it seems like he doesn't want to promise anything. It kind of bums me out. Then again, I liked Esteban, too. I still do. And that would never work out because we don't even live in the same country. Fuck, dating is confusing."

"Tell me about it." Lorena takes a sip of her Coke and stares off into the river for a few seconds. "I want to meet him. Send him a message."

"Are you sure?"

"Why not? I think I should be allowed to meet your boyfriend."

"I just told you he's not my boyfriend, but I'll ask him anyway," I say as I text Connor.

We're quiet for a long time. "Olga was pregnant when she died," I finally blurt. I wanted to wait for another time, but it kept swelling inside me all day like a balloon.

"What are you talking about?" Lorena leans towardme.

"I went through her computer. I found her password, then read all of these emails between her and this old married guy. I have no idea who he is. Their emails were super-secretive. It was like they were both terrified that someone would find out. They didn't even use each other's names or anything."

"No, not Olga. That's impossible." Lorena's eyes widen. "You're lying!"

"I know, right?" It's so ridiculous, I almost laugh—my angelic sister having a steamy love affair.

"And your parents don't know?"

I shake my head. "Can you imagine?"

"Oh my God." Lorena covers her mouth. "Are you going to tell them? What are you going to do?"

A small blue boat called *Miss Behavin'* zips past.

"I haven't decided yet. I don't know what to do. I mean, on one hand, what's the point, right? It's just going to upset them. She's dead, and nothing is going to change that. On the other hand, don't they deserve to know who she was? Wouldn't *you* want to know? There are too many secrets in my family. It doesn't seem right. Why do people always lie to themselves and each other? God, I don't know. I keep going back and forth and back and forth. I just found out about it, and it's gnawing away at my brain like crazy. I feel it's going to come out somehow, sooner or later, no matter how hard I try to lock it up inside."

"Did she want it, the baby?"

Wait, hold on. The waitress keeps looking at us." I gesture toward where she's standing. "I think she's afraid we're not going to pay our bill."

Lorena takes the stack of cash from her purse and waves it at her. "Problem solved. Go on."

I laugh. Classic Lorena move. "She had an ultrasound, so, yes. Plus, Olga was super-Catholic. She definitely would've had it. There's no doubt in my mind."

The waitress suddenly brings us our giant seafood platter. It smells like the ocean. I don't know what a lot of the items are, but I'm going to try them all until I feel sick to my stomach.

"I think you should tell them. I mean, that was their kid, you know?" Lorena is still in shock. She picks at a crab with a fork. "How do you get the meat out of this thing?" She splatters some butter on the white tablecloth.

"But you weren't planning on telling Carlos or your mom if you were pregnant. How is that different? Do you think any good could come from it? You were the one telling me I had to move on with my life and stop obsessing about my sister."

Lorena doesn't have an answer for that.

After lunch, Connor meets us on the corner of LaSalle and Wacker. I already suspected that Lorena wasn't going to like him because he's white and lives in the suburbs, but I'm still surprised by the amount of side eye she gives him.

"Stop it," I whisper to her, when Connor's not looking. "Why did you tell me to invite him?"

"What? What am I doing?" Lorena acts insulted. "I wanted to meet him."

"Come on, you know exactly what you're doing."

The three of us walk along the river in silence until we find a coffee shop. Lorena orders the sweetest, most complicated drink on the menu, and Connor and I both get regular coffee with cream.

"So, um. . ." Connor says as we sit at a table outside. "Julia tells me you're really good at science."

"I guess so." Lorena looks bored out of her mind. She mixes her drink with her straw and stares off into the water.

"She's always helping me with my physics homework. I never know what I'm doing," I say, and smile at Lorena, trying to ease the tension. "And I help her with English."

"So what college are you going to?" Connor takes a sip of his coffee.

"I haven't decided yet. Someplace I can afford for nursing. College is expensive, and some of us can't rely on our parents."

I give Lorena my best death stare.

Connor nods and stands up. "I'll be back. I have to go to the bathroom."

"Why are you being so rude?" I ask Lorena once he's inside.

"I don't know what you're talking about." Lorena shrugs.

"It seems as if you hate him. I don't get it. What's wrong with him?"

"How can I hate him if I don't even know him? Don't be ridiculous. All I know is that he's from Evanston, his parents are rich, and he took your virginity. That's it."

"I really like him, you know?"

"Okay, I get it, but do you actually believe he doesn't look down on us? You don't think he sees us without thinking we're ghetto? I just don't want you to get hurt. You can tell right away that he's rich. You were right. Maybe we shouldn't have invited him."

"He's not like that, though." I look down at my coffee. "He's not like that at all."

"Oh, come on, don't be dumb," Lorena says, and slurps the last of her drink. "You know they all are."

TWENTY-SIX

After school, I take the same buses Olga rode to work the day she died. I'm not exactly sure what I'll do when I get to the office. I don't have a real plan. I just hope to show up and somehow find the man who inseminated my sister.

I sit in the waiting room reading the list of doctors over and over. There's no way I'm going to figure out who he is this way. After twenty minutes of watching me pretend to wait, the receptionist asks if she can help me with something. I wonder if she's the one who replaced my sister. She reminds me of a possum—maybe it's her teeth—but she's still pretty somehow.

"Um, I was hoping to make an appointment with . . . Dr. Fernández."

"Have you seen her before?"

"No."

"Do you have an insurance card?"

"No."

"What kind of insurance do you have? HMO or PPO?"

"I'm not sure." That's a stupid answer, I know.

"I don't think I can help you, miss. I'm sorry. Maybe you should come back with your parents?" she says, and smiles.

As I try to figure out what to do next, a man in a dark suit enters the office. It's him. It's the man from Olga's wake, crying in the back. The one with the gray suit and expensive watch. I guess he wasn't my uncle after all.

“Hello, Dr. Castillo,” the receptionist says. “Your son left you a message about five minutes ago.”

“Thanks, Brenda.”

I crouch to the ground and pretend to look for something in my backpack until he’s gone.

“I think I made a mistake,” I say, and run out the door.

The office closes at 5:30, so I wait outside until he comes out. By 5:45, right when I begin deliberating about going home, I see him walk out the door. He looks powerful in his black suit and leather briefcase. He’s definitely old, but I can see why Olga was attracted to him; there’s something about the way he walks that’s forceful, magnetic.

What am I going to say? What's the point of all this?

I take a few deep breaths and run after him before he gets into his black BMW.

"Hey! Hey!" I yell before he closes his door.

"How can I help you, young lady?" he asks, in a slight accent I can't detect. He has to know who I am. I can see it in his discomfort, the way his eyes shift, as if looking for an escape.

"I'm Olga's sister."

"Oh my God," he says. "Yes, of course. I'm so sorry for your loss. Olga was a wonderful employee. We all miss her very much."

"Yeah, I'm sure you do. Since you got her pregnant and made her think you were going to marry her. . . . And . . . and then she died."

Dr. Castillo sighs and looks down at the ground.

"Why the fuck did you do that?" I'm startled by my own anger.

"Please, stop, let me explain. I'll give you a ride." He leads me to the passenger side with his hand on my shoulder, and something about that is comforting, even though I think I hate him. He smells like cologne and aftershave, like man, just like Mr. Ingman.

The diner is almost empty. Neither one of us says anything for a long time. I don't know where to begin.

"Listen," he finally says. "I know you're upset, but I want you to know that I loved your sister."

"But you were married, and Olga was only twenty-two. That's gross. How old are you anyway? Fifty?"

"When you get older, you'll understand that everything is much more complicated than you ever imagined. You plan your whole life, and nothing works out the way you expect." He sounds as if he's talking to himself.

"Tell me how old you are."

"That doesn't matter." He scratches his neck and looks behind him.

"It does to me."

"Forty-six."

"You're older than our father. That's so fucking weird. Jesus." I can't even look at him.

"Life is incredibly complex. One day, you will see."

"What's so complicated about you lying and taking advantage of my sister? You were never going to leave your wife, were you?"

"I wanted to marry Olga. I swear to you. Especially when . . ." He rubs his face.

"She got pregnant."

He looks wounded, like I just kicked him in the balls. "Yes, that."

The waitress finally comes by to take our orders.

"Just some coffee for me, thanks," Dr. Castillo says.

"I'll have a grilled cheese and some apple juice, please." Might as well get a meal out of this.

Dr. Castillo reaches into his back pocket and pulls out his wallet. He takes a folded piece of paper and smooths it on the table.

There it is, a hazy little outline: a suggestion, a possibility, a blob, a clump of cells. I can hardly make out the shape, but I can almost feel its tiny heartbeat in my hands. “How many weeks?”

“Twelve.”

“What do I do with this?” I say to myself aloud. “How do I bury this, too?”

“What do you mean?”

“I mean, how am I going to keep this secret? Why do I have to be the one living with this shit?”

“Please, don’t tell your parents. Olga never wanted to hurt them.”

“Why wouldn’t I? And why should I listen to you?”

“Sometimes it’s best not to tell the truth.”

“Of course you would say that. You lied to my sister and

your wife. You were playing both of them like motherfucking fiddles."

"I never lied to Olga." He shakes his head.

"What did your last text say? I know you were the one she was texting." I take a bite of my sandwich.

"She told me that if it was a boy, she was going to name him Rafael, after your father."

I don't even know what to say to that. Something about it makes me feel like all my insides are being vandalized.

"So you were never going to leave your wife, right?"

"Yes, I was." He nods.

"Yeah, sure. Look, I read all the emails. Every single one. I'm not stupid or naive, no matter how much everyone wants to think I am."

Dr. Castillo sighs, says nothing.

"You just kept stringing her along, and she kept waiting and waiting, doing nothing with her life."

"When she told me about the baby, that changed everything." Dr. Castillo looks out the window. His eyes are wet now. I don't think I've ever seen a grown man cry before, not even Apá. "I loved your sister. You have to believe that. Her death ruined me. It destroyed me like you can't imagine." He lowers his head into his hands.

"Actually, I *can* imagine. It ruined me, too."

"I'm divorced now. I couldn't do it anymore." He dries his eyes with a silk handkerchief.

"Yeah, well, it's too late for my sister, isn't it?" I crumple my napkin and take a sip of my juice. The waitress picks up my plate and wipes the table. The rag smells awful. There is nothing left to say, so I get up and put on my backpack. I can feel him watch me as I walk out the door.

TWENTY-SEVEN

I still don't know how to talk to my father. I don't want him to know what I know. There is so much I want to say, but I can't. There are times the secrets feel like strangling vines. Is it considered lying when you hold something locked up inside you? What if the information would only cause people pain? Who would benefit from knowing about Olga's affair and pregnancy? Is it kind or selfish for me to keep this all to myself? Would it be messed up if I said it just so I don't have to live with it alone? It's exhausting. There are moments it almost comes out, like a flock of fluttering birds in my throat. But what kind of person would I be if I told my parents? Haven't they suffered enough? Isn't that why Amá never told us what happened to her on the border? I know she'd die with that story still inside her, partly out of shame, but mostly to protect us. And why would Olga need to know that about herself? Apá was her father, no matter what.

Apá is drinking coffee at the kitchen table while Amá is in the shower.

I pour myself a cup and sit across from him. The sunlight pours in from the blinds.

"Buenos días," he says, without looking up.

"Buenos días." I squirm in my chair, thinking of how to talk to him. "Apá," I finally say.

Apá looks up, but doesn't respond.

"Why didn't you tell me that you drew, that you were an artist?" I wonder why I'm so nervous speaking to my own father.

Apá scratches under his mustache. "Who told you that?"

"Mamá Jacinta. She showed me your drawing of Amá. It's really good. Why did you stop?" I twist my napkin in my hand.

"Because there was no point. What was I going to do? Sell my drawings? It was a waste of time." Apá stares at the slices of sunlight on the table.

"It's not. It's not at all. How could you say that? It's art. It's beautiful and it matters." My voice gets loud, even though I don't mean it to.

"Julia, sometimes in life you don't get to do what you want to do. Sometimes you have to deal with what's given to you, shut up, and keep working. That's it." Apá gets up and places his cup in the sink.

I always look forward to seeing Dr. Cooke, even though I often leave her office feeling like someone ripped my chest open.

I never in my life thought I would like exercise, but Dr. Cooke insisted that it would help me feel better—something about endorphins and releasing stress. I swim nearly every day at the YMCA. I used to hate swimming, but now I find it soothing. Life is funny that way. I stopped worrying about all the bacteria and secretions in the water and learned to enjoy it. There's something about it that makes me feel free. I haven't lost any weight, which is fineby me, because my body is tighter and healthier, and I like the way it looks. I have more energy, too. Even on thedays I'm kind of lazy and don't want to go, I make myself do it anyway because I never regret it when I'm finished.

Today Dr. Cooke wants to talk about my relationship with my mom. That's probably our number-one topic.

"How have you and your mom gotten along this week?" She takes a sip of water. She's wearing bright red linen pants, black sandals, and a white wraparound shirt. Her hair is pulled into a tight ponytail. What I like about Dr. Cooke is that she never seems to judge me. I can be my whole self without being afraid. Even when I admit to something that I think is shameful or embarrassing, she doesn't scold me or look at me like I'm a leper. I wish everyone could be this way. I don't understand why people can't just let others be who they are.

"Mostly okay. We went shopping and we didn't fight, which is unheard of for us. I think I can tell that she's scared and doesn't want me to go away, but she never says it directly anymore. It's like she's trying so hard to be supportive, but it also makes me crazy when she doesn't say what she means. I feel like I can tell right away what she's thinking. She's terrified that I'm going away to college. I know her, and I can just sense it."

"And why do you think she's holding back this time?"

"Because she doesn't want to push me away anymore. I think she's scared, you know? I think she finally is beginning to understand that I'm never going to change, and she's learning to accept it somehow. I guess I'm glad, in a way, that she's trying so hard. I'm trying, too."

"Sometimes it's difficult for people to adjust to new ideas, particularly if they come from a very different culture. I can imagine that perhaps your mother doesn't mean to be so repressive; that to her, it's a way to protect you."

"I guess so. Probably."

"Especially after the trauma she experienced crossing the border. Do you ever consider talking to your mother about what happened to her?" Dr. Cooke writes something in her notepad.

"No, I can't. I promised my aunt I would never tell her. Besides, what can I possibly say to her to make it any better? I'm not sure what the point would be."

"Maybe it's a way for you to become closer to her, to let her know you understand a very important part of who she is, to show your empathy."

"I don't know. I mean, even though it's not her fault, I think she feels ashamed. That's why it's a secret. Like, who am I to bring it up and hurt her again?" When I think about what happened to Amá, I get so angry I don't know what to do with myself. How can people do terrible things to each other? What happens in someone's life to make them think that violating someone's body is okay?

"It's something to think about. Maybe not now, but in the future. The same goes for Olga and her pregnancy. Perhaps one day you'll be able to talk about it. When you're ready, of course. It might help you both heal."

"I don't believe in keeping things hidden and buried—because sometimes it feels like poison pumping through me—but at the same time, I wonder if I'll ever be ready to talk about it. I don't know." My lip quivers.

Dr. Cooke hands me the box of tissues.

"You have to look inside of yourself and decide what's best for you. I'm only here to offer options, to give you the tools to make the right choices for yourself. You're a smart young lady. I think you know you can overcome anything. Although you still struggle sometimes, I've seen you change in a short amount of time." Dr. Cooke smiles. "That's something to be proud of."

I'm not sure what it means to be proud of myself yet, but I'm trying to learn.

The days feel endless as I wait and wait for my college acceptance (or rejection) letters. College is all I can think about these days, but no letters come in the mail.

Then, just when I'm starting to think that my applications were so bad the colleges didn't even bother replying, there's an envelope from Boston University waiting for me on the kitchen table.

Dear Ms. Julia Reyes:
We regret to inform you . . .

And then the letters just keep coming and coming.
From Barnard College:

Dear Ms. Julia Reyes:
I write with sincere regret . . .

From Columbia University:

Dear Ms. Julia Reyes:
It is with very real regret that I must tell you . . .

From Boston College:

Dear Ms. Reyes:
We are very sorry . . .

• • •

Lorena and Juanga take me to Lincoln Park Zoo to cheer me up on a warm and bright Sunday afternoon, even though I tell them I'd rather stay home sulking. I can't believe I thought I'd get into those schools. Why did I have to aim so high? What made me think I was so special?

"Don't be sad, Julia. We all know you're as fierce as those beautiful ladies over there," Juanga says, looking at the lions.

The largest one stares at me as if she were in a trance.

"You can always move in with us, you know?" Lorena says, adjusting her flimsy pink dress. "If things don't work out."

"I know, I know. I just really want to go to New York. I need a change. A new start blah-blah-blah."

"Yeah, I get it." Lorena almost sounds irritated.

"Ugh, stop getting sad, and let's go look at the bears," Juanga says, pushing us toward the building.

One of the polar bears just had twins, so there is a crowd of people hoping to get a good look. We worm our way through to the front and see one of the cubs nursing from its mother.

"Aw," Juanga says, putting his arms around us. "Look at its little face."

I put my head against his shoulder. "How's your new boyfriend?" Juanga has been dating a hot guy from Hyde Park for about a month now. They met on the Red Line and have been in love ever since. He's been happy lately, despite his parents being complete assholes. It seems like they kick him out every other week. They can't get over him being gay, and Juanga refuses to pretend he's not. Even if he tried, it would just ooze out of him. He's very much who he is.

Sometimes Juanga stays with his cousin, other times with Lorena. I would offer up our couch, too, but Amá would never go for it. Everything scandalizes her.

"Amazing. Lord, that man is beautiful," Juanga says, fanning himself, as if he still can't believe it. "I just need to move the hell out of my house so we can finally be a real couple. Can you imagine introducing him to my father? Gay *and* black? Ni Dios lo mande. He'd probably burn us at the stake." He crosses himself and laughs. He's kidding but not kidding.

• • •

The next day, right when I begin to consider a career in busking or garbage collecting, two thick envelopes arrive in the mail: one from NYU and the other from DePaul University.

I start screaming when I open them in the living room. Amá and Apá frantically run from the kitchen.

"What happened?" Amá looks frightened. "Is everything okay?"

"I got in! I got in! I got in! I'm going to New York. I'm going to school! *And* I got into DePaul! Holy mother of God!" I can't stop shrieking and jumping. Both schools are hooking it up with a full ride. NYU has accepted me with scholarships, with the condition of participating in a special study and pilot program for first-generation college students.

“Que bueno, mija,” Amá says, even though she looks heartbroken. “I’m very happy for you.”

Apá gives me a hug and kisses the top of my head. “So you’re going to the one in New York? What about the one in Chicago, mija? That’s a good one, too, ¿qué no?”

“Yes, but I want to go to the one in New York. It’s what I’ve wanted for a long time. There is no better place to be a writer. I’m sorry, Apá,” I say, and squeeze his hand.

Apá nods but doesn’t say anything. He swallows and looks away. For a second, I wonder if he’s going to cry, but he doesn’t.

Amá sighs and puts her arm around my shoulder. “Ay, como nos haces sufrir. No se si maldecirte o por ti rezar.”

“You know I don’t mean to, right? I’m not doing this to hurt you. I want you to know that."

"Yes, I know, but one day you'll know how much it hurts to be a mother."

"I don't want kids, so, no, I won't," I say, trying not to sound annoyed. Amá thinks it's funny when I say I don't want to have any children. She never believes me. It's as if she thinks a woman without babies is pointless.

"That's what you say. You just wait and see," she says, and walks toward the kitchen, fixing her braids.

As the end of the school year approaches, I become more and more restless. It's hard to pay attention in class when I already have one foot out the door. All I want to do is be outside eating ice cream, looking at the sky, and listening to the sounds of summer approaching.

I see Connor most weekends. Today we meet at a street festival in Old Town. I don't care for the neighborhood much—too yuppie and white for my comfort—but the festival is free and it's outdoors.

As soon as it gets warm, it's as if the city loses its damn mind. Everyone is excited about life again and wants to be out in the streets. Unfortunately, summer also means people start shooting each other more often. Well, it depends what neighborhood you're in.

Connor and I wander around, looking at the crafts, most of which are terrible. I don't know why anyone would want to buy a watercolor painting of the skyline, for instance, or a woodcarving of the Cubs logo, but I suppose there must be a market for such things.

The day is sunny and almost too hot for May. My new blue dress fits me a little tight in the armpits, but I like the way I look. I've never worn anything with flowers before. I was surprised I didn't hate it when I tried it on. Amá insisted it was flattering, and for once, I agreed. I'm glad I did, because Connor pretended to faint when he saw me walking from the train station.

We share a giant plate of greasy fries at a picnic table by the stage. I don't know how a person can resist fried foods, because I'm a goner every time I catch a whiff of them. Suddenly, the Depeche Mode cover band starts playing "Enjoy the Silence," one of my favorite songs ever.

"Holy shit," I say to Connor, and squeeze his arm. "This song. I can't take it. It's too good."

He smiles. "It's pretty fucking great."

The moment is perfect—the sunset, the fries, the music. I look at Connor, and a wave of sadness washes over me. I miss him, even though he's sitting right in front of me. It's hard to explain, but it reminds me of a haiku I once read: "Even in Kyoto—/ hearing the cuckoo's cry—/ I long for Kyoto." I feel like that a lot. I get nostalgic before I have to.

I know Connor said we shouldn't overthink our relationship, and in my mind I totally get it—we're going away to college, after all. That would make it hurt more in the end. Besides, I try to reason with myself, I should be excited to explore New York on my own. Here is my chance to be completely independent for once in my life.

Connor gets up from his seat and slides next to me.

"I'm going to miss you," I say as he puts his arm around me.

"I'll miss you, too, but we'll see each other again. Besides, we have the whole summer. I'm still right here." He smiles.

"I know, but what about *after* the summer?" I turn away. The sky is beginning to darken.

"I'll visit you in New York, I told you." Connor turns my face toward him.

I hate this feeling, the not knowing. These in-between places are scary, but then again, I understand that nothing is ever certain.

I begin to cry. It's not just because of him, but because of everything. My life is changing so fast, and even though it's what I want, I'm terrified.

"You're beautiful, did you know that?" he says, and kisses me on the cheek.

I'm startled to realize that I believe him.

After summer break

TWENTY-EIGHT

My depression and anxiety have softened with the medication. My moods still dip every once in a while, but there are times I'm actually happy, not just tolerating life. Summer is my favorite season, so that helps, too. The other day I went up to a stranger and asked if I could hug her dog. She laughed and said yes, and the golden retriever covered me with kisses.

Part of it is thanks to my medicine, I think. Dr. Cooke also showed me some techniques to deal with my anxiety. I'm supposed to write what she calls my "mental distortions" in a journal and then challenge them with more reasonable thoughts. Like the other day, I started worrying that I wouldn't do well in college because I'm just a broke-ass Mexican girl from a crappy neighborhood in Chicago. I convinced myself that all the kids are going to be smarter than I am because they went to better schools. I got stuck in this horrible loop. I became completely preoccupied until I focused on my breathing and surroundings, and forced myself to write a list of reasons why that was untrue: 1) The school would not have accepted me if they didn't think I could succeed. 2) I've read about a million books. 3) I'll work really hard. 4) Mr. Ingman says I'm the best student he's ever had. 5) Most people aren't really that smart.

It takes a lot of practice because my mind is so used to jumping to horrible conclusions. There are some days I still feel like the world is an awful, frightening place. Despite that, I want to go out into it and experience everything I possibly can. I'm not sure if that makes any sense.

Dr. Cooke tells me I've made a lot of progress and reminds me how important it is to take my medication at the same time every single day. I've talked to her a lot about my writing, so I ask her if I could read her a poem I wrote last night when I couldn't sleep.

"I'd love to hear it," she says.

I clear my throat and pray that I don't cry because that's what I do in every single session.

"Okay, here it goes," I say. "It's not done yet. I don't know if I'll ever finish it. I've been reworking it all day. It feels good to be able to explain these past two years of my life. It's called 'Pandora.'

"She opened the vault, the box in which she kept herself—old filmstrips of her life, her truth. Broken feathers, crushed mirrors creating a false gleam. She takes it all apart, every moment, every lie, every deception. Everything stops: snapshots of serenity, beauty, bliss, surface. Things she must dig for in her mesh of uncertainty, in her darkness, though it still lies in the wetness of her mouth, the scent of her hair. She digs and digs in that scarlet box on the day of her unraveling, the day she comes undone. She thrives in her truth and travels the world like a nomad, stealing the beauty of violet skies, fishing for pearls, pretty arabesques, paper swans, pressing them to her face, and keeping them between her palms. Forever."

Dr. Cooke smiles. “That was beautiful,” she says. “Thank you for sharing that with me.”

“I’m glad you liked it.” I hug Dr. Cooke, which surprises her, but she hugs me back.

On my way out, Dr. Cooke tells me she thinks I’ll do great in college, and I decide to believe her.

After dinner, Amá asks me to stay at the table and talk to her over tea. At first, I’m worried, but then I realize it’s highly unlikely that anything could be worse than what’s already happened.

“Hija, I want to talk to you about boys,” she says as she puts the kettle on the stove.

"Oh my God, Amá. Please, no." I cover my ears. I can't believe I'm finally having a sex talk with my mother.

"I know you're going to go to school, which is a very good thing. Your father and I, though we don't understand why you need to leave, we're very proud of you for being so smart. We just want you to be careful and protect yourself. Boys are only after one thing, you know? And once you give away the milk. . ."

"Milk? Ew, gross, Amá, please stop. I know what I'm doing."

"You think life is so easy, don't you? You think nothing bad will ever happen to you. I'm telling you that you can't go around trusting everybody." Amá shakes her head as she reaches for the mugs.

"I *don't* trust everybody." I know where she's coming

from with all of this, but it still frustrates me. It's not like I'm some simpleton who doesn't know anything about life. Besides, terrible things have already happened to me. She knows I'm no stranger to trauma. I've seen what the world is capable of.

"You know, I saw on the news that there's a drug some men put in women's drinks."

I try my best to be patient. "Yes, I know about roofies."

"Roofies, ¿qué es eso?"

"Forget it. Anyway, I know what that is. I'm not dumb, I swear."

"I never said you were dumb. I just said you were smart, didn't I? Why do you have to take things the wrong way?"

"Okay, okay. I'll watch my drinks. I'll be careful around boys, I promise. I'll carry mace, if you want."

"You know, you can get AIDS or get pregnant. What would you do then? How would you be able to finish college?" Amá puts her hand on her hip.

Talk about worst-case-scenario syndrome. Now I know where I get it from. "Jesus, Amá! I'm not getting AIDS or getting pregnant. I know about health. I've read lots of books." I don't tell her that condoms are ninety-eight percent effective, or that there is no way in hell I'll ever have a baby, even if I do get pregnant.

"I'm only telling you to be careful." She pours the hot water into our mugs.

"I know. Thank you. I know you're just trying to help, but can we please stop talking about sex now? Do you want to teach me how to cook instead? I really, really want to know how to make tortillas," I joke.

She can't help but laugh at that.

TWENTY-NINE

The morning before my flight, I call Freddy and Alicia to tell them I'm going to NYU. They're proud of me, they say. I wonder why exactly, since I hardly know them, but I promise to call them when I come home for winter break. As I'm hanging up, Lorena walks into my bedroom and sits on my bed. She's enrolled in nursing school and works as a waitress at a Mexican restaurant downtown. She says she has to wear those ridiculous frilly and embroidered dresses, but the money is good. She and Juanga, who now works in the Macy's makeup department, are planning to get an apartment together in Logan Square as soon as they've saved enough for a deposit. I guess the three of us are desperate to move on with our lives.

"Can I help you pack?" Lorena says as she looks around my messy room. She's wearing tiny black shorts and a gray tank top with a silver dollar sign on it. I'm really going to miss her fashion choices. She's finally dyed her hair back to brown, like I've been telling her for years. I've never seen her look so pretty.

"No, it's okay. Mostly everything is ready to go. I just have to clean up," I say. "I know I'm going to sound like an old geezer saying this, but I'm really proud of you. You're going to be an amazing nurse. You have always known how to take care of me."

"Oh my God, shut up. Stop it. You're going to make me ruin my makeup."

"I'm serious. I love you, and I don't know what I'm going to do without you. I'll probably call you, like, ten times a day."

"You'll be too busy with your new fabulous life. You won't even remember me." Lorena puts her face inside her shirt. I have only seen her cry three times before—when she fell and split her head open in the fourth grade, the day she told me about her dad, and right after I got out of the hospital.

"Lies. All lies. You'll see." I start crying, too, but a sliver of me wonders if what she's saying is true.

"I should go now. I have a shift in two hours," she says. "If I get there a minute late, my boss will probably fire me. He's such an asshole."

"I love you," I say again, looking at my dirty floor. A roach crawls under my bed, but I don't bother killingit.

"I love you, too," she says. "Try not to forget about me."

I hug her one last time at the door, then watch her walk away into the blinding afternoon sun. I can't help but laugh at her stick legs in her ridiculous short shorts. Lorena has never had any shame about her body. Now that I think about it, she's never really had much shame about anything, which is partly why I love her.

Apá is wearing the same faded blue shirt as the day he found me. Amá must have figured out a way to get the stains out because she hates throwing anything away. For months, I've tried to forget what happened, but it comes back in flashes and specks, no matter how much I try to drown it out. Apá has never once mentioned it to me, but I can see it in his eyes. There's so much

I wish we could both un-see.

Amá was working that night, and the house was quiet, except for my sobbing and the song I had on repeat—"Todo Cambia" by Mercedes Sosa. I became obsessed the first time I heard it. Everything in the song is true—everything changes, for better or worse, whether we like it or not. Sometimes it's beautiful, and sometimes it fills us with terror. Sometimes both.

Cambia el más fino brillante
De mano en mano su brillo
Cambia el nido el pajarillo
Cambia el sentir un amante
Cambia el rumbo el caminante
Aunque esto le cause daño

Y así como todo cambia
Que yo cambie no es extraño

I heard Apá at my door when I made my first cut. "Mija," he said quietly. "Mija, ¿estás bien?" He was supposed to be helping tío Bigotes with his car, but I guess he had finished early. He must have felt like something was wrong, because, unlike Amá, he never bothers me when I'm alone in my room. I tried to quiet myself by pressing my face against my pillow, but I couldn't. The noise came against my will. My body wouldn't let me silence it.

"Mija, open the door! What are you doing? Please open the door. Open it for your father, please." He tried pushing it open, but I had pressed my bed against it. I heard the panic in his voice, and I felt terrible for hurting him but couldn't force myself up.

I had never loved him like I did at that moment.

My life didn't flash before my eyes. All I saw was the picture of me and Olga, in front of Mamá Jacinta's house with her arm around my neck. I could even hear the birds chirping.

O'Hare is brimming with frazzled people in a hurry. We try to move out of the way as the crowds shuffle past us, but there's nowhere to turn. "I'll have to board soon," I tell my parents. The security line looks endless.

Apá puts his hand on my back, and Amá begins to weep. How can I leave them like this? How can I just live my life and leave them behind? What kind of person does that? Will I ever forgive myself?

"We love you, Julia. We love you so much," Amá says, and presses some money into my hand. "Para si se te antoja algo," she says, in case I crave something when I get to New York. "Remember you can come back whenever you want."

My eyes are faucets now, but it doesn't matter. If there's any place on earth where people should be allowed to cry as they watch their lives transform before them, it's the airport. In a way, it's kind of like purgatory, isn't it? An in-between place.

"I have something to give you." I crouch down to look through my backpack. Amá and Apá look confused.

"Here." I hand Apá his drawing of Amá in her long dress in front of the fountain. "It's beautiful, and you should have it," I tell him. "I wish you'd draw again, Apá. Maybe you can draw a picture of me sometime?" I smile and wipe my face with the back of my hand.

Apá closes his eyes and nods.

I wake up to the New York skyline. I thought Chicago was big, but New York is vast, enormous, overwhelming. I wonder what my life will be like there, who I will become. Connor says we'll see each other again. I'll miss him, but neither one of us knows what next year will be like.

Looking at all the cities and towns below reminds me of borders, which remind me of Esteban and his perfect white teeth. Part of me wonders if he will ever cross over here. It's his dream to live in the U.S., but I almost wish he won't. Even if he makes it alive, this place is not the promised land for everyone.

I know I've come a long way, and though it's hard, I'm trying to give myself credit for that. If I think about it, just a few months ago, I was ready to die, and now here I am on a plane to New York City all by myself. I honestly don't even know how I was able to pick myself back up, and sometimes I'm not sure how long it will last. I hope it's forever, but how can I know for certain? Nothing is ever guaranteed. What if my brain fails me once again? I suppose the only thing I can do is keep going.

I still have nightmares about Olga. Sometimes she's a mermaid again, other times she's holding her baby, which is often not a baby at all. Usually, it's a rock, a fish, or even a sack of rags. Though it's slowed, my guilt still grows like branches. I wonder when it'll stop, feeling bad for something that's not my fault. Who knows? Maybe never.

In some ways, I think that part of what I'm trying to accomplish—whether Amá really understands it or not—is to live for her, Apá, and Olga. It's not that I'm living life *for* them, exactly, but I have so many choices they've never had, and I feel like I can do so much with what I've been given. What a waste their journey would be if I just settled for a dull, mediocre life. Maybe one day they'll realize that.

When I told Mr. Ingman about the responsibility I felt to Olga, to my family, he told me I had to write about it. In fact, he pretty much forced me to do it then and there. That day I sat in his classroom for nearly two hours, crying over my notebook, smearing the ink on the pages. Mr. Ingman never said a word the whole time. He just touched my shoulder and then sat at his desk until I finished. Though most of it came gushing out, it was the hardest thing I've ever written. At the end, I had eight handwritten pages, so sloppy, only I could ever read them. That's what became my college essay.

I pull out Olga's ultrasound picture from my journal before we land. At times, it looks like an egg. Occasionally, it looks like an eye. The other day I was convinced I could see it pulsing. How can I ever give this to my parents, something else to love, something dead? These last two years I combed and delved through my sister's life to better understand her, which meant I learned to find pieces of myself—both beautiful and ugly—and how amazing is it that I hold a piece of her right here in my hands?

MENTAL HEALTH RESOURCES

The JED Foundation is a national nonprofit that exists to protect the emotional health of—and to prevent suicide among—our nation's teens and young adults. You can find more information at jedfoundation.org.

The Life is Precious™ (LIP) program from the nonprofit organization Comunilife offers culturally and linguistically appropriate educational support, creative art therapy, and wellness activities to Latina teens, aged twelve to seventeen, who have seriously considered or attempted suicide, and their families. You can find more information at comunilife.org/life-is-precious.

The National Suicide Prevention Lifeline provides 24/7 free and confidential support for people in distress, prevention and crisis resources for you or your loved ones, and best practices for professionals. You can find out more at suicidepreventionlifeline.org. If you need help now, text "START" to 741-741 or call 1-800-273-TALK (8255).

ACKNOWLEDGMENTS

A huge thank-you to my amazing agent, Michelle Brower, who believed in this book from the start and took a chance on me. I couldn't have asked for a better advocate for my work.

I must acknowledge my dear friend Rachel Kahan, who has been such a fantastic mentor throughout the years by giving me invaluable feedback and opening her home to me. To think we met on the Internet six years ago! Goodness.

My editors have been downright incredible. Thank you, Michelle Frey and Marisa DiNovis, for your incomparable insight, generosity, and support. Your guidance allowed me to write the best version of this book. In fact, the whole crew at Knopf Books for Young Readers has been an absolute dream.

To my coven of boss-ass women, I'm so grateful for your love. This includes Adriana Díaz, Pooja Naik, Sara Inés Calderón, Ydalmi Noriega, Safiya Sinclair, Sarah Perkins, Sara Stanciu, Elizabeth Schmuhl, L'Oréal Patrice Jackson, Christa Desir, Mikki Kendall, Jen Fitzgerald, Andrea Peterson, and so many others.

Eduardo C. Corral and Rigoberto González, thank you for the constant mentorship, camaraderie, and laughter.

A shout-out to Michael Harrington for reading an early draft and providing me with much-needed encouragement.

I'm forever thankful to my family for their unwavering support, even when my life choices puzzled them to no end.

Gus, Cata, Omar, Nora, Mario, Matteo, and Sofia—this book is for you.

I would also like to acknowledge all the immigrants who have risked their lives to come to this country, and the children of those immigrants. *You* are what make America great.